DON'T YOU KNOW WHO I AM?

A Rock N' Roll Hollywood Tale

ROBERT ALLEN MILTENBERG

D1401565

You – I Know As A Literary Comrade.
RAM
5·24·21°

-Qui Petunt Recognicionem-
★Here's To Living The Dream★

CHAPTER 1

This is the story nobody ever gets to hear - the actual fucking truth:

The Orifice of the Oracle burst onto the music scene beating on eardrums at the dawn of the Punk and New Wave era in the mid-1970s. Their groundbreaking 90-second commercial: *We're All Gods (With Amnesia)* played on New York late-late-late night TV in the summer of 1975. It aired intermittently from 2 am to 5 am in between old re-runs of The Cisco Kid and commercials for Crazy Eddie Electronics whose prices were insane and JGE Appliance Stores featuring a short, stocky guy named Jerry who told you what "da story" was.

In 90 seconds the Orifice Of The Oracle declared Mankind wasn't really human at all-but fallen Gods who had lost their identities, now doomed to primal mortality and they, taking over the Orifice: the mouthpiece of the Oracle: the media, were simply pointing out Man's downward spiral - and inviting everyone to rock out to the beat.

The song was simple, fast and infectious. Hard rock chords infused with just enough classical dissonance, electric guitar and synthesizer to make it poppy, sci-fi edgy and danceable all at the same time.

And who wouldn't like to be a God?

Inspired primarily by Erich Von Daniken's *Chariots Of The Gods* with some ancient mythologies thrown in for good measure, The Orifice Of The Oracle claimed they were exposing the truth of Man's real origins and why our society and in fact all civilization was so fucked up.

Lyrics like:
"We were up in the Heavens/And we crashed down to Earth/We lost our wings/ Our right of birth/We're not human/we're exiled Gods/Welcome to the zoo, man/ We're exiled frauds/Heed the Orifice of the Oracle/Forget your amnesia/ It's not metaphorical/We're All Gods/We're All Gods/We're All Gods!"
-said it all.

The commercial showed the band dressed in Mylar togas playing their instruments while falling upright from Mount Olympus in standing positions, landing directly on the island of Manhattan in the heart of the Bowery, hitting the last note as they touched ground in front of the primordial venue for all things Punk and New Wave.

Seeing this, insomniac and chronic late night TV viewer CBGB owner Hilly Krystal booked them immediately. There, they got the attention of Lou Reed. The Proto-Punk Rock God of the Velvet Underground dug their sound and their theatrical shtick enough to get them a contract with Vestal Records. A contract they would rue forever.

The music wasn't the only thing that set them apart. Throughout their careers they wore a variety of costumes starting with the Mylar togas in *We're All Gods*. But the singular look they were most remembered for was yet to come.

Together, they were four average young middle class Americans of their day. Randy was 5'8" of slight build, towheaded with a deceptively angelic face featuring deep blue eyes that had an owlish look to them behind round, John Lennon wire framed glasses. Jeffy stood 5'11", was raven-haired, square-shouldered and square-jawed with a glint of ego's certainty in his big green eyes. Larry was 5'9', skinny as a rail with short-cropped sandy hair and sullen hazel eyes. She had over-sized hands with huge knuckles from all her fights. If she didn't have a cigarette hanging out of her mouth, it was because of a show, a photo shoot, or there weren't any cigarettes around. Joey was 5'10' slightly zaftig but muscular with auburn hair kept in a Beatles bob that stopped just above her bright brown eyes. Typically wearing an inviting smile, she was considered the nicest of the group.

They were unique, taking their art school philosophy, fashion, even language, (calling people things like *sleepwalking-mortals* or *awakening-gods*, among other jargon) and putting it all together into one amazing musical presentation. Quirky minor rock chord progressions and orchestral-worthy melody lines created a futuristic signature sound they could play raw or polished-depending on their mood and song-message, which was either religious and political criticism or teenage angst about getting laid. Only the hardest of hardcore fans really cared much about their philosophy, anyway. Most just dug the tunes.

The Rolling Stone Encyclopedia of Rock put it this way:

"The Orifice of the Oracle-an art band from the 1970s/80s Punk/New Wave Era. A quintet comprised of two sets of siblings out of the American Rustbelt: The Roots and the Jabonnos. The Roots: Randy, co-founder, lead singer on keyboards, plus his brother Larry on lead guitar. The Jabonnos: Jeffrey, co-founder, on bass with vocals and his brother Joey on rhythm guitar and keyboards, plus drummer Skippy Watts. The O of the O (one of many nicknames) combined UFO-Sci-fi- Conspiracy culture with a smattering of ancient mythologies (Egyptian, Greek, Norse) and fused it with pop music and stage theatrics as a device to critique and satirize contemporary society."

Once they signed the contract that signed away 70% of whatever they recorded for the Vestal Label forever, they spent the next six months recording their first album, named for the title track *We're All Gods*. From that, they released a single that brought them national attention. It was a cover of the Beatles *HELP* delivered in a manic, undone, off-key, staccato style. That got them their first tour from coast to coast. They even played Toronto, Montreal and Vancouver. *We're All Gods* went gold in three months.

That's when the world started calling. Their first Euro-tour wasn't what they expected at all, though they hadn't known what to expect. Certainly not being met at London's Heathrow airport by a mob of wild kids, kicking them and yelling and screaming something to the effect of: "Since you're Gods, this can't possibly hurt! Make us Gods, too! Make us Gods, too, you wankers!"

Later, at several concerts, particularly Shepherd's Bush Empire where Charlie Chaplin once performed, Randy caught a mouthful of "nectar of the gods" as the Brit -fans called their spitting, or *"gobbing"* globs of phlegm into Randy's mouth as he prepared to sing. That was a story he was fond of telling (and Jeffy refuting) for decades to come. After that, the rest of the Tour went well, though Paris police briefly interviewed Jeffy after a scuffle between him and three women, (one of them a midget), regarding payment due for services rendered.

Soon after their first European tour, came their first big hit: *Flip 'Em Off* - a tune they claimed was about overcoming obstacles while everybody else thought it was about telling the whole world to fuck Itself-which in part is what made the song a hit in the first place:

"If They Tell You What To Do / Flip 'Em Off / If They Put It All On You / Flip 'Em Off
If The World Tells You You're Through / Flip 'Em Off
Flip 'Em Off-You've Been Ripped-You've Been Stripped-You've Been Clipped
Flip 'Em Off/On A Dare/ Flip 'Em Off-You Don't Care/Flip 'Em Off Till They Stare
-Flip 'Em Off! "

But the song wasn't written for those reasons, at all.

Randy had fun with it, stating before reporters, cameramen and microphones that, "I can see how pointing to the sky with our middle fingers on the album cover would lead people to think that-but all we're doing is giving all the world's leaders the classic rock n roll salute-especially our own beloved President."

After blowing a loud raspberry, Jeffy petulantly added: "And that's so obvious we shouldn't have to even explain it."

The real explanation was even more comical. By the time their *We're All Gods* commercial got them to CBGB, they were wearing their Mylar togas regularly on stage with gym shorts and t-shirts underneath. This was functional as well as theatrical. With all the cigarette smoke, over-packed wall-to-wall sweat-producing pogo-bodies, on top of the already withering stage lights, the heat was as stifling as the music was deafening. Worse still, temperatures rose higher after each show because the pay was nowhere near what the crowd size suggested it should be.

Flip 'Em Off was really about Jeffy's vicious battles with club management over money and those sweltering performances that prompted the Band's joking desire to flip off all their clothes on stage and play naked. Though Jeffy wasn't joking. Jeffrey Brutus Jabonno was a master of the wardrobe malfunction and he exposed himself before thousands every chance he got. "My body needs air on stage." He'd explain.

The Orifice of the Oracle could be thought provoking with anthems like *Give Me Immortality Or Give Me Death! Get Back-To Olympus, You're Every God, (-Rock-n-Rolled Into One)* and *Rise Up From The Underworld.*   They could get down and dirty with tunes like *Lick My Hermes Pillar Baby, I'm Bangin' On Pandora's Box, Icarus Was A Pussy, Kiss This Orifice* - and other such classics.

They appealed to adolescents who wanted to be teenagers and teenagers who wanted to be in their early twenties as rebels looking for causes, angst about the human condition, man's inhumanity to man and the corporate Big Brothers conspiring against everybody. They all came from blue-collar families with hardhat fathers, uncles, mothers and aunts working the General Motors assembly lines that made the city of Flint, Michigan prosper.

Having such a long name, fans shrank it down to their initials: *T.O.O.T.O.,* and then played with it from there. In the 80s they were affectionately referred to as *'the Toots',* which was amusing to them and their inner circle. Everybody knew they spent most of the 80s tooting up lines of enough cocaine to buy the ation of Peru. Of course, to the general public, *the Toots* referred to their most memorable piece of wardrobe.

Though usually called just The Orifice or The Oracle - they had many more names than that from The Double O's to the Gods-Unlimited Band, thanks to their parade of get-ups and choreography. Each of them dressed as different Gods depending on the tour. There was among many, the Zeus Tour, The Thor Tour, The Shiva Tour, The Shinto Tour and the deliberately provocative Jesus Tour - which attracted a lot of angry Evangelicals and required triple the security in certain southern cities.

With all that, in addition to their mannequin-like stances, their jerky, spastic moves (their attempts to act like ancient statues of Gods slowly coming to life) - they were called The Automatons, The Mannequin Men and even The Rustbelt Tin Men of Rock. And because Randy's and Jeffy's sisters were so butch in their own ways, many didn't even realize "Larry" and "Joey" were actually Larissa and Josephine - as the Rolling Stone Rock N' Roll Encyclopedia bore written testimony to. And that was fine with them.

In the early days it was just Randy and Jeffy. Not because they didn't have other band members. But because they didn't have band members they considered up to their standards.

"I want Billy out of the Band."

"Why Jeffy?"

"You mean aside from his shitty playing? I beat off better than he plays guitar." Jeffy paced the Root's basement floor, his bell-bottom blue jeans slapping each other at the ankles, just above his purple platform shoes.

Randy raised an eyebrow, watching Jeffy pace as he sat back in his dad's old Barcalounger, faintly smiling. "I'll take your word on that one. But you're right. He's not that technically tight. But that's what you said about Carl, Jeffy, and that's what you said about Ted before him and Scott before him. We go through musicians the way our moms hope we go through underwear."

"Hey Man, I can't help it if you and I have more talent than all these other gene pools combined. We need players we can trust. Players more like us. Fuck, I'd rather have my sister Josephine in the Band than any of those lowly peons. Joey listens to what she's told and can play more than three chords."

10

A smile grew on Randy's face. Standing up, he tucked his paisley shirt into his red corduroy jeans and tightened his white macramé belt. "You know, JJ, that's really not a bad idea. My sister Larissa plays a mean guitar."

"Yeah...Mean's a good word for her." Jeffy replied smirking. "She's not too keen on listening-but so long as she doesn't beat the shit out of anyone, it could work... And women in Rock? That's revolution."

"Yeah...well...they're so butch, everyone will think they're guys anyway. They don't even like being called Larissa or Josephine - you know that. Forget all that. Larry listens to me. And better yet, she knows a drummer."

It took them a while to get to the name they became known for. They went through a shitload of crazy monikers before landing on The Orifice Of The Oracle. First they were the Somnambulists. Then they were the Sleepwalkers, but they soon learned another band already had that name. The Michigan Sleepwalkers sounded like a bad baseball team. So then, they were the Far Tones, until they realized everybody was calling them The Fart Tones. Then they were the Mute Ants. Then they were the Discharged Angels. Then they were The Falling Angels of Flint. And, for a very short time, they were The Pie Holes.

Then one day, after rehearsal in the Root basement, Joey turned on the portable round Panasonic 9" television they kept on one of the speakers. What appeared was this talking head of a local station manager droning on about dress codes in Genesee County high schools, which they were all products of. Larry, who was not only a tomboy-but an aggressive bully of a tomboy, snarled at the flickering black and white, static-scarred image of the old man and yelled, "YOU DON'T KNOW SHIT, YA OLD TELEVISED FUCK-FART!"

Jeffy laughed and added, "AND YET HE YAPS LIKE SOME FUCKING ORIFICE OF THE ORACLE!" Jeffy's eyes widened. He turned and looked at Randy who looked like a light bulb really hovered above his head. To punctuate that historic moment, Larry punched the TV so hard, it flew off the speaker and crashed to the concrete floor, spitting sparks and puffs of smoke, never to work again.

From then on, they were The Orifice Of The Oracle. And in the beginning, The Orifice Of The Oracle was desperate for work. Part time jobs at sandwich shops and t-shirt stores weren't cutting it. So they didn't practically lie to get gigs. They lied practically all the time to get gigs. They pretended to be whatever they needed to be: a Queen cover band, a Journey cover Band, an Air Supply cover band, a Kool & The Gang cover band, a gig they narrowly escaped from. They could usually fake their way through one or two songs they knew by ear and then they'd either charm the audience into listening to their music - or get thrown off the stage for the next act to follow. But pretending to be a Steppenwolf cover band required medical attention after their brief performance before a group of very unhappy bikers.

Holding ice to her swelled lower lip, Joey mumbled in the back of the speeding van right after they had narrowly escaped with their lives: "Well, this proves two dykes and three dorks are no match for a hundred Hells Angels. Just in case you were wondering."

Larry on the other hand, had totally enjoyed herself. She always gave worse than she got. "Coulda' been worse. I'm just glad no pigs showed up." She muttered.

"Then you're gonna love our next gig," Randy teased: "A Fleetwood Mac cover band at the Police Benevolent Association." Even with black eyes and bruises, they all laughed.

Soon after that, the local bars started to give them auditions. New clubs opened up. Detroit offered even more opportunities, only an hour away. Their goal was the clubs of Manhattan: Max's Kansas City, The Bottom Line, Hurrah and the prize: CBGB.

The Orifice Of The Oracle began to get more gigs and develop a dedicated local following. Soon after that, between the money saved up from those club dates and a loan from both sets of parents, Randy and Jeffy scraped enough together to produce the commercial and buy those late-night time slots for it to air on local New York City television.

That seemed like a million years ago to them by the time they enjoyed their next hit, which came from their second album, "Kiss This Orifice." The blockbuster

"Blow It Out" reached 11 on the charts. This was a defining moment that transcended the song itself, or even the album going platinum, because *Blow It Out* introduced their seminal look. The signature ensemble of a sparkling gold space suit complimented by a gold and purple conical crown sporting wings on its sides with a hole at the top is what they'd always be remembered for.

They called their hats *MegaHorns*. Critics called them *"Traffic Cones With Wings."*

Every time he heard that said by reporters or anyone else for that matter, Jeffy would rant almost involuntarily: "It's the fucking MegaHorn, you pathetic, sleepwalking mortals! THE FUCKING MEGAHORN!" Jeffy got more upset over that than Randy ever did.

They were more than just window-dressing, though. They were instruments. Randy and Jeffy used them as megaphones to shout out the chorus throughout the song. Then, at the very end, the entire band blew through them like Polynesians sounding conch shells at sunset or as journalists universally reported, "like Rabbi's with rams horns, signaling evening's prayer." It was one of those memorable Rock moments. And live, it drove the crowd crazy.

They personally thought it hilarious being compared to Rabbis with ram horns. None of them were Jewish. In fact, both Randy and Jeffy had their own separate obsessions with Hitler and Nazi regalia. For Jeffy, it was bad enough they were calling what he considered his and Randy's invention literally traffic cones with wings and in more vicious circles: *"dunce caps."*

Randy used the ridicule of the MegaHorn to hone his real talent, which was putting a spin on anything. Usually just for the fun of it. Like the time he explained part honestly and mostly not, exactly what the MegaHorn was all about:

"We call it the MegaHorn -patent pending- because we use them as megaphones to sing the chorus and then as horns at the end of *Blow It Out,* hence the name: *Mega-Horn*. It is actually based on a design for a power grid by the great scientist, Nicolai Tesla. It draws natural electric power out of the air and pours it directly into your brain. The wings on the side symbolize enlightenment and the way back from man's descent into mortality - through the teachings of The Orifice Of The Oracle."

As for the song itself, the lyrics were fairly straightforward:

*"Blow It Up/ Blow It Out/Clear The Air/Twist & Shout/Show Some Flair/Blow it Out!
On A Dare/Yell & Swear/Give A Scare/On A Tear/Not A Doubt/-Blow It Out!
Chorus:
Blow It Up/Blow It Out/Break It Down/Twist & Shout
Blow It Up/Break It Down/Twist & Shout/-----Blow It OUT!!!!"*

The Orifice of the Oracle's mystique continued to grow. The song was widely interpreted as promoting terrorism and blowing up buildings. Randy, in his own way had even more fun with that than he had with explaining the MegaHorn.

"These are facts." He explained straight-faced to reporters. "UFO's, what *you* call UFO's, are powered by methane gas specifically created by people. When the aliens came here and did probes on first cows and then us, they realized that the methane gas created by cows is not as potent as the gas created by us because of our inherent God-DNA. So all these alien visits and probes over the years have been to research and develop processing our gas as the fuel for their spacecraft. Soon the aliens will be back to enslave us and turn us all into one giant gas station. So we better realize our own God-powers, blow out all our petty differences, unite, and get ready to confront them before the Earth ends up looking like an Intergalactic Texaco."

Thanks to all the controversy, (the preferred fuel of rock n' roll) offers poured in. TV specials, TV Talk shows, movies, commercials and even corporate sponsorships. It was all there for the picking. For a time it looked like it would go on forever. But after their next album, the hits just didn't keep on coming. *Go To Hell For The BBQ* was eagerly anticipated until its release. All Rolling Stone wrote about it was "The Orifice Eats It."

By the fifth album, *Stimulate Your Godhead* everything started to dry up, just like the merchandise revenue had over the years until it basically just paid for itself, leaving what Joey quipped was "just enough quarters for the Laundromat."

Album sales dwindled. Concert promoters stopped calling. The public at large stopped listening. All their domestic equity was spent. They were getting zero radio airtime and everything started to wane.

Tours to Brazil, Japan and Australia, where they were still big news, became more than important. They became survival. Thanks to the monthly expenses all of them had racked up since moving to Los Angeles, it was life or death.

The reasons why haunted Jeffy. Randy really couldn't care less-though he would later try to. Their next to last cd, a hardcore fan fave long-forgotten indictment of Christianity: *Jesus, What's Your Hang Up?* was so ignored by the distributors as well as the disc jockeys, most copies of it were now collecting dust in Randy's many storage units. That was the fate of what Jeffy had desperately hoped would launch their comeback. What was sure to be their last album had been prophetically entitled *What's Ever Left*. Rolling Stone was even less kind than before: "The Orifice Of The Oracle: Enema Time For The 80s Art Band."

They were once as big as The Ramones, The Talking Heads, the B-52's or Devo. Some say The Orifice could have been much bigger than that, if it weren't for their own individual orifices. The Band was one thing. The band members were quite another. The reason for the Band's decline into passé oblivion was simple. The sum of the whole was greater than its parts. So from once literally a million fans, their audience shrank down to a die-hard and devoted one tenth of that, at best.

Now, decades past that, Jeffy was listening to Randy give him one word answers as if he were just another mere mortal like one of their geeky, lowly fans.

"No."

This was the only story Jeffy was getting from Randy nowadays:

"No."

It didn't start like that. Back in the day, he'd dazzle Jeffy Jabonno with tales of their unending fame and fortune to come.

"Jeffy, we're going to take over the media, from radio to television and revolutionize it all. You and I together can do it. With our vision, we'll usher in 3-D television and movies. -Radios with holograms. -Concerts with aerial platforms that we'll fly around the arena on like skateboards while playing our songs! The future is ours! Once we make it big, we'll move to L.A. and start our own anti-corporation-corporation! We'll make it like a commune for artists! And we'll make millions and millions doing it."

Jeffy's eyes would glaze over. He had dreamed of starting his own revolution since he was 14.

"It'll be just you and I as partners, Jabonno. *That* will never change. Let's make it a pact. We'll sign it in blood."

Jeffy still had that long-ago sanguine-signed oath, but he knew it wasn't worth the blood it was written in. Not anymore.

That had been over forty years ago, back in Flint, Michigan in the basement of Randy's parent's house. Now, in LA, in Hollywood, at the mouth of the Sunset Strip, Jeffy thought about that, looking at Randy look back at him blankly. He couldn't help but pace back and forth in front of him as he digested Randy's answer to him.

"No."

"No?"

"You heard me."

Nestled in his conical Horn O Plenty building on Sunset at the start of the Strip, right across from the famous Chateau Marmont where John Belushi shot his last 8-ball, Randy Root controlled the narrative, the Band and Jeffy Jabonno. Root was now the acting God in their relationship and Jeffy, the mere measly mortal.

The Horn O'Plenty was a conical marvel Root bought in early 1990. He had it painted gold with purple polka dots. It resembled a horn reaching into the sky in a twist of stucco and concrete that turned the head of anyone driving by. Randy loved to tell everyone that the three-story building was designed by Frank Lloyd

Wright to be the headquarters of a defunct record store chain in the 50s, claiming it was homage to the Victrola phonograph horn. And because the cone reminded people of the Guggenheim Museum that Lloyd designed, people believed him.

In truth, the building's real architect was Charles Luckman, who designed the "Horn" in 1968 for a Dr. Abe Rattrop. Rattrop was known as "the Vet to the Stars" back then. He made a fortune bilking millionaire pet owners in the Hollywood Hills by worming their pets whether they needed it or not and selling them what in the trade is known as Elizabethan collars: cones for their dogs to prevent the animal from licking their wounds, especially their behinds. So the good doctor had Luckman, the same architect who designed the famed Los Angeles Forum, build a veterinarian office in the shape of what had made him his fortune. To his friends and family Luckman laughingly referred to his creation as the building that "dog's assholes built."

After the Doctor hung up his worming gloves, the building passed through several hands, housing a florist and an avant-garde furniture store. When Root bought it, it had been vacant for two years. It had been on his radar since the Band had moved to Los Angeles from Flint permanently, right after *Blow It Out* became a hit. It had caught his eye for obvious reasons.

Now, after all the albums and all the concerts and TV appearances, it had unraveled into revivals, county fairs, several private corporate parties and once, even a bar mitzvah. It was all old hat - literally. For Jeffy, The Orifice Of The Oracle performing live was his only real way to make decent money anymore. He'd blown every other opportunity he'd had. And he'd had plenty.

Thanks to Horn O Plenty, Randy didn't need the Band. He also now hated wearing the spacesuit and donning the MegaHorn - as much as he'd forever use both whenever possible to get more jobs composing music for TV shows and films, or, more accurately - getting lackeys to compose the music and then putting his name on it.

Joey Jabonno would laugh, telling friends about how Randy's eyes glazed over the first time a fellow ex-rocker turned-composer told him he could legally pay someone else to compose the music and then put his name on it. Yes, he could claim he directed where the composition went. But that was only true in the sense of approving what the composer he had hired did and whether he considered it "worthy" of him putting his name on it. He was a master manipulator who had the gift of looking innocent while exploiting those around him. People so admired him for his early work that they overlooked this - until they were the people he was doing it to.

By the time The Orifice was no longer getting bookings or airplay or really anything like they used to, Randy had already networked his way through Hollywood and landed several composing jobs for a variety of Saturday morning kid shows and commercials. His first job was for a cartoon called *Hercules, God Of Strength & Heroes*. From then on, it was kid-shows from pre-K cartoons up to high school juvenile comedies and dramas. He began doing these projects at his house up in the Hollywood Hills, where he already had a private recording studio.

As for the Horn, the moment escrow closed, he remodeled the interior, put in recording studios and started a music production company he named Horn O Plenty. He promised the rest of the Band that this was their new headquarters as they transitioned to the times. He told the same thing to several magazines that published photos taken of the Band standing in front of the V-shaped building. It was there during that interview and photo session Root first told his fairy tale about Frank Lloyd Wright designing the building.Of course Root always told the better story whether it was true or not. He told that story so much it turned up on other websites as fact and even as the cover story for an issue of LA Architecture. People literally gobbled up Randy's bullshit like Christmas pudding and then begged him for seconds.

Jeffy's days of dining at Randy's bullshit banquet table were long over. He shook his head as he kept pacing behind Randy, who sat at his computer perched on top of his soundboard, now pretending to work. Jeffy angrily chewed on Randy's "No." It left a bitter taste in his mouth.

"I've got too much to do here to be putting on that monkey suit and hopping around a stage singing the same old set of tired old songs we've sung for the last forty years." Randy tucked his blue polo shirt into his grey khakis for emphasis.

Jeffy cringed at hearing that. He straightened the lapels of his self-designed, single-breasted two-toned green silk suit that reminded people of a comic book super-villain.

"Well" he replied. "You don't seem to mind it when it helps get you one of your teenage romance movies or kiddy cartoons."

Root shot Jabonno a dirty look as Jason Barter, Root's latest associate-composer/arranger, came into Studio Zero, the main and circular studio at the Horn. Barter was 6'1' but his hunched shoulders and stooped posture made him appear smaller than he really was and quite unsure of himself.

"Ok," Root said, ignoring Jabonno and turning his attention to Barter.

"Randy, can we talk about that increase you promised me six months ago?" Barter pleaded with his eyes, trying to keep any hint of whine out of his voice.

Root glared at Barter, pointing with his eyes at Jeffy. "Later, when we can talk in private. Now listen carefully. This is the theme I want for "My Teeny Bopper Baby Daddy..."

Root then whistled the old Popeye the Sailor song. Barter's eyes widened. "Now, go compose the main theme twisting it out from that. Come back by tomorrow with a three minute track cue of it for me to review." Slightly bowing Barter nodded and practically shuffled out of the room backwards.

"Now-" Root, said, not even looking at his old partner, his eyes glued to a computer screen filled with antique pornography from the 19th century. "As you can see, I'm composing.

"A tour opening for KISS for three shows at a hundred thou' -each- and you're too busy??" Jeffy clenched his hands into fists. Then he took a deep breath. "Tell you what. How about we do one show? That shouldn't interrupt your "composing" that much."

"No."

Jeffy continued angrily pacing until he suddenly stopped and looked down at his shoes. "Dammit! I just stepped in yet another mound of your dog's *art* that's all over the fucking floor! Do you have any idea how much a new pair of Amedeo Testoni's from Italy cost?"

Nipper, Randy's four-year-old Whippet was laying at his feet. It looked up at Jeffy indifferently. Randy always brought the dog with him to the studio. He named Nipper for the dog on the RCA Victor label. In Jeffy's mind, the mutt was literally sneering at him.

Randy, as always, looked innocently at Jeffy. "Hey, I thought it'd remind you of Hilly's dog at CBGB. Remember? You couldn't take a step anywhere without sliding in that mutt's fudge-mountain? Kinda like a nostalgic slip down memory lane, huh?" Randy giggled and turned back to his computer screen.

"All it reminds me of is how Hilly's crazy wife was always ripping us off and how it seems that someone, somewhere, somehow is *still* ripping *me* off, one way or another."

Jabonno looked at Root's back for a second and then walked out in frustration. Root didn't even turn around. "Now I know where he gets his ideas for his sculptures." Jeffy said to himself.

Randy had been sculpting with clay since his art school days. While he did small caricature busts of people in a *Robert Crumb meets Big Daddy RatFink Roth* sort of way, for the most part, he was totally obsessed with making endless renditions of clay vaginas about the size of postcards that he displayed around the Horn. "They're like snowflakes!" Randy would joke. "Not one of them is alike!"

Walking by Barter's small studio, Jeffy could see Randy's mentally indentured slave forlornly stare into space, whistling the old Popeye tune. Jabonno shook his head. Jeffy was more hip to Root's business model than anyone. He'd witnessed it in practice (and approved it when it benefited him) for years: #1: Lowball everyone. #2: Make it a privilege to work for you at low wages with zero-benefits by insisting everyone be independent contractors. #3: Work them like full-time employees.

And finally #4: If they try to increase their compensation in any way, publicly declare they're stealing from you to justify your complete exploitation - and firing of them.

Randy paid typically half of what was the industry standard for 99% of his workers, with the elaborately expressed promise to increase their wages for good results. But he rarely did, except for Tina Drekk, his second wife.

Walking down the Lucite staircase as each step lit up in reverse prismatic order from violet to blue to green to yellow to orange to red, Jeffy eyed all the old supermarket kiddy rides from the Pony Express to the Formula One Race Car, the Skee-ball machines and all the other carnival accouterments Randy had all over the Welcome Lobby for clients to marvel at and play with.   It reminded him how much he hated his childhood.   Pushing through the revolving doors and leaving the Horn, Jeffy was so frustrated he seriously thought about getting into his Alpha Romero and driving directly to TMZ and then calling Rolling Stone, The Hollywood Reporter, Variety, The National Enquirer and anyone else who would listen about Randy Root and tell them everything. EVERYTHING. -Especially with what was happening in the news.

"That would be the end of Randy Root!"

But by the time he got in and turned over the engine, he sighed. The once brave revolutionary was now afraid of being sued for libel and slander.

"How can the truth be libel and slander?" He asked himself out loud. "When the asshole you're exposing has a five-star attorney on retainer at a million bucks a year. That's *How*." He answered himself, hitting the steering wheel as he put the car into gear and drove off cursing Root.

Driving up Sunset before heading back to his home in Venice, Jabonno decided to call his favorite dining establishment. It was the most exclusive eatery on Pacific Coast Highway between LA and Santa Barbara.

"Le Beau Dilettante, good afternoon. How may I help you?"

"Yeah, I want a reservation for two at eight tonight at that little corner table-"

"I'm sorry Sir, but we're all booked up."

"What do you mean, you're all booked up? This Is *Jeffy Jabonno*. There is no 'all booked up' when it comes to Jeffy Jabonno. Just add another table for me."

"I'm sorry Mr. Jabonno, we don't do that. And again, we're all booked up."

"I don't give a fuck if you're all booked up! Don't you know who I am??"

"Aside from telling me your name, it wouldn't matter if I really did anyway, Sir. We're still all booked up for tonight. Now, if you'd like to make a-"

Jeffy hung up as he suddenly swerved to avoid hitting the car next to him. "MOTHERFUCKER!" He screamed, hitting the steering wheel. He was still thinking of Randy.

CHAPTER 2

"IT'S THE 1984 CBS HALLOWEEN SPECIAL!
STARRING THE ORIFICE OF THE ORACLE!
SPONSORED BY IDA-OR POTATOES: THE NO-OTHER-FROZEN CHOICE!"

Dexter Dille III opened with a wide shot of the Band using camera one. The Orifice of the Oracle were all standing on separate plexiglass platforms covered by billowing clouds of dry ice so they appeared to float between three and four feet in the air. Each platform was timed to slowly shift up and down creating a wave affect as they played their instruments.

Dille cut to camera two to show Randy dressed as Zeus, playing a lightning bolt shaped electric accordion. Then he cut to camera three on Jeffy as Ra all decked out in silk robes and a pharaoh's bejeweled head crown playing a sphinx-shaped bass. Camera four was on Larry as Mars all in classic rose-gold Roman battledress on lead guitar playing what looked more like a bazooka than a Fender Stratocaster. Camera five covered Joey as Shiva showing both her shoulders adorned with two motorized mannequin arms swaying above her own two appendages as she rocked a rhythm guitar resembling a Vedic battle axe. Camera six was all over

Skippy Watts as Poseidon, banging on giant clam shell-shaped drums with trident-like sticks.

This was all in front of a sky blue seamless matte. Symbols from every civilization known to man were strewn around the stage just below their hovering presence. Jugglers and acrobats dressed in different period costumes danced, flipped and cartwheeled beneath the Band like fevered acolytes running in between Roman columns, Greek arches, Egyptian pyramids, Easter Island sculptures and much more.

They were playing *Trick Question Or Shock Treatment!* A Root/Jabonno song they had written just for the Special. It had a menacing creepy-cool mock-scary melody with a beat intended to get viewers into the Halloween spirit. It was working. The audience was whipped up into a shriek fest. The sound was pumping out of throbbing giant pumpkin-shaped speakers at deafening decibels. The whole look of the show had a time traveling circus quality to it. The cameras were all over the set getting great close-ups, full shots and every choice angle.

Dille puckered his lips like he was kissing his boyfriend. It's what he did by reflex when he was happy. Everything was working perfectly. Everyone was having a fun time.

And then:

"Stop! Stop Everything now!"

Dille's puckered mouth dropped open. Jeffy stopped playing bass in mid-beat turning Randy's accordion chords sideways which slammed into Larry's guitar riff which smashed into Joey's rhythm which left Skippy in a long snare roll thinking this was his solo, until he realized it wasn't and stopped with a cymbal crash. The gruesome aftermath of dead air silence followed. The jugglers, acrobats and dancers froze for a second and then ran offstage right to their dressing rooms and stayed there. The only thing heard was the humming of the platforms still rising and lowering and rising and lowering. And Jeffy.

"This is not how it's supposed to go!" Jeffy howled, looking right up at the director's booth. Randy looked meekly at Larry. Larry glared at Jeffy. Joey was shaking her head, her extra arms shrugging. Skippy had the same puzzled "*Where am I?*" look on his face he usually wore.

At first, the studio audience thought this staged. They laughed and applauded until Jeffy started screaming. "It's not funny, you measly mortals! Besides the rhythm and melody being off, I can see the camera work is all over the place! What is wrong with you up there??" Jeffy pointed to the director's booth. "Yes, *YOU* up there!"

Dille shook his head with raised eyebrows as Jabonno went on. "What happened to the directions I specifically gave *YOU*??"

"I'll never forgive them for this." Dille muttered under his breath. He didn't just blame Jabonno. He considered them all snide jerks. All week in rehearsals they had acted liked he worked for them, talked behind his back and made fun of him. They ridiculed everything about him. Not just the way he directed. They got personal. His goatee. His height. His dressing in polyester suits with bright colored ascots and sockless loafers. His Oxford educated accent. His posture.   How   he walked.   Even the cologne he wore.   -Dior Eau Sauvage Extreme, or, "*Swish-Lube,*" as he overheard Randy murmur a bit too loud to Jeffy the first day of rehearsal.

This disaster was just final proof to him of how they were all to blame. And now they had signed their own suicide note as far as the Network would be concerned. In fact, Dexter Dille III was certain no other network would ever take a chance on them after this.

"Cut to commercials, now!" Dille barked.   Immediately the phone rang.   Dille picked it up and just listened without saying a word. Instead he just nodded his head. "I understand. I'll inform everyone immediately."

While Jeffy ranted on about the whereabouts of the dancers, the Network execs informed Dille that the show's live feed had been cut and switched to a repeat of last year's "A Very Merry Monster Mash Halloween Special" which came on the air after the commercial break following a sign reading "*Sorry! Our program has been preempted by technical difficulties!*"

Dille wasted no time turning on the house lights and flipping on his microphone informing everyone onstage and in the audience that the show was over.

"What?!" Screamed Jeffy. He jumped off his platform onto the stage disappearing into the dry ice mist. He popped up, his Pharaoh's crown teetering over the left side of his head. "We haven't even done *Roasting Weenies On The Burning Bush*, yet! WE HAVE A CONTRACT!"

Jeffy woke up in a cold sweat. His 40 years younger wife mumbled "Wedding Photos..." rolled over and continued sleeping.

Not far from Jeffy's Venice Beach home up in a part of the Hollywood Hills known as Mount Olympus, Randy Root laid in bed tossing and turning without sleeping at all.For once, he was happy he and Tina slept in separate rooms. Randy pulled out an old photo. He stared at it longingly. Then he put it back where he'd gotten it from and sighed.

He didn't regret a thing. It was ridiculous to be ashamed or feel guilty - especially for someone of his status. -Guilty for what? There were Popes who probably did worse. In antiquity it was considered natural. In some cultures it still was. -But not in his. Fucking Philistines, he thought. And because of the nature of his work, he would really be in a world of shit if it were ever found out. And still it was all he thought about. He missed it. He dreamed about it more than his recurring dream of being in a sea of puffed wheat and swimming to a glistening pink oyster shell holding a golden pearl.

"Boy, would Freud have fun with that one." He laughed to himself. Then he frowned.

Lately, he'd been having the other dream. It had been a while, but it always came back: He's sitting in a production office with Roman Polanski. Polanski offers him some blow and then begins talking to him about scoring a movie he's shooting, which is the story of why he had to flee the United States. Then, so Randy can really get the feeling, Polanski offers to demonstrate. That's when he'd always wake up.

Ever since the Weinstein Scandal and the *#Me Too Movement*, let alone the whole Epstein thing, he hadn't been able to sleep through the night. He found himself looking over his shoulder a lot more than he used to. And not just because of hearing loss in his left ear.

He unlocked a bottom drawer, pulled it out and looked into it for a moment. -The Travelers checks. -The passport with another name and his photo on it. -The throwaway phone. Everything was there. Just in case. It was his emergency kit. He closed the drawer back with a quick shove and relocked it. He'd probably never have the balls to use it. But it made him feel better to have it.

Lately, when he thought of all the things he'd done, no one was more surprised than him that he had gotten away with it. -So far. He seemed invulnerable. Or invisible. He didn't feel like a superman. He felt like a soft, pudgy hamster who knew how to look harmless.

He was a master at looking innocent. He always had been. He saw Innocence as a form of invisibility. After the legions of stars and star-makers caught, exposed and destroyed, he remained unscathed, unsullied, silent, safe, and smiling sweetly. Randy stoically reasoned, that that's just the way it was meant to be.

"Some people are just lucky and I just happen to be one of them. And I can't say I don't deserve it."

After all the drugs and all the wild sex and all the crazy out-of-his-mind parties there on Mt. Olympus rivaling anything done in the 1920s at Fatty Arbuckle's house, *nothing*. No repercussions. No recriminations. After all the excesses and abuses and all his mistakes, he was suspected of *nothing*. Mistakes sounded so much better than crimes. It did beg that question that needled him as much as his gnawing hunger chewed on him.

"Can I still get away with it? There must be more like me in this town that don't get caught. That never got caught." After all, what he'd done used to be the right of tribal chiefs and ancient kings, even feudal lords. "So what harm was really done?" He said out loud to himself. "All it cost was a house n' cash. Hey, you got off cheap. Ha. Got off, cheap." He laughed at his double entendre. "Good one."

He took a good look at himself in the mirrored doors to his walk-in closet. By this time, Randy had aged from the fresh faced young "up and comer" of the 1970s to resemble Joe Flynn, a long-forgotten 1960s TV star in a sit-com called McHale's Navy, he looked the part down to the thick black Clark Kent glasses with short clipped more gray than blonde hair. And, like Pete Townsend of The Who, he'd lost the hearing in his left ear from all those years of playing in front of deafening five and six-foot speakers. Still, he wasn't always looking over his shoulder because of his hearing loss. But it was an effective cover for his justifiable paranoia.

He shook his head with a grim look fixed on his face thinking about expenses and how Tina was always finding ways to increase them. "She just had to have her anchor babies. Not for love. -For leverage. -Too selfish to have her own. She'd rather buy them. Like her talons weren't into me deep enough already."

He would bitch about it to himself, but Randy always gave Tina Drekk whatever she demanded and always would. Just like the $250,000.00 sexual harassment suit she had brought against him and won while he was still married to Lacie. Just like there not being any prenuptial agreements to protect his assets after divorcing Lacie and marrying Tina. Just like all the money he threw away on Tina's vanity projects she called *companies*. For years, he paid out large sums of cash for her to have her own offices until in the last few years as money got tighter he had her move into the Horn's third floor. From her nest up there, she chased away anyone she sensed threatened her influence on him with a smile on her collagen-plump lips and a deadly look in her cobra-like eyes.

It didn't matter that they rarely fucked anymore. She still maintained a vice-like grip on him. He still loved to hide behind her coy overbearing and aggressive presence and subtle venomous viciousness made even more viperous by a mesmerizing blonde countenance, strong sharp jawline and an even sharper, more cunning intellect. It worked with Randy's own desire not to confront people directly. He'd much rather have someone else do his dirty work for him. Tina was perfect.

Tina had started working at the Horn O Plenty as a music supervisor in the mid-90s. Christina Andrea Drekk, who professionally went by the name C.A. Drekk was called Tina by people who knew her personally but didn't really qualify as friends.

Her personal creed and business model simply came down to: *"I'd rather be paid than be right."* She lived by those words. And they worked well for her. So not so surprisingly, she'd be accused of stealing jobs, positions, clients and even husbands in her illustrious career as an entertainment manager. Before long, she was giving Randy Root blowjobs and whatever else he wanted in the bathroom up on the Horn's third floor.

"Boy, was *that* a long time ago..." He murmured.

His first wife, Lacie St. Louis had met Randy as a super-groupie in the early 80s. Lacie was known around LA rock circles as *The Original Punk Pocket Rocket.* She was a doe-eyed 5'2" dark-haired prince valiant cut ball of energy prone to dress in tight plaid miniskirts, bright t-shirts, fluorescent knee-high socks and Dr. Martens work boots - a standard for many punkers of the day. The moment she met Randy at a Madam Wu after-party, she had taken him aside and hiked up her skirt showing him she wasn't wearing any panties. She then sang a song she had written about herself in intimate detail.

The combination was too much for Randy and they were married one month later in a ceremony in Malibu at a beachside villa then owned by Vestal Records owner Dick Grahamstone. It was at the height of the Oracle's success. Randy and Lacie started off happy with great promise. As time went on and Lacie's acting career went nowhere despite Randy's support, they settled into an affectionate but exhausted routine that had less and less passion fueling it.

So when Lacie realized Randy was playing with Drekk, almost by involuntary reflex, she demanded Randy fire her immediately. And Randy obediently fired Tina. Tina then hit Randy with her sexual harassment suit the next day like she'd been waiting to be fired. The interesting part was, after Randy settled, willing to pay whatever he had to, Tina didn't go away as Lacie expected. Instead, she began showing up at the Horn O Plenty entrance, knocking, banging on the locked revolving door, yelling, screaming and crying Randy's name, ringing the intercom buzzer over and over with repeated proclamations of love and destiny, demanding to be let in.

After close to two weeks of that, Randy let her in. The blowjobs resumed and Lacie filed for divorce. Randy bought another house on Mt. Olympus and Tina moved in with him. Subscription magazines like *Newlywed Monthly* began showing up at the Horn, soon after. The moment his divorce with Lacie was final, Tina began making wedding plans and Randy quietly went along. They were married in Kansas City, where she grew up, the daughter of a mobster who had made a fortune in fertilizer and her Dallas Cheerleader mother. After the wedding they honeymooned in Tahiti, turning their five-star ocean hut into a tropical version of the Horn's third floor bathroom. They never had as much sex again.

Now they had separate bedrooms. They often only saw each other at work or dealing with the kids. He took care of Nipper. Tina was basically addicted to Botox and spent more alone time with her dermatologist than she did with Randy. And every time Randy tried anything with her anymore, she'd shut him down, saying she was feeling symptoms of the MS she'd been claiming she had for years.

"Funny how that seems to come out only when I come on to her. Yeah," he mused wistfully, thinking about that bathroom on the third floor of the Horn, "that *was* a very long time ago."

The next day at the Horn, Randy was having a conversation with Larry about developing a theme song for a sequel being developed for *Head Lice,* the long running animated series that had made Randy a fortune. This kid-comedy had grown so popular with children and parents there had already been two follow-up feature films, so far. The sequel series the KIDZ Network was developing followed the same cartoon characters as young teens.

"Listen, Larry, I'm giving you *Toe Jam*, just like I handed *Head Lice* over to you. And I expect stuff at a quality level that represents me. Us. This stuff you just played for me doesn't do that. It makes my dick shrivel. So, please, go back to the drawing board and bring me several options for show themes in a couple of days. I'll review your tracks, pick one and we'll share the thing fifty/fifty."

Larry was staring at the floor. She glanced up at Randy and grunted, "How were you able to tell your dick shriveled?" nodded and walked out. Randy looked after

---

30

her with a mixture of resentment and resignation. Jeffy brushed by Larry who grunted acknowledgement to him as he walked past the framed gold and platinum singles and LP's adorning Horn O Plenty's second floor hallway. Those aging accomplishments shared the walls with movie-posters, revolving magazine racks holding small art books, postcards and greeting cards. He sidestepped an assortment of chairs looking like giant Venus fly traps and two antique sculpted naked wooden women coffee tables from the 1920s, their spread arms and legs supporting the glass top while revealing all below.

Jeffy walked into the main studio carefully, looking all around. "Where's Nipper? Bring him today?"

"At the vet. He's got worms. What's up? I got a new kids show to review." Randy briefly smiled and half-turned his back.

"We got a new tour offer."

"What's it this time, opening for The Archies?"

"Ha-Ha. Thought cartoons were your specialty. Was a time you would have jumped on that. No, this is something a little more serious: *The Titans Of Yore-Time Twist Tour.* Eight cities: Miami, Atlanta, New York, Chicago, Seattle, San Francisco, San Diego and here, Los Angeles. -A Mil' for this, Randy. -A *Mil'*. I already talked to RoyBob Fratello about tour managing. He's available. C'mon. We haven't appeared in over five years since Japan. And things have been tight. I need this."

"When is this? What are we talking about? I can't be out of the Horn for more than a week. See if you can cut it down to six cities and I'll ask Tina what she thinks."

"Tina? According to you, Tina turned down tours with Aerosmith, the Smashing Pumpkins, Jane's Addiction, and more. How about The Palooka Bazooka Tour? What about The Wham Bam Thank You Ma'am Tour? Can't you tell me what *you* think?"

"All those were my decisions!" Randy snapped but quickly recovered. "None of that shit worked with my schedule. What was I supposed to do? I had two feature films and a new TV show to score. I wasn't just sitting around waiting for tour offers! Tell you what, make it four cities and maybe I'll do it."

Jeffy turned purple and started to shake. "Even if they agree to that we're talking half the fee. And I need that money, Randy. Things are tighter all the time. Even *Flip It Off* isn't getting used in commercials like it used to."

At one time that one song could be counted on for a minimum of a million in licensing fees per year for years in a variety of national ads. -Everything from pancake mix to cigarette lighters. But as time went on the generation of copywriters and art directors that knew and loved that song were getting old and being replaced by young advertising creatives with very different ideas and taste in music.

"Let me discuss it with Tina."

"What if I told you Dille was looking for a new composer and he'll be shooting this thing as a documentary?"

Dex Dille or "3-D" as he now called himself had become one of the most celebrated directors in Town. The Oscars had just happened and his film *The First Shogun* had won in every category, including best original film score, written by Derek Scorch of the Rhode Island Band, The Lip Readers. And for an obvious reason, Randy had always felt a competitive twinge towards Scorch. Going all the way back to their CBGB days. Especially since Scorch was continuously achieving Randy's goals while Randy was stuck doing kid TV shows and movies. And Scorch being considerably taller than Randy added to it, not that he'd admit that.

For several years, Randy had been the "go-to" music composer for Easton Amberson, a spindly, quietly nervous director of note with films deemed quirky classics like *Sock Puppets, The Common Evergreens*, and *Everest* - for which Randy received serious praise as a "Master of the Eccentric." But when Easton walked in on him at a spotting session where music cues must be placed in the right spot (hence the name), there was Randy playing with clay for his prolific *Snowflake* project, while Joey who had been his engineer and studio manager at the Horn since Randy bought the building, was the one actually directing the session. From the first moment the director had crept silently into the room, watching behind them, Randy didn't look up at the screen once or pay any attention to anything but the clay in his hands.

Root instantly went from being Amberson's *Go-To Composer* to Amberson's *Gone-From-Composer.* So any chance he had of breaking out of his kiddie show-pigeon hole more than interested him. But he half-dismissed Jeffy with a crisp wave of his hand.

"He's hated us for years, Jeffy, what's the point. He's the head of the Gay Mafia here in Town. Anyone whoever made a gay joke is on his black list."

"I read he was impressed with your film work with Amberson. He actually called it 'gifted scoring.' "

"Really? Where'd you read that?"

"Shoot Magazine. -Last month's issue. You didn't hear about that?"

"Hmmm.... No...I hadn't.... You know, eight dates isn't completely out of bounds now that I think about it more. But remember, I got a company to run."

"Oh I remember. I remember when you told us it was going to be *Our* Company. All that fuss you made for the press about *Our* Company. You promised us Horn O Plenty was for the Oracle. But it's so fuckin' the other way around, man."

"What's the damn difference, Jeff?"

"Your word, Randy. That's the difference. You promised us a piece of the Horn."

"You could have bought in at any time."

"Bought in at any time. Are you fucking kidding me? That's bullshit. You tell me this *now*?"

"I had to tell you?"

"Yes, Randy. You did. Then. Not now. We were all waiting for you to tell us our pay-in and you never did."

"That's not how I remember it."

"Yeah. That's the thing I've noticed. -Your memory. The Orifice Of The Oracle Incorporated, remember that?"

"Alright, well let's say we do this. We'll need a drummer. Who you got in mind?"

"Wish we had Skippy. He was one of a kind, alright..."

"The Immaculate Percussionist."

"I remember when you came up with that." Jeffy laughed. "And then dressing him up as Jesus Christ during that Easter Tour? Man, that was fun, for what it lasted, thanks to Larry smashing that irate fan's hand to hamburger with her Doc Martens when that Christian clown tried to take the stage. What'd Larry's stomping fest cost the Band that day? Oh yeah. -One point five million."

Randy laughed, shaking his head. "That *was* freaky. What I remember is Skippy, covered in tomatoes, eggs and what looked like actual shit dripping off his nose and he kept drumming even after the cops dragged Larry off the stage."

Jeffy stared into space, remembering another moment. "Skippy always kept drumming. He was a trooper."

"Yeah, even when you shut him down that time for trying to say something on his own on the Shecky Green Show. Heh, he took most things in stride. Even that."

"We all had agreed *I* was the Band spokesman." Jeffy whispered defensively.

Skippy Watts was sadly long-time solid gold rock n' roll gone for a multitude of reasons.

"I miss him, too. Hey, that reminds me. You hear about Dick Grahamstone from Vestal is starting an airship cruise line? Fucker is bringing back Zeppelins. Supposedly safe, modern super-Hindenburgs with theatres, restaurants, shops and swimming pools, man. Cruise ships in the sky. Hey, that guy always did have wacky ideas. Like that time he tried to match up Billy Bumhole of the Love Muscles with us. You weren't there as I recall. He had this super weed that got me and the other three higher than we ever got on old Michigan Mitten dirt weed. I mean, we were really fucked up. So when Grahamstone suggested the matchup out of the blue and Skippy asked, "Who's Billy Bumhole?" We couldn't stop laughing. Hysterically. And the best part is Bumhole was in the next room waiting to be introduced! Ha! By the way, where were you then, doing some interviews for MTV?"

"No Randy, I was there, too."

"Huh. I don't remember it that way. I thought you were somewhere else. Anyway, let's get Luke Wharm, if he isn't on tour with the Pagans. He's the closest to Skip of any of the drummers we use. And call Fratello, oh yeah, you already did that. Good."

Jeffy decided he had to get out of there. "Ok, he managed to say evenly, "I'm going to get all the details on the tour. I'll tell our chief geek fan Milkner to do his thing, get the merchandise in order, our props. I'll call Wharm. Just remember saying yes to this gives you a shot at Dille."

"Good idea. Get Shaggy on it."

Peter "Shaggy" Milkner was the greatest Oracle fan in the world. He was more accurately the band's chief archivist. He had collected and saved every bit of historical memorabilia for the Band since the early days. Several local papers where he lived in Georgia had done stories on him being *the* quintessential Oracle Fan. But his subservient adoration of the Band and appearance and wide-eyed kid-like behavior earned him the Scooby Doo nickname. It made him more of a gofer both Randy and Jeffy completely took for granted.

Jeffy left the Studio. Randy followed him out. That part of the hallway leading to the kitchen featured multiple shelves displaying Randy's ever-expanding array of ceramic vaginas in a variety of colors and swirls, again all the size of a postcard.

But instead of going into his snowflake analogy for the work, if anyone, especially a female visitor to the Horn asked Randy what the sculptures were he'd simply reply and sweetly smiling as if it were obvious, "Why, *rosebuds*, of course."

As the two of them walked past the kitchen and went by the dining room, Jeffy saw Joey having lunch. She had just finished some recording sessions for Head Lice. Jeffy nodded at her. She nodded back and then rolled her eyes, glancing at Randy. The big screen TV was on and tuned to a news channel:

"Today in New York Superior Court, Harvey Weinstein was indicted for-"

"TURN THAT SHIT OFF!!" Root yelled louder than he meant to. Joey just ignored him and continued to eat her lunch. Funny thing was when anyone brought up those subjects, which was being talked about everywhere in Hollywood, Randy would just mirror the mock-shock and disgust of whoever was expressing it, as if anyone in Hollywood didn't know what was going on. He would blink innocently, never letting it show how it actually scared the holy shit out of him.

Jeffy knew this. He smirked to himself but didn't look behind as he continued down the flashing-in-sequence rainbow Lucite stairs past the kiddie rides and circus mirrors and all the carny crap that symbolized Randy to him. Jeffy gave the door a shove and walked out. Every time Jabonno left the Horn O Plenty he told himself he had never been more pissed till that moment and now was no exception. By the time he got into his Alpha Romeo he was already on the phone with Shaggy Peter Milkner.

"Wow, Jeffy! That's so cool! One month from now, huh? This is the first tour since Japan '14! What a tour that was. Remember when they lost your guitars on the way back?"

"How could I forget?"

They had just gotten back from a 14-hour flight from Tokyo. Everyone was standing around Baggage Claim #23 getting their luggage. -Everyone but Jeffy. Suddenly his cell phone rang.

36

"Hello Mister Bono? This is Trans-Asia Airlines Lost & Found."

"Lost and Found? And the name is Ja-Bonno. Jeffrey Ja-Bonno. Where the Hell is my luggage? Where the fuck are my guitars??"

"We understand you demanded special treatment for your luggage and apparently the instructions you gave at Narita Airport were confusing and all your luggage was sent to Venice, Italy."

"Italy? Venice-Goddamn-Italy?? Why the fuck did you send it to Italy?? I clearly said Venice, *California*!"

"Apparently our Japanese colleagues were confused and that's how the mishap occurred."

"Mishap? You call this a mishap? This is a fucking disaster! Those are priceless guitars! My name is on the cases! They should have known from my name alone, it's Venice, California!"

"Know from your name alone? How would that be, sir?"

"Don't you know who I am?" "No, Mister Bono, I don't, Sir."

"JA-Bonno! Jeffy Jabonno of The legendary Orifice Of The Oracle! I'm immortal you tedious troll! You'll be forgotten. I'll be remembered forever! I'm a God and you're *nothing*. So get me my fucking guitars and don't you dare niggerize me! I have been niggerized enough through this fucked-up ordeal!"

The voice replied softly and measured. "Well, Mr. Bono, your luggage should be returned to you within the next five business days unless *you* as a God can get it back here faster than us mortals. Thank you for your patience." Then came the click.

Jeffy shook off the memory with a shrug. "Thanks for reminding me of the times I've been shit on, Peter. Remind me to return the favor. Just get all our props together. Get the merchandise in order, too. Let me know how we are on t-shirts and MegaHorns."

"You got it. Where you guys gonna rehearse? The Horn?"

"Probably. I'll let you know. We'll do two rehearsals. We'll make the second one the dress rehearsal. Now get to work on the merch'. I have other calls to make. Thanks, Shag." Then he hung up while Peter was still talking, telling him he could count on him to be in every city with them. Everything Peter did was at his own expense, never once compensated for his complete devotion. It never entered Jeffy's head nor Randy's to ever ask Peter if he needed any help.

"Now for Wharm..." Jeffy searched through his phone and found the journeyman drummer's number in his iPhone's contacts and called him.

Luke Wharm was a journeyman drummer mostly known for the neo-punk band The Pagans. When The Orifice Of The Oracle asked him to perform with them at the MoonSong Film Festival in '96, he was a polite and amicable 21 year old just grateful to be playing with "Legends" as he put it. Twenty years later, that kid was gone and in his place was a snide, arrogant elitist who now felt it was *their turn* to be grateful he would still perform with them. Those he was the most polite to when he first felt lucky to be with the Band now saw someone else entirely.

"Yeah, I'm available for that. You guys are lucky. Hey man, Sorry to hear about you losing that gig with that robot just because of some fucked-up wedding photos. What bullshit. Man, that would have been historic! Funny, but not funny, huh?"

Jeffy had been working on a project he was sure would gain him attention on his own, free of Randy and The Orifice Of The Oracle for once. Dr. Donald Hinton founder of Hinton Robotics had created a humanoid with a revolutionary level of AI, artificial intelligence, named Eve. Eve was already a celebrity. She had appeared on every late night talk show and more than held her own with the hosts, joking and chatting and even flirting.

Seeing this, Roy Robert Fratello who had managed the last few Oracle tours over the years, came up with the idea of the world's first duet between human and humanoid. A duet of the one classic Orifice song Jeffy sang lead on (Because as Randy claimed, Jeffy couldn't sing and play at the same time): It's A *WonderFool Life*. It turned out Hinton was a fan of the song and a deal was made for a video to be shot of this first of its kind duet. And it would have truly been historic. RoyBob, as the Band called him, had been an advertising TV producer before becoming a Tour Manager. His Brooklyn Italian dad taught him the finer points of bullshit and his Long Island Jewish mother taught him patience and a love of Chess.

But Jabonno's desire to make true music history was sabotaged by his politics. He claimed himself a Marxist-Leninist but acted out an insatiable lust for capital his whole life. So he took every opportunity to make political statements that appeased his monetary guilt.   Which didn't make him very different from most of his Hollywood contemporaries. Randy would nod to concur with Jeffy's spouting off and occasionally at press conferences add a few words.But he'd do it in such a meek way only Jeffy's stridency was noted.

Like virtually everyone in Hollywood at this time, Jeffy and Randy sported "compensational politics." The guilt that motivates rich people who make pretense for a living to support political policies that would ultimately destroy them, but they'd look good doing it, like post-modern Robespierres. So many in Hollywood claimed to be members of the proletariat and actively advocate socialism, until you took their table at Spago or worse - interfered with their money. Neither Jeffy nor Randy was an exception to this Hollywood rule.

And while Jeffy insisted he believed all the pretentious rhetoric he spewed, Randy didn't really believe in much of anything, except himself. He would tell you he did until you were blue in the face. But he really didn't. Here was a group of people all living in high security homes, often with bodyguards, always expecting to be given special, elitist preference. So calling for the most radical and destructive policies a free society should never suffer, pretty words that sound good but in reality produce the exact opposite results was just a matter of public relations for the early 21st century Tinsel Town crowd. Only those at the level of A-list legends could tell the Hollywood "Politically Correct" to stick their bullshit politics up their sanctimoniously phony asses.

So when Jeffy wedded Mindy Willow, a woman 40 years his junior, he came up with the idea of a wedding reception he vowed people would not soon forget. A vow he'd soon regret.

Parodying the assassination of JFK seemed fun when he thought it up. But by the time his bride was dressed exactly like Jackie on November 22nd, 1963 up to her pink pillbox hat, it wasn't. Jeffy dressed as JFK, had his best man dressed as Lee Harvey Oswald. A hired actor dressed as Fidel Castro gave the bride away. The wedding cake was a coconut with raspberry jelly bust of JFK's head -after the second bullet loafed it open. Raspberry jelly blood actually pumped slowly out of the cake head. The plates had autopsy photos of the 35th President, served with forks in the shape of the Carcano rifle Oswald was found with. The paparazzi had a field day. Poor Mindy looked at all the smirking photographers and did her best to smile. Her wedding photos would later show she looked deadpan.

Beginning by saying this all made the band, the Dead Kennedys look respectful by comparison, TMZ labeled it the worst taste in a wedding ceremony and reception *ever*. -Worthy of shaming in perpetuity.

Reading all about this online, Faye Fong, the marketing manager for Hinton Robotics raised her eyebrows practically off her forehead as she picked up her office phone and pushed a button.

"Cancel the Eve/Jabonno Project immediately."

Jeffy still couldn't understand why. He shook his head thinking about it as he made a left on Sunset out of the parking lot headed back to Venice.

Randy was looking out the dining room window, watching Jeffy drive off. He turned around and made his way to the third floor where Tina was sitting at her desk, talking on the phone. Without looking up, she said, "I'll call you back in a second." Then she cleared her throat. "I'm busy. I need to call Bela Marconi back. What do you want?"

"A tour is coming up."

"Another stupid tour?"

40

"No this one has decent money, is only eight shows *and* Dexter Dille is filming the tour for a documentary."

"I thought he hated you."

"That's more Jeffy than me. He recently complimented my film work with Easton."

"Hmmm...What's the money?"

"A million. But I care more about Dille. Scorch got an Oscar with him."

"Well. You're right...Dille... It's the least *The Ori-Feces of the Ora-Dull* can do for you at this point. Of course I'll come along to help." Tina stood up buttoning the top of her white silk blouse and then straightened the belt in her red pantsuit as she smiled, squinting at him.

"I wouldn't have it any other way, Tina." Randy muttered as he left, looking briefly at the bathroom door.

CHAPTER 3

"By the summer of 1973," the celebrity narrator began, "John Lennon and Yoko Ono's marriage was on the rocks. And, as a rather strange solution, Ono suggested that Lennon have an affair with their assistant, May Pang. That put Lennon directly on a collision course with his infamous "Lost Weekend," a legendary disaster capping a string of disasters throughout the eighteen months the legend lived with Pang in her New York apartment and a rented home in Los Angeles."

Mindy Jabonno sat curled up on the white Natuzzi Italia Positano leather couch in her gold silk pajamas, nibbling lightly on her plump lower lip. The remote control was nestled in her lap. Twirling a cherry-red bang absentmindedly with her right index finger, she stared intensely, her green eyes scanning every flickering image like she was searching for clues from the 72" flat screen HD TV. "Eighteen months...that's a year and a half." she said sadly to herself.

"Musically," the narrator continued, "it was a very productive period for the ex-Beatle. Lennon recorded three albums: *Mind Games, Walls and Bridges* and *Rock 'n' Roll* and also produced LPs for Ringo Starr and Harry Nilsson. There was even an impromptu jam session that would mark the very last time he ever recorded with Paul McCartney. Few remember that."

Jeffy had just gotten home from the Horn and pulled into the garage.

"What people remember is John Lennon's outrageous behavior fueled by an ocean of booze and a mountain of blow. Rolling Stone put it succinctly in its February fourteenth, 1974 issue: -John Lennon went to the Troubadour to hear Ann Peebles, and for the occasion he wore a Kotex on his head."

Jeffy was still thinking about the Tour as he got out of his car.

"And with eleven people in his party; Lennon didn't leave the waitress a tip."

Walking up the stairs from the garage, Jeffy heard a voice that sounded familiar.

"And in response to her scowl, John said, 'Don't you know who I am?' 'Yes,' the waitress said. 'You're some asshole with a Kotex on your head.' "

Mindy half-giggled. Then went back to biting her lip. "Is he tired of me already? Maybe." She was surprised to hear herself sound so certain.

"A memorable answer, isn't it? So-" The narrator's inflection teased with the tension of a pitcher's measured windup.

As Jeffy climbed the stairs getting closer to the living room, he recognized the voice.

"Consider this:" the narrator delivered his point like a screwball with teeth: "If that's what a true legend like John Lennon got for asking that question, just think of all the answers you'll get, *Jeffy - whether you have a Kotex on your head or not!*"

"What??" Jeffy couldn't believe what he heard. Did he really hear what he clearly heard? He stood frozen for a split-second before rushing into the living room startling Mindy. He looked intensely into the TV, still not sure that what he thought he'd heard was really what he had heard and then stopped right in front of her, turning around, blocking the screen. Flashing a look back at the TV once more, he turned facing Mindy. "What are you watching? What is this? Was that Kelsey

Grammer narrating?" And then more to himself, "Did he really say that last part to *me*?"

"What? Um, it's a documentary on John Lennon when he left Yoko. I wonder what happened to May Pang..."

"John Lennon, huh? ...Really...John Lennon...Hmmph..." He took a deep breath in an attempt to regain his composure. He had to get his mind back on business. But business always ran through a minefield of Root grievances. "It say anything about John Lennon coming up to Randy at CBGB's in '76 and giving him a pair of his sunglasses, telling him he'd look more rock n' roll wearing frames like his?"

"Huh? No..."

"That's 'cause it never fucking happened! Just like all of Randy Root's Goddamned bullshit stories." Jeffy began to pace in front of his now confused wife.

His voice grew louder with each new word he spat out. "He tells all these fucking stories that I know *never* happened. Just utter total horseshit. Because I was there! -I was Goddamned there! So what does he do more and more? He claims I wasn't there and people believe it! They fucking believe every fucking, fucked up lie he fucking spews - and somehow I'm *never* there!"

"Where were you, honey?" Mindy was even more confused.

"THERE! GODDAMMIT! THERE! I WAS ALWAYS THERE! I'M FUCKING SICK OF THIS!" Jeffy stopped in mid-rant and took a good look at his wife. "Why   are you in pajamas?"

"Well, we really haven't seen each other for awhile and I thought-"

"I have a tour to plan. We can play later."

"I'd be happy if we could just talk."

The phone rang Jeffy's favorite ringtone, the opening notes of the *Workers Internationale.* "Yeah. RoyBob?   -Good. Hey. Yeah, let's talk about the Tour." He walked into his office and closed the door.

___

While Mindy sat on the couch staring at the screen without looking at it, still wondering what to make of what she found in the bedroom closet earlier that day, Randy Root was having an early dinner with Ricky Rudolph, the music critic for the New York Times. They were sitting in Charlie Chaplin's corner booth right by the front window at Hollywood's oldest restaurant, the famed Musso & Frank Grill on Hollywood Boulevard. A landmark since 1919, Ricky had gotten there early and decided to check out the homey time capsule-like interior.

He was new to his job and new to Los Angeles. This was his first time in the place. He walked into the "New Room" built in 1955 and marveled at the long elegant bar straight out of film noir. So was the bartender, dressed in a classic red jacket, making change out of a cash register resembling some 1920s styled typewriter. His eyes scanned the rich, warm setting all around him. The dark chocolate toned wood booths and lush red interiors. The brass coat racks and mahogany stands and gold tinted glass lamps dotting the coffee and almond parquet walls, topped by a green and tan pastoral scene in a wrap-around-the-room mural. He looked up at the arched redwood ceiling beams above it all, ribbing the roof. His eyes finished sweeping the room just in time to see Randy and Tina arrive. He walked over to them, introduced himself. The maître 'd then led them to their booth in the original room.

Tina would never let Randy go on any halfway promising opportunity without her. She sat in between the two of them. "You know," Tina began like a high-end tour guide for Ricky, "they say when this place first opened, Chaplin would race his friends here on horseback and the loser had to pay for lunch. He always insisted on sitting in this booth 'cause it's the only one by the window so he and his friends could keep an eye on the horses."

"And over there-" Randy interjected, pointing at the dining counter by the grill. "That end-chair on the right was Steve McQueen's when he was shooting *Wanted Dead Or Alive*.

"And I hear," Randy segued, "Steve McQueen was a big Rolling Stones fan. So dig this: When the Oracle was recording in London back in late '77, early '78, I once *accidentally* crashed a Stones recording session at Abbey Road. I was just walking around, checkin' out the place, lookin' here, lookin' there. Poking my nose down different halls and rooms and there were the Stones in Studio Two, working on *Some Girls* album tracks. I see Keith Richards working on a hook, melody line, something. So I walked right up to him and complimented him on his guitar. Beautiful thing. Richards broke his concentration, took one look at me and asked me if I'd like him to shove that *Micawber*, 50s built butterscotch blonde blackguard Telecaster right up my wanker's ass. And that's how he put it: *Right up my wanker's ass.* Man, that guitar was a thing of beauty. I think Clapton had given it to him. So I told him: 'Go ahead and do it, Keith, 'cuz that's about as good as I could play it anyway, compared to you.' He laughed, thanked me and said, kicking me out with a shove, 'Now get the fuck out, ya fucking four-eyed wanker!' Which reminds me of something that happened with John Lennon-"

Tina turned to Ricky before Randy could go on. "That's what I love about Randy. He's fearless when it comes to his music and his art."

The waiter came over looking like a pissed off granduncle with zero patience. The 70-year old veteran of the old Hollywood eatery glared at Randy. "You ready to order or you got more stories to tell?" He had an accent hard to place, somewhere between Eastern Europe and the Latin World. "Hmmm?" He prompted Randy, raising his eyebrows like an impatient professor.

Randy smiled at the man forgivingly. "You remind me of a waiter I know at Katz's Deli in New York."

"That's my baby brother. He's the nice one. -Your order?" Uncle waiter replied, unimpressed.

"I'll have a burger. -Medium rare."

"Oh, an aristocrat..." the waiter quipped. -And you, your Highness?" He nodded at Tina.

"I'll have the same."

"Me too." Rudolph smiled pleasantly at the waiter who squinted back at him. "No drinks?" He said in a disapproving tone.

46

"I think we're fine with water." Randy answered. "Thanks." Ricky nodded in agreement.

"And I'm fine with my wine." Tina added.

"Big spenders." The man grunted and walked away, scribbling on his pad.

Randy got up. "I'll be right back. Duty calls. Hey, I understand you're both from Kansas City." Then he left.

"Oh yeah? KC?" Tina purred, sliding over the plush red leather closer to Ricky. "Where'd you grow up?" She literally pried into his eyes with hers.

Ricky shifted slightly away from Tina, feeling himself suddenly become very warm. "Um, I grew up in North Blue Ridge. You?"

"Oh...I grew up in Sunset Hill West."

"Wow. That must have been nice... You know this is the first time I've been to Musso & Frank's. I'm kinda spoiled about burgers. I'll be surprised if they live up to the burgers in KC. I just ordered that 'cause Randy did. I'm totally in awe of him."

"They're OK here. But you're right. Nothing beats a Hayes double chili cheeseburger."

"Oh man! Hayes! Or how about one of those Jess & Jim's giant plate-sized steak burgers-"

"-with the grilled red onions, yum! Remember the Flea Market Burger?"

"The greatest burger dive in the world! Tina, you're making me miss Cowtown."

"That's where Randy and I got married. In the house I grew up in Sunset Hill. Nice Oracle t-shirt you got on there, by the way. -Very colorful. And you wear it well." It was Skippy dressed as Jesus crucified on giant drumsticks in the shape of a cross.

"Thanks. I had to special order it. I can't even begin to tell you how much I admire your husband. I've been a big fan of the Orifice Of The Oracle since I was a kid. To me, Randy is a Rock God."

Tina tilted her head and smiled. "He's come a long way since those days. You might say I've helped steer his career as a composer. Right now we're about to engage in talks with Dexter Dille on his next project, but that's off the record, for now."

"Hmmm. I totally understand."

"Randy and I've been collaborating on one of my new ventures to bring attention to the plight of species threatened with extinction: Endangered Animal Gummies in a variety of organically grown all natural fruit non GMO flavors! We had an ad campaign: *Eat 'Em While They Last!* Really bringing attention to the plight of those poor creatures. Of course I also manage other talents such as Bela Marconi. One of the hottest composers around today." Rudolph smiled at her blankly. But she was dauntless. "So what's your article going to be about?"

"Well, what I'm really interested in and what my article's about, is simply what Randy's up to now as an established Hollywood composer of children's shows and, you know, what does it look like from an old Rock God's view living up there literally on Mount Olympus."

Tina looked him in the eyes and beamed. Ricky again grew quite uncomfortably warm.

Randy returned to the table motioning with his thumb behind him. "I think Uncle Grumple's coming back with our food."

Uncle Grumple gave Randy a dirty look and served them each the same dirty look, along with their food. When he left, Randy winked at Ricky. "Welcome to Hollywood."

"Old Hollywood." Tina added.

"Old indeed." Randy agreed.

"And I was just telling Tina I'm new to Musso & Frank's. So tell me." Ricky suddenly grew serious, putting on his writer's hat, trying to be professional as he sat inches away from one of his rock n' roll heroes. "What's new for Randy Root? What is the co-founder and front man for one of the seminal rock bands of the 70s and 80s doing now? A new kids cartoon? A teenage TV show? A full-length kids film feature? Anything in the works like your old Amberson stuff?"

Randy and Tina looked at each other. "Well," Tina started. "Randy's been working on a very serious, very important film by Latvia's leading film maker, Lotvo Schlomo-"

"It's called *Discharging General Schmutz*. Randy finished.

"Ah ha..." Ricky smiled politely.

At the same time Randy was telling Ricky this, more than anything, Randy was wishing he could actually talk about his working with Angelina Jolie on a film project of hers coincidentally entitled *Flip It Off!* But he couldn't. The problem was Jolie needed to call meetings at any time of the day or night as it fit her production schedule - and she had made this very clear to Randy from the beginning. But after one early morning and two late night meetings, Tina told Randy she didn't like Jolie calling meetings whenever she needed and demanded Randy tell the film star, activist, director, producer, icon that he would only meet with her at pre- arranged times from 9am to 5pm. So he did.

Jolie didn't say a word. She just smiled, said, "OK, I understand. I'll call you at nine tomorrow morning." Then she left.

Later, nodding confidently, Randy told Tina, "I think AJ's gonna be fine, now. It's all worked out."

That next morning promptly at 9am, Randy got a call from Angelina Jolie's personal assistant. "Mr. Root, Ms. Jolie wishes for me to relate the following as she is in a meeting at the moment: *'Regarding our conversation last night: If you can't work with me when I need you to work with me - then you can't work with me.'* I'm sure you understand and we apologize for any misunderstandings or inconvenience."

Then she hung up while Randy was still speaking. "OK, please tell her-" Randy stopped when he realized he was talking to the dial tone.

Instead, while all that played in the back of his head, Randy managed to steer the conversation in another direction. "You know I heard you refer to this place as Musso & Frank's before. Everybody does. But did you notice the sign on the roof of the place when you got here? -Or the sign in the lot by the valet booth? It reads *Musso & Frank Grill.* But everybody calls it *Musso & Frank's.* We add the apostrophe to places and things all the time. Just like we called CBGB, *CBGB's.* Like we need the name to possess the place or maybe *itself.* An apostrophe is a powerful thing."

Ricky's eyes widened. "I love that. That's a great quote to start off the piece. And you made me think of Frank Zappa's classic solo album, *Apostrophe.* His unique way of saying the album was all his. -A total musical declaration of Him possessing himself. Just like you did on *Flip It Off.*"

Tina winked at Ricky. "We're all possessive about something."

Randy saw his opening and took it. "Would you like to know what I possess? And also possesses me? Key to this story you're writing?"

"Tell me."

"Over two thousand classic rock n roll ceramic pieces, sculptures all done by me for an upcoming exhibition. Stuff that captures feelings and historic moments from a lifetime of rock n' roll."

"Cool! But before we get into that, I have to ask: Any plans to work with Kevin James again like that one funny Vegas movie you did with him in the early 2000s? *Four New Jacks And A Drag Queen?*"

"Oh, um...yeah, yeah of course there's the desire, but our schedules just haven't meshed in a while. Like I was saying, I'm planning this major exhibition all based on the rock n' roll experience. -Very autobiographical of my music career. Some of it will show how I came up with many of the things the Orifice of the Oracle are famous for, like the MegaHorn. I think it's perfect for your story." Randy went on like this for some time as Ricky took out a pad and pen and began taking notes.

When the check came, Randy paid the bill, giving the waiter a 15% tip. Used to at least 20%, the old garcon looked at the tip and sarcastically replied, "Oh, what a *generous* tip, Sir. Thank you oh so *very* much, *Sir*..."

Only half-listening and tone-deaf to sarcasm anyway, Root replied with a wink and a nod: "And well deserved." As they walked away, Uncle Grumple made a final parting gesture at their backs and then grumpled onto his next table of unworthy diners.

Outside in the back parking lot, standing under the hunter green canopy leading out, they all said their warm goodbyes while waiting for their cars. Tina's sky blue XKE came first. She got in the car and sped away. Randy's red convertible '58 Mercedes 190SL came next. Before he got in he turned to Ricky. "Come over to the Horn in a day or two-we'll keep talking. Call me later, we'll set it up." Then he got in his car and took off back to Mt. Olympus, opening his left hand wide out the window in a farewell gesture as he hit the accelerator.

Jeffy sat at his office desk, talking with RoyBob about the Tour. "It's called *The Titans Of Yore - Time Twist Tour.* I'll put you in contact with the coordinator. You probably know her."

"Already on it, Jeffy. Yeah, I know Andromeeka Abalone from way back. As a matter of fact, we spoke. She says they were considering London and Rome for the Tour, but the dates didn't work. Think Randy would have said Yes to that, anyway?"

"If Dexter Dille wanted to shoot Randy performing in Satan's asshole, Root would have a jet chartered for Hell before you could say *Blow It Out.* Yeah, I think he'd say yes to anything. Been a long time since the Oracle performed in London..."

"Randy tells me you guys were working at Abbey Road at the same time the Stones were. Told me this hilarious story about his running into Keith Richards. Ha." RoyBob snickered.

"That's what he told you? He really told you that moldy old crock a crap about the Stones at Abbey Road, did he? Motherfucker. Well guess what? The Stones *never* recorded at Abbey Road, RoyBob. *Never.* Just another lie by the Root Of All Evil." That's the first time Jeffy thought of his nickname for Randy. It just slipped out.

"What? Really? Wow. Well, maybe he got that experience confused with another time. He did say he was the only one there. Funny nickname, Jeffy." Ever the diplomat his job forced him to be, RoyBob wasn't exactly sure what to say, so he laughed.

Jeffy, not finding Randy's lies as charming as others did, found nothing to laugh about. After five seconds of dead air from Jeffy, RoyBob tried to change the subject.

"So how's married life treating you? Good time to be married with all this *hashtag Me Too* stuff going on, huh?"

"I'm fine. We're fine. Hashtag Me Too... There are women who are always looking for slights and sexual insults so they can feel powerful bringing some poor horny hapless schmuck down. Nowadays, they can lie with impunity. Which makes it harder for the women who have really been abused and could tell the truth, but don't. It's like talking about the Almighty Randy Root always getting his fucking way."

"I remember that chick who tried to pull that shit on you on the last Tour in Tokyo. I mean, running down the hotel hall naked. The cops. What was her name? Reminded me of Morphine...Delpheene! That's it. Delpheene. Man...Yeah...I think Mindy's way better. Delpheene actually scared the hell out of me, Jeffy."

"Me too, RoyBob. Me too. Some people are looking for offenses around every corner and make up one if there's nothing for them to play victim to. Ok, let's talk tomorrow after you get the whole itinerary from Andromeeka. And touch base with Shaggy. I'll speak to you later, bye."

He hung up, got up and walked back into the living room. Mindy was still sitting on the couch staring at the big screen. It was now showing a documentary on The Monkees. But she wasn't watching it at all.

"Get dressed, we'll go to dinner."

"We could order in, I'd like to talk."

"About-?"

"I was making more space in the closet for some things and I found your poster."

"My poster? What the fuck Mindy? A poster?"

"This poster." Mindy picked up a 3'x3' photo poster on thick foam core showing a guy on a white seamless matte, wearing a Batman costume performing fellatio on a guy wearing a Robin costume. "Is this why we haven't fucked in months?"

"What? Why would... Hey, I'd forgotten I even have that! I've had that for years. It's a joke. Don't you get it? It's reverses the power dynamic. Instead of Robin blowing Batman, which everyone would expect, Batman's blowing Robin! Isn't that funny?"

"People would expect Robin to blow Batman? Really? I never saw that in the movies. Is that what you really like? I remember you once saying if a girl wouldn't let you go anal, you'd rather have a boy and since I haven't been into that-"

"Look, I have a lot on my mind. This new Tour is vital to us. I really don't want to fight over a fucking poster. Let's just calm down for now, OK? Let me order us some Thai food in and I'll tell you all about the Tour. How's that?"

"Ok," Mindy said, resigned to letting it go for now. "But we still need to talk."

After leaving Musso & Frank, Tina had wasted no time in calling Bela, barely taking a breath ranting: "Yes, I brought up your name. It didn't matter. The guy was another Oracrap-nerd. I can't believe this geek works for the New York Times. Talk about a decline in standards. You should have seen this twerp: Puppet lines running down both sides of his mouth. -Bags under his eyes. Balding. And he came on to me, too. Shifted closer to me the moment Randy went to the bathroom. Ugh. He stunk of Hai Karate or Brut mixed with body odor. And he was wearing this super-tight tacky Oracle t-shirt. -Another thirty-five year-old boy going through puberty. I mean most every fan of theirs you meet is pathetic. And *they* think so, too! Yes, the Band was legendary, but so what? That was over thirty years ago. They're getting old. Nobody cares anymore. You should have seen them at Coachella with those stupid gold dunce caps humbly in hand, dressed in those ridiculous gold costumes, begging, literally begging Taylor Swift at her trailer door to do one of their songs. She wouldn't even let them in. I swear, Bela, they should change their name to the Cringe-Worthies. -And Josephine, that Bull Moose? You can tell what she had for breakfast, lunch and dinner just by looking at her shirt. And those candy corn teeth of hers? I think she eats cocaine for breakfast and washes it down with a big glass of crystal meth. And that's Randy's chief engineer here. -For now. I have plans for that behemoth, and those other losers he's kept on for years. Meet in 10 minutes? -Your place? I'll be right over. I can say I had a contract to discuss with you."

Randy turned off the spyware on his laptop and slowly closed it. He sat there in the Mercedes, thinking about something that happened one week before the wedding in Kansas City.

He was standing in the basement of the Horn, behind the oval rehearsal space directly below his studio, directing Jake and Bertie, two of his apprentice composers' attention to the dozens of large unmarked boxes filling up half the space there. The rest of the basement was packed with plastic covered rolls of old Orifice Of The Oracle concert posters, boxes upon boxes stacked high with merchandise ranging from Orifice Of The Oracle Mylar togas and God-costumes to Orifice Of The Oracle stickers, Orifice Of The Oracle collectors buttons, Orifice Of The Oracle license plate frames, Orifice Of The Oracle key chains, promotional pens, action dolls, MegaHorns, old unsold cds like *Jesus What's Your Hang Up?* And *Kiss This Orifice*, on top of dvds with live performances dating back to the 1970s. And as much as Esmeralda, the Horn's cleaning lady dusted once a week - the dust was winning.

"Now that I'm getting married to Tina, I have magazines and books I need to get rid of pronto. All those boxes over there must go. -All of them. You can keep them yourself. Some of them are very expensive. You can give them away. You can throw them away. But whatever way, just get rid of them."

So as Bertie and Jake assured him they'd just throw it all out in the dumpster in the back parking lot, Randy walked over to one box and pulled out a few publications to show. The magazines were a mixture of little girl kiddie porn from all over the world. This was a collection that took years and years to amass and now he wanted it gone in the course of a day. Some of it was from France and Germany, even Scandinavia. But most of it was from Asia. Some of it was anime. Most of it was real. Bertie and Jake couldn't help themselves and saved several richly bound editions with exposes of Asian and African girls all well under 18 years old. A favorite range of Randy's as all the guys in the Band back then knew and tacitly approved by looking the other way. Now thinking of Tina's mouth on Bela at that very moment, Randy deeply regretted ever getting rid of those boxes.

That memory taking all of five seconds, he grabbed his laptop and got out of the car. He sighed playing back in his head everything he'd just heard Tina say. He had little use for Bela and didn't hear a word he'd said. He didn't need to. He knew Marconi was like everyone else in Hollywood. It's all about what you can get. And it's always at someone else's expense. Always. That's how it's played here. And most of what Tina said wasn't new to him. He'd already heard it directly from her many times. The only difference was, he wasn't the one she was sucking and fucking after saying it.

As he came into the house he heard splashing, girls laughing and a woman with a Jamaican accent sternly say, "Don't you leave the soap there, now Silly. That's not where it goes!"

The next thing he knew both girls ran past him, their wet skin glowing pinkish gold, wearing nothing but soap bubbles, screaming and laughing.

"Bathsheba! Khungit! Come back here, girls! You're all slippery wet!" Solita, the nanny, chased them waving two thick towels in her hands, leading them towards their room. She turned her agile, 5'11" muscular frame around to greet Randy.

"Oh, Greetings Mista Root. Blessed Welcome home, jah! Just getting' the little ladies ready for bed." Tiny gold curls covered her head and framed her bright brown eyes, eagle nose and full-lipped smile of a face. Few knew she was in her sixties.

Randy just stood there watching the girls run into their room. What ran through his mind was what it had taken just to see those girls run through his house. -All the needling from Tina to save someone, anyone from the African Famine. -All the lawyers and forms and fees and interviews and government agencies and embassies and consulates and child services and orphanages and doctors. -The applications for birth certificates. -The applications for passports. -The airline tickets back and forth from Addis Ababa. -All the time at the Hilton Addis Ababa watching those crazy game shows. -And so much more. He broke off his stare, turned and smiled at the nanny. "Hi Solita, everything good?"

"Oh yes, Sir. Good girls, today. And I got Nipper from the vet. He's in the back."

"Very good." His phone rang with a blocked caller ID. Thinking it could be Ricky Rudolph wanting to ask a few follow-up questions and set up the next interview, or Tina who sometime blocked her ID, he answered it, despite his general policy to never answer any call he didn't recognize.

"Ricky...Tina-?"

There was silence for several seconds. Then a female voice sang in a whisper.

"Double Your Pleasure?"

Then another female voice sang in a whisper. "Double Your Fun?"

Then both voices sang in tauntingly loud harmony.

56

"Double Mint, Bubble Bum!"

"Who is this??" Randy asked, his voice betraying more fear than anger over some juvenile crank call.

"*Click.*"

"Who the fuck was that?!" He yelled stupidly.

He knew who it was.

CHAPTER 4

"JESUS GOT A WOODY!

FOR MAGDALENA'S GOODY!

THE QUESTION WASN'T SHOULD HE?

THE QUESTION WAS WHEN WOULD HE?

JESUS GOT A WOODY! - JESUS GOT A WOODY! - JESUS GOT A WOODY!

COULD HE? - SHOULD HE? -WOODY!!!

COULD HE? - SHOULD HE? -WOODY!!!

COULD HE? - SHOULD HE? -WOODY!!!

-JESUS GOT A WOODY!!!"

The music stopped with a blast of squelching feedback. "All right then." Randy tightened the gold lamè strap on his Telecaster. Joey toyed with the treble on her Gibson. Larry kept slapping the whammy bar absentmindedly on her Ibanez while Luke Wharm's pale countenance and tall, thin frame hunched over his Ludwig drum kit, tightening the top wing nut on his high hat and then pulling back on his long stringy dark hair. The band's usual crew of roadies, Philly Phingers and Keith Utz had spent the last three hours setting everything up in the Horn's rehearsal space directly below Studio Zero. Now they stood around waiting to be useful.

Keith Utz was 5'9" with wiry dark brown hair, everywhere. -Especially the back of his hands and his knuckles. He had pale blue eyes, which blinked half as often as most people. Both he and Philly were gifted guitar techs Randy claimed could string and tune a guitar faster than most people could sneeze.

Soundboard man Truck Copland (the guy who made sure the audience heard everything right) and backstage mixer Scruffy Diggins (the guy who made sure the band heard everything right) stood taking mental notes, their arms folded and their feet tapping. Truck was tall and blonde. Seemingly sullen, but solid on the job, he was legendary for kicking back shots of Crown Royal like lemonade. Scruffy lived up to his name with an unruly mop of black curly hair and a gruff yet disarming positive exuberance that could win over even the biggest of star-level assholes shining at the brightest magnitude. He could even play drums decently enough in a pinch.

The rehearsal space, an oval room walled off in front of the Horn's basement storage area had not seen a drum kit, or mic's, or stands, or amps or guitars or keyboards or speakers set up there in a very long time. All of the road crew standing around debated exactly how long it had been. "Seven years?" Pondered Philly.

"Nah, more like six." Grunted Utz.

"A little less than that. You're forgetting Tokyo." Scruffy answered back. Remember, I had to fill in for Luke on drums?"

"Oh Yeah." Deadpanned Truck. "Who could ever forget that?"

RoyBob, who had just showed up, chuckled. "Yeah, there you were, dressed to look like Buddha, but the audience were all saying in Japanese you looked like a starving sumo wrestler." They all laughed on that one.

The tour cases were all out in the lobby ready to be packed and loaded. Joey, being the chief engineer at the Horn O Plenty had arranged the Band's rehearsal set-up, making sure to put the drums in the middle a bit back with her and Larry on each side and their brothers to the left and right in front of them forming a half circle.

"C'mon!" Joey had barked, orchestrating it all. "Let's get this set up before Randy realizes Dille will never give him a shot at a major film project. Let's go!"

As they warmed up, Shaggy was going through storage boxes with June Lucey, the Band's super-devoted lady ultra-fan, gathering CD's and other merch' for the Tour. He whispered to her excitedly. "This is historic! The first time these guys have rehearsed in years!" June giggled by reply.

Randy looked around the room. "Not a bad start. We'll work out the entire set as we go along. Me n' Jeffy discussed this already. Speaking of which, where *is* Jeffy? -You guys seen him?"

Both Philly and Utz shook their heads left to right. Shaggy and June Lucey, who had come on her own dime to help Shag sell Oracle merchandise on the Tour, stopped moving boxes of MegaHorns, cd's, buttons, stickers, shirts and other memorabilia to shake their heads "No." So did the Horn's personnel who had come down to watch. For the most part, everyone there wore their own takes on the casual dress of the day: t-shirts, jeans and running shoes. The crew. The staff. The Band.

Randy looked at them all and shrugged. "Said he'd be here at four. Well, let's finish this practice run on *Woody*. As much as we've all played this a ga-zillion times, it's been a while and that was kinda loose. I know we're missing bass right now, but let's review: standard rock progression in C, four-four time. -G2 to G4 to C-back to G2. Got it? Follow me into the instrumental on the third bar. Then second verse and end with chorus. Ok, on three, two, one:

60

"WALKIN' ON THE WATER
OR ROLLING HIS STONE
JESUS GOT A WOODY
THAT STANDS ON ITS OWN
IT'S BIG AND THICK AND HARDER THAN THE HARDEST BONE
YEAH-JESUS GOT A WOODY / THAT EVERYBODY'S BLOWN
HIS WOODY GIVES NO SPLINTERS/ HAS A GOLDEN TONE
HE PUT HIS SERMON ON THAT MOUNT/ AND MAN DID MARY MOAN:
JESUS GOT A WOODY!
JESUS GOT A WOODY!
JESUS GOT A WOODY!
COULD HE? SHOULD HE? -WOODY!!!
-JESUS GOT A WOODY!!! -JESUS GOT A WOODY!!!"

"Ok-" Randy stopped, tapped the mic, turned around and played with his amp for a second. That's when Jeffy walked in holding a towel to his forehead.

"Where've you been, man? The rehearsal *you* called started thirty minutes ago."

Philly Phingers ran over and set up Jeffy's spot. Phingers was a legendary roadie from Liverpool. A heroin addict with a silver tongue, he had a talent for getting trunks packed and unpacked from any truck, which he could then pack and unpack and repack in a matter of minutes. And it didn't matter what you had. Philly always managed to get everything in no matter how much the Band had to haul. "If you need ten pounds of shit put in a five pound can," Randy was fond of saying, "Philly Phingers will give you a hand."

"Hold on, oh Godly one." Philly's Brit accent usually never failed to charm. He plugged in Jeffy's black Steinberger bass, adjusted the volume, switched on his amp and ceremoniously bowed. Jeffy wasn't feeling so charmed, even as Philly comically moonwalked away.

Jeffy dropped the towel for someone else to pick up. "Traffic sucked, but your parking lot sucks more."

"My parking lot?"

"Yeah your parking lot and the lunatic you got living back there! When did that start? I parked back there against the trees and this guy or simian thing swings down from a branch yelling at me that I'm in HIS spot. So I ask him where his car is. I'm trying to reason with him. The next thing I know, he throws an orange at my head while I'm telling him who I am. He starts screaming *'Who are you? Who the fuck are you?? For all you know I'm God, bitch!'* Then he turned and shot a moon, the scarring image of which I should have some hypnotist acid-wash out of my brain forever. So I moved my car to another spot and came in here. We need to move the dress rehearsal to S-I-R. You can stop laughing like a hyena now."

Randy Root had this high-pitched tremolo of a laugh that only came out when he was genuinely amused. But Jeffy wanting to move the dress rehearsal didn't please him much so he didn't indulge in his tittering as long as he would have liked.

"S-I-R... That's a pain in the ass to go three miles away, plus the rental cost-"

"Oh yeah?" Jeffy countered. "Can you see Dille filming that fucker in the back? Oh, that'd be great, huh? How's that for a pain in the ass? Make you look real good."

Randy gazed at Jeffy expressionless. He continued what he'd been saying as if he hadn't been interrupted. "But, on the hand, we do need practice getting everything together...Ok...sure...why not...We'll talk about all that later. I wanted Dille to see the place. -That's why I got rehearsal going on time, waiting for you to get here. We need to be 1977 razor-sharp when he comes to film. Wanted that to start here. But it doesn't have to be the Dress Rehearsal. He's shooting that first. Maybe it's better to have it there. Looks more prestigious having the S-I-R people kiss our ass. Better Dille comes here another time for his film. So have it your way. And you got a point. Tarzan might not make such a good impression on Dille as he did on you."

62

Randy and some of the others laughed loudly. Jeffy didn't. Randy cleared his throat. "I'll get Paulette on that tomorrow. Right now, we got people here. The equipment's all set up. Let's get to it. We still have to work out the rest of the set."

"Yeah, I wanna talk about The Intervention, too."

Randy let out an impatient sigh. "That thing? Every year you ask me, and what do I tell you? I don't have the time. I'm lucky to have the time for *this*..." He gestured with arms outstretched waving across the band set-up. "Anyway, we just warmed up with *Woody*. Remember on The Easter Tour we followed up *Woody* with *Divine Intervention*? Always was a good mash up. And since you kinda mentioned it, let's work on it." We'll segue from *Woody* into that. I'll do the keyboard intro."

Randy took off his guitar and was exchanging it for his Yamaha Sonogenic Keytar with Keith Utz when Jeffy jumped in.

"Right. I'll follow on bass. Larry and Joey, lead and rhythm. Then on the fourth downbeat, Skippy, I mean Luke, you do a snare roll into the first verse.

"Knew that." Wharm said smugly as his right foot tapped on the bass drum pedal for emphasis.

Jeffy continued. "Larry, take your solo after the first chorus on that-and Joey just keep us moving."

"Alright then," Randy said, shooting a look at Jeffy. "Heavy Rock. Four/four time. C to B to C, then C to G to F - right? Right. On four, three, two, one:

CRONUS SCREWED URANUS

THEN ZEUS SCREWED CRONUS TOO

THEN HERA SCREWED ZEUS'S LIGHTNING BOLT

AND THAT SCREWED ME AND YOU

-DIVINE INTERVENTION! -IT DEFIES ALL CONVENTION-

-IT DESTROYS ALL PRETENSION -YEAH- DIVINE INTERVENTION-

MOSES LIKED TO GET HIGH ON A BURNING BUSH

THE SHIT HE SMOKED WAS BETTER THAN THE STRONGEST KUSH

HE ROCKED OUT WITH GOD POWERS FROM THE TABLETS TO THE SEA

HE MADE THE PHARAOH KISS HIS ASS - AND SET HIS PEOPLE FREE!

-DIVINE INTERVENTION! -IT DEFIES ALL CONVENTION-

-IT DESTROYS ALL PRETENSION -YEAH- DIVINE INTERVENTION-

-SAY DIVINE INTERVENTION -YEAH- DIVINE INTERVENTION!"

They all stopped, Larry last with a first-string twang. "OK." Randy took a swig of water from the bottle Utz had put by his stool. "That wasn't bad. And I guess we're gonna do it, but I'll say it to make sure: Under the present circumstances, I say we leave out the Muhammad verse, you know, the Muslim thing. Rather not get a fatwa over the fucking song on a has-been tour."

"Yeah Randy, right." Jeffy shot back, fists on his hips. "We are leaving it out, obviously. But try not to say that when Dille is there at the dress rehearsal. Not sure that would clinch the deal for his next film project."

Root shot Jabonno another dirty look that was starting to get obvious to everyone around them. Standing in a corner, out of the way, nobody noticed it more at that moment than Ricky Rudolph, who was well aware of the tempestuous relationships in famous rock bands. It was the kind of thing that made the proverbial saying "like an old married couple" the cliché it was. Randy then turned his attention in Keith's direction, holding up the water bottle squarely in the roadie's face.

64

"*This* is room temp!"

Ricky had gotten there early. He hadn't seen Tarzan when he parked so he felt a mixture of relief and disappointment when he heard Jeffy's story. Randy had introduced him to everyone and when Jeffy showed up, he wanted to introduce himself to another hero of his, but he waited. Shaggy had taken him on a tour of the Horn before the rehearsal. He walked around ogling at the kiddie rides and the circus mirrors and the gold and platinum records, the wacky furniture and everything else like a kid set loose in Willie Wonka's Chocolate Factory. Right after they finished the song, he couldn't wait a second longer and went up to both Randy and Jeffy.

"You know, they say Divine Intervention was an inspiration to Tarantino's Pulp Fiction." Ricky turned to Randy. "You worked with him - once. How was that?"

"Well... That was in Q's early formative days. He wasn't as focused then...he was feeling things out...trying this n' that. You know, testing the waters..."

Ricky then turned to Jeffy. "I trust Randy told you about me. -Ricky Rudolph music editor for the New York Times. What an honor to meet you, Mr. Jabonno."

"Yes. Pleasure to meet you, Rick. Call me Jeffy, please."

"You know, I've always thought White Zombie's *Dragula* sounds conspicuously a lot like *Divine Intervention*."

"I've heard that said myself by some very serious musicologists." Jeffy said a little too lofty. "I've been told Rob Zombie is a very big 'Oracle fan. Honored, of course."

"Well you've certainly influenced a lot of Bands. It must be of great pride to you."

"Pride? Yeah. Got a lot of that. Fuck Pride. I'd rather have more money."

Randy pretended not to hear Jeffy and smiled a Cheshire cat smile.

Jeffy's answer was meant to shock Ricky. He had said it deliberately. He didn't care it was the New York Times. To Jeffy, Ricky looked like a kid on his first visit to Disneyland. That annoyed Jeffy because it was all about *RandyLand*. -As usual.

The Horn O Plenty was a wonder to the first-time visitor. Ricky turned back to Root. "Wow, Randy. The Horn is amazing. 8224 Sunset Blvd. Right at the mouth of the Strip. -Across from the Chateau Marmont. Marilyn Monroe stayed there. John Belushi died there. So who built the Horn? Can you tell me the real story behind it?"

"Well" Randy began, "It was designed by Frank Lloyd Wright in the 50s for a record store chain in the 50s, early 60s..."

"What year? Wright died in 1959."

"You can read about it in LA Architecture Magazine. It's all documented there. I'll get you a copy. Later, maybe RoyBob can give you a tour of the Horn."

"Shaggy already showed me around."

"Good to know he's good for something."

They all laughed, including Shaggy.

"I live to serve." The long-suffering super ultra-fan declared.

Suddenly the rehearsal room door opened and Nipper, who had just been wormed, wandered in wearing the Elizabethan collar the vet had given him.

"Wait. Is that how Nipper just got in? Milkner, you let the dog in while you were playing tour guide??" The Whippet mulled around the room along the wall trying to sniff out places he'd marked, but the cone wouldn't let him as he scrapped and bumped against the wall. "Come on, Shaggy, take him back up to Tina. He's 'sposed to be with her on the third floor."

Staring at Nipper's cone for some reason reminded Ricky of the remarkable building he was in. Sensing Randy didn't want to go into that at the rehearsal,

Ricky quickly changed the subject back to what he had really wanted to ask before he'd been distracted by Nipper.

"Randy, let's get back to *Woody* for a second. It's probably one of your most controversial songs. Certainly caused a riot at that one concert where Larry got arrested. -The record burnings. -The protests. -The concert siege by the Eastboro Antioch Baptist Church Commandos. -Larry's counter attack. What did you make of all that?"

"Yeah, people got buggy on that one. Really misunderstood us just telling the story of Jesus dying on the cross in our own postmodern way."

There was a *Jesus Got A Woody* video. It aired on MTV. Once. It showed Skippy Watts as Jesus on a giant-phallus-looking crucifix that turns into a phallus-looking shaped woody-station wagon with Jesus at the wheel and Magdalena by his side. They drive along the Trail Of Tears back up to Calvary Hill, where the station wagon turns back into a crucifix of Skippy's drumsticks, also very phallic.

The uproar from Mothers groups was deafening. Of course Randy loved it and explained that it was all metaphors for the crucifix, which after all was made of wood and Magdalena's goody was her sin. And humans who deny their inner-God are doomed. But nobody but the hardest of hardcore fans bought that.

"Ricky, for the record, it's simply our way of saying Jesus said *be* like him, so die for your own sins, and wake up to your own god powers!"

Randy loved saying things like that. Joey came up to Jeffy from behind and whispered in her brother's ear. "I think he really gets off on saying that shit. Look, I think he's got a hard on."

"I'll take your word on that one." Jeffy whispered back.

Ricky was taking in Randy's explanation at the same time he was taking note of everything else he knew about the song and its infamy in the back of his mind. But rather than follow up on that, he pivoted, asking something completely unrelated.

"I understand Dexter Dille is going to film the dress rehearsal."

Randy took a beat, making a slight gulping sound. "Actually, he's filming the entire Tour. I'm looking forward to working with an old friend once again."

Much of the staff at the Horn had been walking in and out during the rehearsal. Chiefly among them was the office manager Paulette Matthews. She came down several times from her office to hear a few of the songs, discuss a few matters with Randy, basically check on everything and then about 15 minutes before the rehearsal finished, she came back one last time to say goodbye, putting on her red driving gloves that matched her candy apple red Maserati. Then she sauntered off like a dusky supermodel on a Paris Runway in her tight designer jeans, rhinestone studded shirt and ebony pumps. Her long black braids cascaded left then right with the rhythm of her engaging stride as she exited the building. In years past, Randy had referred to her as his "Chocolate Barbie."

The sweet and earthy receptionist Mei Ling Yen hung out longer, answering the phone down in the rehearsal room, when she could hear it ring. She was a pint-sized feline marvel partial to patent leather mini skirts, halter-tops and sandals. -The perfect host to welcome all to the Horn. -Especially for the first time. Unbeknownst to anyone at the Horn, RoyBob and Mei Ling had been secretly dating for quite some time. About the same height, they made a good match. But Scruffy was convinced by RoyBob's mannerisms, his shaved head and the gold ring in his left ear that he was gay - and he told everyone his suspicions.

Randy's two apprentice composers Bertie and Jake stood around for a while, talking to Phingers and Utz, Truck and Scruffy, until they saw Randy giving them The Look. The Look meant get back to his work. Jason Barter knew The Look all too well too and avoided eye contact with Randy for the five minutes he came down to see what was going on.

Solita showed up halfway through the rehearsal with Bathsheba and Khungit all over her like a tree. The girls wiggled, wriggled, twisted, jumped, rolled, ran up, ran down and all around Solita, making the woman look like a sleep-deprived alley cat frantically chasing her own tail dressed in beige work clothes and orthopedic shoes.

Ricky had showed up at the same time Shaggy had with June Lucey so they had all come in together. Neither Shaggy nor June was ever paid a penny for their tirelessly devoted service. But they did get free tickets to the shows. It was typical of all Rock bands to have an inner circle of people close to them made up of family, friends, business associates and decorated ultra fans, attend rehearsals. This was considered a very high privilege that every band cultivated among their circle.

At one point during the rehearsal, Jeffy stopped and called Philly over. "Phingers, do me a favor. Go in the back and check on my car. I don't trust that lunatic motherfucker back there."

"Who? Oh, you mean Tarzan." Philly chortled.

"Yeah, that's what Randy's calling his backyard pet. It's bad enough to step in Nipper's shit. I don't need to step in the human kind. Just check on the car, please. You know which one it is, right?"

"Sure, I know your wheels. The blue Alpha Romero."

At the same time Jeffy was talking to Philly, Luke Wharm snapped his fingers at Shaggy and June Lucey, standing a few feet away. "Go and get me a cold bottle of water and a paper towel so I can wipe your cooties off. That is what you live for, isn't it, if I heard you right before? Serving? Later I'll sign your arms if you're both good boys and girls."

June looked at Shaggy and smiled. "He means well." She lied. Shaggy shook his head. "I can remember when he used to call me *Mister Milkner* and *Sir...*" June scratched her thick thatch of dark blonde curls and hauled off another box of MegaHorns to sell on tour as Shaggy ran up to the kitchen to get Wharm his water.

After going through several more songs that included *Flip It Off*, *Blow It Out*, *Help, We're All Gods*, *Trick Question Or Shock Treatment*, *It's A WonderFool Life*, *Delphi In Hi-Fi, Jesus, What's Your Hang Up?* with *Kiss This Orifice* as the finale, they had their set list complete. Randy turned to Jeffy and for a very brief moment, it felt like it did in the old days. -For both of them.

"OK, that's a good thirty-minute set." Randy looked at Jeffy. "What about the encore?"

Wharm, always wanting to be seen as more than a journeyman or a "musical utility infielder" as all roadies put it behind his back, piped up: "Hey. What about something unusual like the *Age of Aquarius* done in a twisted Oracle way. *Aquarius* is right in there for the Orifice philosophy."

Randy laughed. "Man, we are a LONG way from Hair. Something else...

"How about *Who Are You?*" Someone whispered in Jeffy's ear.

"*Who Are You*?" Jeffy would have never suggested that in a trillion years. He had said it in disbelief and thought he'd just said it in his head. He didn't mean to say it out loud. But he had.

"Hey...I like that." Randy nodded. "Cool Song. No one will expect that from us."

Jeffy tried to get out of it. "Well, maybe it's not right for us."

"Hey man, you suggested it. And it's perfect Oracle material. It literally asks the question we brought up in *We're All Gods:* We're Gods. Who are you? Aren't you one, too? It's perfect. Done."

As much as he wanted to, Jeffy couldn't argue that. And in his head he could hear someone snickering and muttering, "Oh man-" with an English accent. He tried to ignore it. But he couldn't. It intrigued him. It sounded like John Lennon.

While all this was going on, the volume got so loud, Solita decided to take the girls into the lobby. Bathsheba tugged on her arm with all her weight.

"Want wa-ter stu-pad."

"You know my name, baby and it's not *Stupid*."

Khungit looked up at Solita confused. "Mommy, Daddy say so.

"Do they now?" Solita eyes widened, then she squinted for a second, smiling. "Hmmm."

At that moment, Tina came down with Nipper on his leash. The plastic cone wobbled around on the dog's neck.

"Here," Tina grunted, shoving the leash into Solita's hands. "Make yourself useful and look after our third child. You *are* the nanny."She chuckled at her own wit, going back into the rehearsal room, putting one hand on her hip and the other already to her ear with her phone in between.

Both adopted daughters were caramel-toned beauties worthy of the typical description given Ethiopian females: stunning faces with Euro-features, sharp noses, high cheekbones and full lush lips. Both had brown-green eyes. Bathsheba's shoulder-length reddish auburn hair shined in sunlight. She was short and still had her baby fat, which gave her a cherubic, pixie-like look. She was precocious bordering on the downright devilish.

Khungit, who was a year and a half older, from another tribe altogether, had a hearing disability. She was slender and tall for her age with a jet-black mane halfway down her back. She was shy and tended to look at the ground in front of everyone but Solita. Both girls were still learning English.

Both girls were a handful even for a skilled nanny like Solita. So it wasn't long before Nipper found his way into the rehearsal room again, jimmying open the door and promptly walked over to Ricky and sat on his foot, wiggling his backside into the toe of his left shoe.

"That means he likes you." Randy joked. Everyone laughed. So did Ricky, moving quickly backwards away from the dog as fast as he could. "Hey Shag, take Nipper back out to Solita in the Lobby. She's supposed to be watching him now."

Dropping another box of merchandise he was taking out to somehow stuff into his already packed car, Shaggy shot Randy a thumbs-up and led the dog out of the room.

As Solita tried to entertain the girls on Randy's kiddie rides, first putting Sheba in the sparkling yellow mini Ferris wheel and then Khungit into the bright green kiddie sports car, it was impossible to control Nipper, who had been scratching at the rehearsal door after he'd been put out by Shaggy. So Solita didn't notice Nipper walking behind her and hunching down with an extra reaction to his vet's earlier worming, leaving a loose puddle right by the revolving door.

Tina came back into the lobby, saw what Nipper had done, grabbed the girls and proceeded to push the revolving door out as she barked at Solita. "Is that how people live where you come from? -In a pigsty? -Like a pig? There's a mop in the bathroom down the hallway on the left. Please take care of Nipper's accident now. I can't believe you let this happen. We'll see you back at the house in time for you to make the girls dinner."

With both children now crying, Tina grabbed them in her arms, flashed her trademark smile at Solita one last time and was gone. There wasn't anything Tina Drekk Root could not say with a smile. A smile made with cunning, cynicism, precision, condescension and a teaspoon of pure contempt.

Cursing to herself, Solita went upstairs to find a mop and disappeared up the rainbow staircase just as Jeffy was getting ready to leave for the night. He found himself pontificating to Ricky who had cornered him and was asking as many Oracle questions as he could think of, which right then was on the virtue of having two rehearsals before the Tour for songs they wrote and had played over a lifetime.

"Wouldn't one intense rehearsal be enough at this point, Jeffy? Just do the dress rehearsal at the same time? You've done this a lifetime."

"Rehearsals are like guns, Ricky. I'd rather have one and not need it than need it and not have one. Actually, I'd rather have the gun for that asshole in the parking lot. Though, *of course* I'm for gun control...Ok, let's talk more, later. You have my number now. Call me tomorrow in the late morning, round eleven."

Jeffy then turned to Randy and tried to make one last appeal. "Just think about the thing. It happens right after the tour. After that last date in LA, I'll fly out to Flint. We're talkin' like four weeks from now. Consider coming with me. It'd be like the old days. You could see your folks, old friends - the old neighborhood. The fans would go nuts if you came."

"The fans are nuts. You know that. I'll sign some posters, some photos, some MegaHorns. They always dig that."

"Randy, you've never been to one of these."

"Jeffy, I got better things to do than waste time wearing a "I'm so happy to see you all!" bullshit look plastered on my face in front of those dweebs. And even if I wanted to, I'm planning a series of art exhibitions then."

Jeffy left the rehearsal room walking into the lobby towards the revolving door, muttering to himself. He was thinking about calling Mindy and asking what she wanted to do for dinner when he suddenly found himself sliding a foot and a half and almost falling on his ass.

"That goddamned dog!"

He stood there just outside the Horn entrance trying to shake Nipper's finest off his right shoe. He started thinking about Tarzan in the back and whether he was still lurking in his tree, waiting for him with another half-rotten orange and another full moon. The whole episode replayed in his head. He hadn't told Randy the whole story. How it terrified him. How Tarzan looked like Big Foot coming out of the tree right in front of his car, totally naked, shaking his manhood at Jeffy while grunting. The moon shot had been Tarzan's punctuation point. And while what Jeffy had described as trying to reason with the man actually sounded more like: "Get the fuck out of here, you animal! Nobody shakes their shit at me!"

Tarzan yelled back. "Fuck You! Fuck Hole! Who are you? For all you know, *I'm* God! So who the fuck are you?? I'll dance on your fancy car if I want! I'll piss all over it if I want, you elitist fuck!" Then he had pulled out that orange out of nowhere and threw it hitting Jeffy right on the forehead.

Jeffy, slightly in shock, ignored that, moved his car, beeped its alarm several times and then walked quickly into the Horn. Tarzan screamed at the top of his lungs to Jabonno's quickly retreating back: "EAT MY SHIT, YOU BIG SHOT! I'LL BE WAITING FOR YOU!"

Thinking about that now, he stepped out into the night air. Jeffy could hear the noise of the Strip alive with partiers and tourists all mingled together. A late Sunset Strip Night, any night was packed with people filled with food and drink and the desire for fun. Jeffy cautiously walked toward his car, ready for Tarzan to jump out at any moment. He sighed a breath of relief, realizing the ape-man wasn't around and his Alpha Romeo was fine.

But as he unlocked the car, he jumped to the right at the sight of a young woman in a complete drunken stupor squat peeing by his front left tire. The pungent urine ran in a steady stream directly in front of his car door hitting the same shoe Nipper had gotten.

"Your parents must be very proud." He said to her. She was barely aware of the surroundings, let alone him. As he got in the car he said to himself. "Dress rehearsal definitely at S-I-R. Fuck the Horn. Maybe we should all be wearing cones."

Everyone who knew the business knew you rehearsed at SIR if you wanted to be known at all. *Studios Instrument Rentals* was the premier rehearsal space in Hollywood. Any band worth at least one top 40 hit wouldn't rehearse anywhere else. Any band struggling to be worth at least one top 40 hit did everything they could not to rehearse anywhere else. The pale green stucco building numbered 6465 on Sunset and Wilcox that took up two-thirds of the block east towards the next cross street of Cahuenga, was a monument built on musical hopes, dreams and desperate whims.

Jeffy struggled to maneuver through the narrow entrance to the L-shaped parking lot in the back. He could see Joey was already there with Roy Bob, Shaggy and June behind the truck they rented. They were both directing the guys unloading the equipment. The parking lot was tight and the only spot he could find was the farthest one away. By the time he parked and got out of his car, he could see from how Phingers and Utz were on the back loading dock with Diggins and Copland helping, they were putting everything into Studio Two.

"WHAT THE FUCK? GODDAMMIT! MOTHERFUCKERS! COCKSUCKING ASSHOLES! YOU SHIT ON ME! YOU PEE ON ME! I AM TIRED OF BEING NIGGERIZED!" Jeffy screamed in a Tourette's-worthy reflex. He got a hold of himself quickly and gave a sigh of relief, figuring he was still far enough away that only a security guard passing in a golf cart had heard him. As he got closer he could see Randy was also there walking into the studio. He caught up with him just inside as the guys were setting everything up and visitors started coming in as well.

"Hey man, what is this? Why are we in Two? I specifically asked for One. I told Paulette to get ONE last week!"

"I know. She told me. I changed that. Two is easier with its loading dock for the guys to load and unload from. You know that. Everyone knows that. Plus it looks cooler for Dille, gives him more editing options on the full rock n roll picture...I wonder if he's here yet... Hey! Anybody seen Dille yet? He's 'sposed to be coming with his crew."

"Randy, I wanted One because of the vibe there, man! You just changed it 'cause I wanted One. -Big deal about the fucking loading dock. I should have said I wanted Two and then you would have had it changed to One!"

"Will you cool it? Dille will be here any minute. And you just as much as me want him to see The Oracle in the best possible light, so let's change into our gear and make this as important as our first gig at CBGB."

"Who's in One? Maybe they'll change with us."

"Forget that, man. I'm telling you Dille's about to be here. Give it the fuck up, Jeffy. This is no time to get all bitched out about which studio we're in."

As much as he wanted to, Jeffy realized having it out with Randy here was the wrong place at the wrong time.

"I've told you a million times I play better in One. I like the acoustics in One better. But I guess you don't remember that either. Yeah, let's get into our gear and make this work for all our sakes."

They both walked into the bathroom to change without saying another word to each other.

As Randy and Jeffy had decided on a set that comprised much of their early classic work along with more recent stuff, they of course came dressed in their signature look: the sparkling gold space suits with their winged MegaHorns.

People were constantly arguing the pros and cons of both Studio One and Two. Both were theatre style with a maximum capacity of 350 people. Both had stages. Both had excellent acoustics. While the dimensions between both weren't exactly the same, the major difference was Two's loading dock led out to the parking lot, making it the easiest place to get in and out of. There were seven studios altogether, but the premier rooms were One and Two. Two was a typical music theatre space. Open with a two-foot high stage and six playback speakers studding the foot of the stage. The first four feet of the walls were red felt acoustic panels all around the room, a wrap around black counter top with eight foot grey felt acoustic panels above that. People started to mill around. Some hung out on the loading dock, smoking various substances from weed to clove cigarettes, cigars and hand rolled cigarettes.

By the time Dille showed up with his production crew, which consisted of him, his Director of Photography also acting as the cameraman, the sound technician and Dille's personal assistant, the place was packed to capacity. The Band's equipment was all set up. Copeland and Diggins manned the monitors while Philly and Utz turned on amps and tuned guitars.

Dille was working the room, filming every notable, recognizable face at the same time he was soaking in the sweaty cloying mist of people all sweetly wanting something from him. Randy was more subtle. Jeffy went up to Dille the moment he saw him enter the studio with his crew. Greeting him politely, Dille smiled but never once looked Jabonno in the eyes. Randy remained on the stage, pretending to futz with equipment and review the set list sheet taped to the floor until Dille came up to him.

———

76

"Why if it isn't the Divine Randy Root from a God's mouth to my ears."

"Been a long time Dex. Great to see you again."

"I supposed both of those statements could be a matter of opinion. But it's nice to see you again, too, Randall."

"Really admired your success over these years. I look forward to this project with you. Maybe the start of many to come, eh?"

Dille just looked at him and smiled. "You have a good crowd here." This will *look* good, I promise you that."

Jeffy came up at that moment smiling. "We're ready to go. Dexter, we're really happy you're here. This is going to be historic. Great crowd, huh?"

Dille offered Jeffy a cold head-tilted glare. "I'll just be interested to see you perform without any interruptions."

"That was along time ago, D." Jeffy answered sheepishly.

"Funny how some things seem just like yesterday." Dille replied crisply.

The place was packed with DJ's, rock stars, actors, models, posers, groupies, local bands, tech company execs, producers, friends, acquaintances, business friends, wives, girlfriends, boyfriends, baby mamas, baby daddies and kids. Randy had made it clear he had too much work to do for Bertie, Jake and Barter to attend the dress rehearsal. "Besides," he had cleverly added, "I feel better with you guys holding down the sonic fort." Which made them want to stay.

Mindy showed up, having come in her own car and after driving around the block three times found a garage two blocks away. Solita and the girls were there and never far away was Randy's fixer-attorney, Avi Greenblatt. -A small, quiet man in his late 50's who looked older. He quietly studied everything. The SIR staff made their appearance, shaking hands, slapping backs and kissing ass. "Visit our bar after the rehearsal and get your complimentary glass of wine on the SIR House!" announced the manager.

There were old band managers, club managers, tour managers, agents, old band friends, new band friends, roadies, friends of roadies, girlfriends of roadies, other roadies, friends of other roadies, friends of groupies, wannabe friends of wannabe groupies, actors, producers and of course, Dexter Dille and his crew were weaving through that sea of bodies. Ricky Rudolph stood off in a corner, noting it all down on his small legal pad.

Tina worked the room, schmoozing with everyone and glommed onto Dille when he first got there, telling him about Bela Marconi. Dille had developed a talent for shooing people away pleasantly, which is what he did with Tina the moment she mentioned Bela.

Amongst many notables in the crowd was Tara Thyme, once the Queen of the 80s Pop and Dance Scene. In her 70's now, her face was a beautiful work of preservation. She wore gloves and a silk Italian scarf around her neck to hide what she could not control.

The legendary Tara Thyme. Singer. Dancer. Choreographer. Actor. She had one major number one hit that stayed at the top for three weeks: *Yo-Yo Nicky!*

Tara Thyme's life was an object lesson in how fame doesn't necessarily lead to fortune. And the lesson was how being the most remarkably talented person in one field doesn't mean you know everything-least of all -Business. Here's how you can have a number one hit and still get screwed: *Yo-Yo Nicky* had been a pop song originally entitled *Licky-Licky*, by two starving British versions of Tin Pan Alley songwriters. Tara came across it and realized the basic song she had written worked in the song she found. It went like this:

YO! NICKY-NICKY MINE/YOU'RE SO HOT AND SUPER FINE!
YOU DRIVE ME WILD ALL THE TIME!
YO-YO NICKY! YO-YO NICKY! YO-YO NICKY! NICKY MINE!

Performed dressed as a cheerleader, Tara had created the ultimate cheerleader chant, which became the most famous cheerleader chant of all time virtually over night. *Yo Yo Nicky!* rocketed to number one and stayed there for nearly a month. In time the chant was put into commercials, Broadway shows, two television series and even a bunch of box office blockbuster movies. It was covered in eight languages. Then after writing it and performing it and making it not just worldwide famous, but a bona fide anthem, Tara Thyme didn't get one dime of its real money. Not one red cent. And why? Because her manager had failed to negotiate a much-deserved writer's credit for Tara with the two British songwriters when he first negotiated use of their song and she had innocently trusted him to protect her interests.

That added up to over 30 years of no writers fees on a song that would be redone and redone and redone over and over and over again to the tune of hundreds of millions of dollars. All Tara got was the occasional performance fee and fame from having a Number One Hit. Outside of that, all she had left was the ability to boast that because of her early choreography for rock shows like *Hullabaloo, Shindig, Where The Action Is* and the early Beach movies, she had been Paul McCartney's girlfriend. "Well," she clarified, "I wouldn't say I was Paul McCartney's *only* girlfriend in those early days. But I would say I was his *LA girlfriend*..."

When the Fab Four first played The Hollywood Bowl in August of '64, Tara had been the choreographer for the opening act. A chorus line of early Go-Go Dancers warmed up the Hollywood Bowl before the Beatles came on to 19,000 screaming fans at 9:30 that hot August night and by midnight Tara and Paul began seeing each other whenever he was in Los Angeles, over the next two years, indeed qualifying her as *Paul's LA Girlfriend*.

"How is Paul?" Dille asked Tara, getting a long shot of the aging Pop Queen dressed in magenta taffeta.

"I haven't heard from him in years, Dear."

"Okay!" Jeffy started tapping his mic. The crowd quieted and faced him. Here, he was certain people knew who he was. Here, he felt celebrated. Here, he felt invigorated. "It's great to see you all here to bear witness to the Gospel According to the Orifice of the Oracle!"

With that, the Band launched dramatically into "We're All Gods" and soared brilliantly through the entire set to deafening screams and cheers. It got so loud the band rehearsing in Studio One for the same Tour came by to visit. It was Band of Pigeons. But Randy's eyes widened at the sight of Derek Scorch of The Lip Readers, talking with Dille.

By the end of their performance, despite all the drama and despite all the bullshit, the dress rehearsal itself was stunning. The five of them as a unit were spectacular. They performed with all the edge and all the ferocity they'd had when it all began. Randy, seeing Scorch in the audience played with a determination that even had Jeffy turn and look at him during *Kiss This Orifice* where he seemed to be playing right to his old rival.

Jeffy himself felt rejuvenated on stage. You could see it on his face. It was a drug that took effect immediately. Though later, his back and neck would always make him pay for it. Whatever else might be said of them, they were consummate musicians and superb performers who cared very much about their craft. The toughest part for Jeffy was the encore. When they played *Who Are You?* he started thinking about how he heard Kelsey Grammer on TV and then John Lennon in his head and how he didn't want to hear anyone between his ears except himself. Now every time the song would be sung or even mentioned, he would think of Lennon.

Right after, people mobbed the stage as Dille and his cameraman got every angle and perspective possible. He made sure to have his DP zoom in on Randy's face when Derek Scorch came up to greet him. He towered over Randy.

"Randy, been a long time. That was great! Really brought me back!"

Randy put on the happiest smile he had. He slowly looked up, extending his hand. "Derek Scorch. God, when was the last time? -Hilly's?"

"CBGB. That's right. -Great to see you and the guys. -So cool. Hey, you know my kids dig a lot of your stuff. They can't get enough *Head Lice*."

"There's stuff at the pharmacy for that." Randy said with a twinkle in his eye.

Scorch caught and returned the twinkle with a soft laugh. "Really best of luck to you, Randy. Really fun to see all you guys again. Brings back old times."

"Take care, Derek. See you soon!" Randy's smile dimmed as the light from the camera shifted back to the crowd. He turned around to face Luke. "You know you were late on the bridge in *Gods*, right?"

Even after a near-perfect performance, it had been a long-standing tradition for Randy and Jeffy to critique their show, no matter where they were.

"And you were early on the solo on *Kiss*-" Jeffy added, raising his eyebrows at Luke who just snorted with a sneer he thought was a smile.

"Maybe you guys were too fast on *Gods* and too slow on *Kiss*."

Randy and Jeffy looked at each other and laughed. "No." Jeffy said, chuckling.

"But that was funny." Randy added.

Tara came up to them. "Congratulations, you guys. -As great as ever. If you need any dancers or choreography, I'm here for you." She gave Jeffy a longer look and then shuffled away.

Back in the 80s long before Tara realized precisely how colossally financially screwed she was, she had been hired to plot out the choreography for the *Jesus Got A Woody* video. That quickly led to her plotting out other moves for her and Jeffy at her country house in Topanga Canyon, not far from the famed Will Greer's Theatricum Botanicum, until her famous actor husband came in from a shoot in Italy to surprise her, only to be the one who was surprised. Jeffy and Tara's relationship had been on and off ever since.

Tara was forever scheming of ways to get writer's credit over 30 years after the fact. Then, when first making the deal, it could have been easily done. But now, Tara refused to accept the fact there was no way two Cockney boys who grew up in the worst part of London would ever share in the millions they made from that one song alone. Ever. Jeffy looked at her walk away and wished there was a way to help her.

Studio Two began to thin out and as Jeffy and Randy went to change, Larry and Joey stayed behind to get their equipment packed properly and direct Philly, Keith and the rest to load up the truck.

As they filmed all this, Dexter carried on a whispered-conversation with his DP, Haskell Howell. "You know, they actually sounded great. But man, they look old and gray and silly in those space suits."

"Kinda overweight. Like baked potatoes wrapped in gold foil." Dille's production assistant hissed.

"Cartoon versions of themselves." The soundman added.

"Ah..." Dille sighed. "What once looked cool, eh?" Dille looked basically the same with a few facial lines, some gray and few pounds, himself.

"A far cry from their heyday, D. -Visually. That's for sure." Answered Howell. "But they did sound sharp. I used to follow the Toots back in the Day. And they were really their old selves tonight, if I closed my eyes."

"Yeah, not while filming darling. Keep those pretty peepers of yours open. And, trust me. I know them better than most. The truth is the sum of their whole is greater than the individual parts. Come. Let's get our complimentary Merlot. Enough of this for now." Dille waved his hand back and headed for the door, leading his entourage.

Haskell chuckled, turning off the camera as they all started leaving the studio for the walnut paneled bar featured in the Main Room. Randy came running up from behind him.

"Dexter! Uh, -D! I wanted to catch you before you left. Hope you got some good stuff."

"I did."

"Well I'd love for you to come over to the Horn O Plenty. I think you'd love the place. A lot of filmic opportunities there."

"Filmic opportunities, huh? I like that. Yes. Easton told me about your place. We'll get around to that, I'm sure. In the meantime, I'll have my assistant Tonda call you when the time is right. We'll be in touch. See you on Tour." Dille winked. "Toodles!"

"Toodles...." Randy replied feeling weird saying that as he stood there watching them walk away. Then he walked away shaking his head. "Toodles..."

Mindy Jabonno had basically stayed by herself throughout the show, saying hi to people who said hi to her. She had already congratulated her husband, kissed him and headed for home. "I'll order something easy for dinner. We still need to talk."

Jeffy kissed her on the cheek. "See you at home." He watched her walk out. Then he picked up his bass and slipped out the loading dock, nodding at Joey and heading for his car. He walked all the way back down to the top of the L-shaped lot. The Lot was still packed. The lot was always packed. He got in his car and began to back up-when the golf cart driven by the security guard he had seen when he first got there, drove right behind him and stopped, blocking his idling car. Jeffy looked in his rearview mirror, shook his head and got out of his car in a huff, stomping over to the guard.

"What are you doing? Can't you see I'm leaving? You're blocking me. Please move that thing."

"Your ID, Sir. Been a lot of thefts here lately."

"Don't you know who I am? Don't you know how often I've been here over the years? I'm a paying customer. I don't need to explain anything to you."

"No Sir. I do not know *who you are*. If I knew who you were I would not be asking who you are, now would I?"

"I don't know because I don't know you either Sir. Maybe I should ask for your ID."

"Sir, when I come on to your lot and start cursing around like I own the place, you can. Until then, your ID, please or you ain't goin' nowhere."

Deciding it easier to just show him his ID than go back into SIR and complain which would only take longer, Jeffy took out his drivers license and showed it to the guard. The man took out his flashlight.

"Mis-ter Jef-fer-ry Ja-Bon-o..." the guard read.

"Close enough. Satisfied?"

"You have a pleasant night, Sir. And try not be *niggerized* from now on - if you can help it." The guard flicked off the flashlight, handed Jeffy back his license, got back in his cart and putt-putted away keeping his eyes on Jeffy until he slowly rolled off into the night.

Jeffy got into his car, backed up and drove away, shaking his head.

"Maybe if you'd had a Kotex on your head, he'd have known who you are. Ah, don't bother yourself, Jeffy-Luv. *I* know who you are." Jeffy shook his head harder, almost running over a fire hydrant as he made a clumsy left on Wilcox and a short right on Sunset. "No, it can't be." He said to himself. But he knew better.

It was impossible for Jeffy to mistake John Lennon's voice.

CHAPTER 5

The poster read:

!THE TITANS OF YORE -TIME TWIST TOUR!

FEATURING

THE ORIFICE OF THE ORACLE

BAND OF PIGEONS

RECTAL THERMOMETERS

THE BELCH

CLONE OF A CLONE

THE RENT-A-COPS

MIAMI NEW YORK*ATLANTA*CHICAGO*

*SEATTLE*SAN FRANCISCO*SAN DIEGO*LOS ANGELES*

JUNE 19 - JULY 2

AN EIGHT-CITY CELEBRATION OF EIGHTIES ROCK GODS

FROM RIGHT COAST TO LEFT COAST

THIS NEW WAVE/PUNK TOUR ROCKS THE MOST

!THE TITANS OF YORE-TIME TWIST TOUR!

A PURESHYTE PRODUCTION

"Hey, this looks cool, Randy!" Jason Barter held the poster outstretched in his hands. He had been walking by and Randy called him into the studio to check it out. It was a thick gauge of glossy coated three feet by two feet stock. It shined metallic gold with green and red highlights. "I like the backdrop of those giant guitar-wielding rock god silhouettes. -Really cool. Perfect for you guys! Uhm... I've been meaning to ask you. Is it possible you could get tickets to the LA Show for me and my wife?"

"We'll see." Randy replied, staring intensely down at the carpet. "There's only a limited number of free tickets each band member gets to give out per show and LA's a tough one seeing it's home. But we'll see. How's the Baby Daddy Momma Drama theme going? Got that worked out yet like I asked?"

"I'll have it for you this afternoon. Just have a few tweaks-"

"You know what my three year-old daughter did last night?"

"Who? Bathsheba? No. What, Randy?"

Randy suddenly turned, staring intensely into Barter's eyes.

"She ran up to me totally naked and said: *'Daddy, come smell my sweet clean pussy!'* "

Barter jerked back in reflex at Randy's words and the look on his face. "She-she knows English that-that-that well already, at three?" was all Barter could manage to say. He blushed lobster red, dropped the poster back on the stack sitting on the client couch set behind Randy's perch at the soundboard. He felt weirdly violated. He slowly moved backwards towards the door. Randy went back to staring at the floor.

"Ok then, I'll get that track to you right after lunch."

"See you then, Jason." Randy replied, still staring past his shoes, past the floor, past the rehearsal space and deep into the core of the Earth.

86

Barter went straight into Paulette's office, closed the door and told her what happened. Paulette rolled her eyes. "Oh, Randy..." she sighed.

"Why'd he say that to me, Paulette?"

"To blow off steam, I guess. He has a lot of complicated pressures to deal with."

"But why of all people, me? I'm not exactly his confidant. That was just weird."

"That's exactly why he said those things to you. Who's going to believe *you* over him, darling?" Paulette spoke with a cultured, dusky voice. Her clipped, light Bahamian accent made people think she was British.

"I'd never say anything outside of here. I'm a loyal guy."

"Oh yes. He knows that. And more importantly for you - I know that."

Paulette had started as a receptionist for Randy years ago and had helped him keep Horn O' Plenty Productions a functioning and profitable concern since the '90s. She ran the Horn as if it were her own company and kept a professional discipline that Randy had depended on for years. She was the only one in that building Randy paid properly plus full health benefits.

Paulette was number one on Tina's Hit List.

"Well Jason." Paulette said with a faint nod. "If I were you, I'd forget all about what Randy said. I assure you - he probably has already. Just get back to work." With that she turned around, faced her computer and started typing.

Jason thought about that a moment, nodded knowingly. "Thanks Paulette." Then he got up and went back to get his track ready to present to Randy.

The Tour was about to start. Randy was packed and ready to go. So was Tina. Randy kept staring a hole into the carpet until he wandered out onto the Strip for lunch. Lately he'd been going to Bushido Sushi two blocks down from the Horn.

While he sat there munching on his second Spicy Tuna Roll, his phone chirped. It was his attorney.

"Randy. Thought I'd catch you at lunch."

"Avi. You did. Been waiting to hear from you. What'd you find out?

"Our guy reports they're like clockwork."

"We're leaving for Miami tonight on a red eye. Make sure he keeps tabs on Marconi. I wanna know if he stays for something else, or follows us out. Also, I got a weird call from the Girls a few nights back.

"*The* Girls?"

"Yeah."

"Been a while. They must need more money."

"Yeah, I'm not so sure that's all this time."

"Well, if it isn't I'll let you know."

"I'm sure you will."

"And the other thing?"

"Leave it alone for now. That's a last resort."

"As I've been telling you now for the last eight months. I told you to get a pre-nup."

"Thanks Avi. Call me tomorrow at the hotel. Paulette gave you all the info. I gotta get back to the studio."

Finishing his third roll, Randy strolled out of Bushido Sushi and ambled over to Book Stew, where he milled through *art* books for a half an hour, bought a few and then browsed magazines at the newsstand right by the Horn, before finally going back to the studio. Once back, he sat down at his laptop and resumed staring at the floor. One heartbeat after that, Jason Barter knocked on the door jam to the studio and came in, as he had promised.

"I got the track here, Randy." He handed Root a flash drive.

Randy plugged it into his laptop. Clicking "Play" he turned to Barter. "Ok. Let's see what you've done then." He listened to the track staring at Barter without saying a word. Then he played it a second time.

"Hmmmmm." Randy lifted his head and looked at his associate composer. "That's not bad. I like what you did, inverting the hook notes on the Popeye theme. Really pops! Got that hip hoppy thing. Now I want you to add the Three Stooges theme. You know, the verse portion of *Listen To The Mockingbird.*"

"I thought their theme was *Three Blind Mice.*"

"That was later. No. Do a spin on *Mockingbird.* Add it into your bridge. Change the piano line to harpsichord. And add more cowbell. A lot more cowbell." With that he got up. "I'll be in touch. I fly out tonight with Tina. We'll be at the Fontainebleau on Miami Beach for two days if you need to reach me. Paulette has my itinerary."

"Good Luck!" Barter said, smiling too big, still shaken, as he uncontrollably replayed Randy's earlier outburst in his mind.

"Thanks." Randy said blandly and left.

"Uh, Hey, could I get you and the guys to sign one of these posters for me?" Barter called out to Randy's shadow, which didn't answer back.

The Tour began in Miami.

After RoyBob got them their rooms at the Fontainebleau, the first thing the guys had to do to kick off the Tour was a press conference at the Hard Rock Stadium, arranged by the tour promoter. It was the first the Band had had in many years. There they were, performance-ready dressed in their sparkling gold space suits and winged MegaHorns. There were reporters from the local news stations and newspapers as well as some bloggers and even a reporter from Rolling Stone magazine and a few online publications. Dille was there, filming away. He had positioned himself and Howell so he could cut between the reporters and the Band.

"How does it feel to embark on your final tour?"

"FINAL TOUR? WHO SAID THAT??" Jeffy exploded. Muffled laughter could be heard around the room. Jeffy glared back."No. This is NOT our final tour. Who said it was? Who?"Jeffy turned to Randy, whispering, "Stop kicking me."

"Dille's filming. Be cool." Randy whispered back. Then he addressed the reporter. "Ah, honestly we like to keep our options open."

Luke Wharm always desperate to be seen as a true member of the Band, piped up expectedly. "This ain't over as long as they got new blood here. You might say I'm the heir-"

"Apparently-" Jeffy said, cutting Wharm off brusquely. "-Whoever told you that was totally misinformed. We never say quit. And we definitely never say die. Whoever said that was giving you hype. Definitely Fake News." He shot Luke a nasty look sideways. "-Next question."

"An oracle is supposed to predict the future. What'd you guys ever predict?'

Randy smiled. "That we'd get asked even dumber questions in the future than we did in the 80's. Look it up: Village Voice, October 31st edition, 1984. Welcome to the Future. -Next question."

"Why aren't you guys in the Rock N' Roll Hall Of Fame yet. The Ramones. The Cars. They say Devo is next. So many of your contemporaries have been inducted. Why not The Orifice Of The Oracle?"

"Our time will come." Jeffy answered honestly and confidently. "-Next question?"

"What do you think of the MeToo Movement and what's happening between Harvey Weinstein and now the suicide of Jeffrey Epstein?"

Randy looked back at the questioner and blinked with all the innocence he could summon to his eyes. "We must rise, as we always said in our songs, to a Godly level where such depravities are no longer..."

"We've always sung out about corruption and immorality in our society. Randy's right." Jeffy stepped in. "-Any more questions?"

"Jeffy, You were recently married and several news organizations pronounced your Kennedy Assassination-themed wedding as possibly the most tasteless ceremony and reception ever witnessed in recorded history. In retrospect, would you agree?"

Jeffy turned purple, but kept it together. "First off. I was framed. That's not how it was supposed to really go and secondly, I was drawing attention to the fact that over a half-century later and we still don't know the truth of what happened that day in Dallas!"

"Ok, yeah, we'd all like to know that, sure. But why make that your wedding theme and how were you then *framed*? You arranged for the exploding Kennedy head cake, which I hear was delicious, by the way. Dressed your best man up as Oswald, yourself as JFK, and an actor dressed as Fidel Castro gave your bride dressed as Jackie Kennedy away. Didn't you?"

"That's all been taken out of context. -Any more questions?"

"Yes. There's only one other band I know that designed their own hats-"

Jeffy shot up from his seat. "Stop right there! There's *NO* comparison. We didn't design a *hat*. The MegaHorn is *not* a hat! It is a musical instrument conveniently located."

Randy nodded, chuckling. "Yeah. Try playing their hat."

Jeffy had had enough. "-Any more questions? No? Thanks. See you at the Show." They then ended the press conference the way they used to at their height. They all got up in unison, put their MegaHorns to their mouths, blew a loud F note and walked off to their dressing room.

"That went well." Randy said smirking. "Just like old times." Randy always enjoyed press conferences. They gave him a chance to sell an image that sold tickets and sold records and drove producers in their cars to the Horn to have Randy do the music for their movies and shows. Jeffy was different. He was a true Orifice of the Oracle believer.

After the press conference, the guys hung out in their Hard Rock Stadium executive team locker-suite. The suite was part dressing room and part game room with four full bathrooms, a pool table and a Jacuzzi. It was furnished with plush couches and upholstered chairs. There were several well-stocked refrigerators and coolers filled with chilled bottles of water, soda, energy drinks, wine and beer placed around four long tables topped with fruit platters and veggie platters and sandwich platters and pizza platters and pastry platters. Larry had grabbed a beer, twisting off the non-twist cap in her hand. The guys started to check out the spread and settle down and relax before their sound check. They hadn't been there more than five minutes when this short, bald, tan Tasmanian devil in a shirtless white linen suit and matching sockless loafers burst in.

"Hey Hey! There they are! Superstars! The Orifice Of The Oracle! -True Eighties Rock Gods! I'm Trippin'! I'm back in Time! It's a Time Twist! Oh Man! Look at you guys! Spectacular! Fucking spectacular! -Morrie Pureshyte, Pureshyte Productions." He said, shaking everyone's hand furiously, spinning this way and that. "You like the room? You guys got what you need? Wow! This is going to be amazing! And do we have an after-party planned! Oh man, you're going to totally freak! Everything good? Everything cool? Everything Great? -Great! Any problem, just have RoyBob get my assistant, Andromeeka." A short slender woman with a crew cut wearing horned-rimmed glasses and playing card tattoos up and down her cinnamon arms nodded authoritatively holding her clipboard.

Pureshyte went on. "Lemme tellya: YOU Toots are in classic company! Yeah, originally we wanted to get Flock A Seagulls with you guys, but they were all booked up so we got something even better: Band Of Pigeons! Huh? Yeah? You remember their hit: *I Sat?* You know: *I Sat So Close and Stayed*? Charted the top 40 *at* 40! Gonna be an awesome show! Okay. See you guys backstage. I gotta visit the other bands before the show. So! Have a great one out there guys. I know you will. You're beautiful! You guys haven't aged a day! I mean, Wow! -The Oracle of the Orifice! Wow!" With that, the promoter left with Andromeeka right behind him.

Larry growled. "One more minute and this Tour would have been without a fucking promoter."

Randy nodded chuckling. "Whadda you guys wanna bet he's now in the Pigeons' executive team locker-suite telling them how he tried to get The Lip Readers instead of us."

While everybody laughed at that, Tina laughed to appear supportive, sitting down in one of the green leather chairs. In her head, she said: "That would have made for a better Tour, for sure." But out loud she said, "Derek Scorch doesn't have half your talent, baby."

Mindy had come in with Jeffy after the press conference. She was dressed like a Go-Go Dancer from the 60s, complete with White Go-Go Boots. Jeffy took two bottles of Pellegrino sparkling out of the cooler and handed one to her. She handed him a slice of pizza. She looked at Tina staring at Randy, she assumed, adoringly. She turned and whispered to Jeffy. "Tina's like Yoko Ono."

"Jeffy chuckled lightly. "Yeah, Tina's like Yoko Ono, from the Netherworld."

"I didn't know she was Dutch."

Jeffy smiled at Mindy. "How's your pizza?"

While Jeffy and Mindy carried on their whisper conversation at the catering table, and everybody else was laughing with Randy, RoyBob walked to the center of the room and cleared his throat. He held up like a poker hand several shiny laminated playing card-sized badges.

"Here's your guys' All Areas Access Passes. I got one for everyone, including wives and girlfriends!" He handed the shiny metallic, green and red miniature version of the poster with "AAA" printed at the bottom out to Tina and Mindy, as well as Larry and Joey's current girlfriends, then the crew and then the guys. Each was attached to an orange lanyard so it could be worn around the neck for easy viewing.

Shaggy took his and June's from RoyBob and got down on one knee, half bowing and handed it ceremoniously to his associate. "Your very first." He said with all the majesty he could muster. He smiled, but she could tell something was bothering him. June took the pass carefully and held it reverently in her hands staring at it like she'd found a golden ticket under the wrapper of a Wonka chocolate bar. In her mind, it glowed exactly the same.

The fabled **A**ll **A**reas **A**ccess Pass was the coveted key to the Rock Kingdom. - The passport to ShowBiz Heaven. The very sight of it could a make three hundred pound muscle bound guard twitch and bow before you. It could part a sweaty sea of sardine-packed people and make them wonder who you are and how you got that pass as you pass them by.

That little plastic coated piece of paper gave you access to every part of the venue: Backstage. The Cantina. The Band's dressing room. All doors opened to you. For ten days, June Lucey would belong to an elite class with an exclusive set of privileges never granted the general seating public. Privileges totally taken for granted, except for people like Shaggy Milken and June Lucey.

About an hour later as the Band began to prepare for their first sound check of the Tour, Tina had gone off to make a call to Bela and when she returned, Randy was not in the executive team locker-suite. No one was in the executive team locker-suite. Not even RoyBob, who basically used it as his office and made and took countless calls from there. Tina was hungry and decided she wanted to grab a bite at the Cantina. But to do so, she needed one of the meal-stubs Andromeeka had given to RoyBob. At that moment, Joey came in and grabbed some bottles of beer out of a cooler, she smiled at Tina and was about to open the door and leave.

"Hey Joey."

"Hey Tina. How's it goin'?"

"Do you know where my meal ticket is?"

"Oh, yeah, Tina. If by 'meal-ticket' you mean Randy? He's on stage. We're about to do our sound check." With that, Joey smiled and left.

Tina just stared at the closed door with slit-lids and constricting pupils in her cobra-like eyes.

The first sound check went off without a hitch. It had been so long since they had one, it all sounded good to them. They were back in the locker-suite in twenty minutes. A minute after that there was a knock on the door. RoyBob answered. It was Andromeeka.

"Hi Doll. I need a copy of the Band's set list. I'll have the stage manager get someone to tape yours in front of the drum riser by the center mic, before you come on."

"Here you go." RoyBob smiled as he handed her the list. Thanks, "Meeka!" The production coordinator winked, threw him a kiss, turned around and left.

Each Band's play set revolved around their biggest hit and in some cases, their only identifiable tune, giving them the pejorative title of One Hit Wonders. The Pigeons, another Aussie, AC/DC-like Down Under band had as Pureshyte pointed out, *I Sat. (So Close And Stayed)*. The Rent-A-Cops had *AgnesAnn! (You Don't Have To Put On The Black Lite.)* Rectal Thermometers were known for *She Deafened Me With Alchemy*. The Belch had *Rock The Clam Bar*. Clone Of A Clone were big in the Day with a number of hits, though *Horny Like The Moose* was what most people recalled.

The Orifice Of The Oracle were seen the same way and were consigned to the same fate with *Flip It Off* even though their set list was filled with a variety of hits and songs considered anthems by their most devoted followers. These bands were remembered for their most maudlin tunes, instead of their best. Technically, the maudlin tunes had become maudlin by being over-played. They were over-played because they were popular. Though some would claim they were popular by being overplayed. Either way, that's why people typically remembered the tune and why each band was branded by their biggest hit.

One thing Randy left for Jeffy to do all by himself on tour, chiefly because Randy saw little personal gain in it for himself, was visiting the local rock stations and offering free concert tickets. Starting in Miami, this routine began with a short interview by the DJ where the questions and answers usually went something like this:

"Hey! I am here with The Orifice Of The Oracle co-founder, Jeffy Jabonno! Jeffy! Great to see you, man! Thanks for coming on the Jimmy Jam-Jam Show."

"Great to be here, Jimmy."

"Jeffy's in town with his band The Orifice Of The Oracle on the Titans Of Yore Time Twist Tour! How's it goin', Jeffy?"

"Great Jimmy."

"Awesome Jeffy! We'll be listening to a few of The Oracle's greatest hits while you're here and I hear you've brought free tickets to the Titans Of Yore Time Twist Tour for our first five callers! -Is that right, Jeffy?"

"It is, Jimmy."

"Well, we'll get to that in a sec. Let's talk for a minute. Tell me, Jeffy: What's it like working with such a genius like Randy Root? I mean the songs are one thing. But his coming up with something as iconic as the MegaHorn raised you guys to a whole new level!"

"What makes you think Root designed the MegaHorn all by himself, Jimmy?"

"Hmm. Sorry, Jeffy. I thought I heard that Randy had done that all by himself. I don't know why."

"Well, being the guy who co-designed the MegaHorn and first came up with the idea and also named it, I don't know why you said it either. Let's get on with the ticket giveaway, Jimmy Jam-Jam. I'm sure your listeners are waiting for that."

"Right on, Jeffy. But first, let's *Blow It Out!*"

If the interview didn't go that way, it tended to go this way:

"So Jeffy, I always wanted to ask you about your solo album, *I'm A God - What The Hell Are You?* I loved it myself. But why do you think people in general, *flipped it off?*"

"Ha! Good one. Flip It Off. Good play on our song. Clever! Well, Lemon Head, Lemon Head, right? People were just not ready for the next step in musical evolution. So like my mom always said, if you're not failing - you're not learning. Just like you're learning right now about how to conduct an interview, huh, Lemon Head?"

"Ok! -Let's give away those tickets now."

And when it didn't go either of those two ways, it went like this:

"Hey Jeffy, I remember when you had your own designer line of customized suits! Very Orifice of the Oracle back in the day."

"Yes, Thank you Guaca...molius... That is what you said your name was, right? -Guacamolius? Yes. I'm very proud of that. That was our fashion subdivision of the Orifice of the Oracle."

"What was the name of your sharkskin suits? The Immortal GodsHair Selection?"

"The Immortal *GodHead* Collection. Single-breasted with double vents and Double-breasted with a single middle vent. Made of a rare spider silk and Egyptian linen blend and available in black, red, green, gold or purple."

"I had one of your suits!"

"Had?"

"The wife gave it to Goodwill, unbeknownst to me..." The DJ squeezed a clown horn for comic affect. "HONK!"

"Well, Guacamolius, that's awesome and a perfect segue into our ticket giveaway for the Titans Of Yore, Time Twist Tour..."

In the early days of The Oracle's success, Jeffy could be as obnoxious as he wanted and everyone had to kiss his ass and call it ice cream. But all that kissing his ass made him so intolerable that by the end of their peak, everyone else in the Band couldn't take his complaining and bitching and directing either. They just ignored him and walked away, leaving Joey, basically the same height as Jeffy and a bit heavier, to give her brother some tough love by pushing him up against a wall and advising him with the sweetest tone in her voice to "calm the fuck down and shut the fuck up."

When The Oracle's fame began to wane, Jeffy started a line of suits. As Jeffy was generally credited back in the beginning with designing the Oracles' space suit, at first there was great interest in his designs. -At first. It even led to him becoming a runway director for a variety of designers from Los Angeles to Miami to Paris. That is until Jeffy's control freak tantrums and impulse issues had him touching the models too much, changing their clothes two, three, sometimes four times in a row and even going out on the runway during a show to tell a model her rhythm was off. Jeffy Jabonno's fashion industry career didn't last much longer after that.

All the tirades followed by the tantrums followed by more tirades and more tantrums added up to zero people wanting to have anything to do with him, let alone actually work with him. His reputation as a designer and runway director, along with his self-celebrated GodHead Collection clothing line quickly went the way of the Nehru jacket.

Small wonder why he needed every "One-Hit Wonder" and "Where Have They Been?" nostalgia tour offered the Oracle. When you choose to let every opportunity that comes your way get sabotaged by your temper, your tenor, your tenets and worst, your lack of tact - you have no choice.

So no matter how much it pissed him off. No matter how much he imagined strangling the DJ, or stabbing the DJ or shooting the DJ, or his favorite: poisoning the DJ, Jeffy managed to act magnanimous and laugh off every fucked up question with a smile and one modestly snide remark. His favorite snide remark was:

"Thanks for having me on your Show. It's been like getting a lobotomy from a proctologist."

The DJ's dug it. To most people in the rock n' roll world, the ruder and nastier a rock star acted, the cooler. It was actually one of Jeffy's last places to feel that people really knew who he was. The only thing troubling was when he began the station visits, as the Tour began, he began hearing John Lennon singing *Who Are You?* -And loud. "That's a *Who* song." Jeffy muttered to himself. "Bollocks!" replied John. "*I cant'* do covers? Remember *who* you're talkin' to. I was doing covers when you were playin' with ya wanker *under* the covers, Jeffy-poo." Jabonno shrugged and shook his head. "It's me, talking to myself... Playing with myself... Fuck, *Stop it!*"

After their first sound check, Tina finally found Randy as he was leaving the stage and suggested they take a walk around the Hard Rock Stadium, just to check it out before they let people in. The massive football field's retractable roof was open to a bright Florida day. The field was shimmering green. The blue sky was cloudless. The stage was set on the line of scrimmage. Speakers stacked fifty feet high flanked the stage. Guitar and organ blasts and bleeps and blangs came out from time to time along with snare rolls, bass drum kicks and cymbal crashes as different band's crews tested their equipment and worked out their sound checks. The sound pumping through the air could be felt from forty feet away. Walking around the front row seats, Randy looked up at the speakers.

"Hey, Remind me to wear my earplugs onstage. I sometimes forget."

"Well you can hear me now, right?"

Randy sighed. "Yes..."

Honestly, I think the Horn O Plenty studio could be run a lot more efficiently."

"We've had this conversation before."

"And we'll have it again until you get my point."

"C'mon, Tina, I got history with her."

"History. Yeah that's a good way to put it. She should be history. Joey Jabonno represents the Horn at its worst, Randy. She's slovenly. She's overweight. She cares little about her appearance. You can tell what she had for the last eight meals from the shirt she's been wearing for the last two days. She's got those candy corn teeth from all the coke she's done over the years. What kind of impression do you think that makes on your clients, hmmm? Don't be so sentimental."

Deep down, Randy felt exactly that same way, but would never bring himself to express it if Tina hadn't expressed it for him first. That was the one thing Tina still did for Randy that really worked for him: Her ruthless business sense. Her balls to say and do things he would rather only think.

"Finding someone for the same money will be near impossible. And she is a great engineer."

"Whatever it costs, it'll be worth it in image, believe me. And there are plenty of great engineers out there. I bet for what you've been paying her, you could get two young hungry engineers eager to please. Get rid of her. One thing has nothing to do with the other. You're running a business. Not a charity." Randy looked straight ahead and nodded.

Roughly fifty yards away from Randy and Tina, Dexter Dille was filming June Lucey backstage. She excitedly went on at a mile a minute about The Orifice of the Oracle and her life-long dedication to the Band as a super-ultra-fan. Getting a medium head shot of her wearing her own MegaHorn with all the Band member's signatures on it, including Skippy's, Howell then zoomed in to an extreme close up on June's wide-eyed face. Her glowing green eyes rolled around as she made the most of her fifteen minutes of fame.

"Hi! My name is June Lucey! I've been an Orifice of the Oracle acolyte since 1977. That's what we super-fans call ourselves: Acolytes. I've got all their albums. I've been to all their Tours, so this is a dream come true! And when I first heard they were touring again I thought Wow! They'll be in their Mylar togas like in the very beginning, you know? And then I thought, No, maybe they'd do the Zeus tour, you know? -From '79? Dressed like Greek Gods? Then I thought, wait, no. Going to Atlanta, maybe they'd do the Atlantis tour there and the Thor tour in New York, the Jesus Tour in Chicago and the Shiva Tour in San Francisco. The Mayan Tour or the Ra Tour in San Diego. The Shinto Tour or the Gilgamesh Tour in Los Angeles. But then I realized: No. They'll go with their classic gold space suits and MegaHorns and you know what? I was right! They did! They are!"

Shaggy had been acting subdued all day compared to his usual self. The only time he sounded halfway like the Shaggy everyone knew was when he gave June her AAA pass. He had gotten the merchandise table set up in the front of the venue and had made sure June was enjoying her first experience on Tour with the Band, though there were times where he looked like he was going to cry. June noticed it and decided to ask him. "You look so sad and I'm so happy. You've been sweet all day but I can tell something's bothering you. What's wrong, Peter?"

Shaggy looked down at the ground. "Oh...nothing. Just Waffles, my dog died... He was fourteen. He was my best friend. He just died this morning before we got here. I had to take his body to the vet for disposal before getting on the plane. I can't afford one of those pet cemeteries. And when I got here to the Stadium and met Randy, he yelled at me for some box of merch' not showing up. I told him about Waffles and he just kept yelling about the box having collectibles in it-he didn't care about my dog at all..." Shaggy choked on his words, afraid he was about to sob in front of June. He took a deep breath and slowly let it out as June hugged him.

"I'm sorry Peter. Sometimes our heroes don't live up to their hype. But I forgive them for their less than God-like and sometimes less than human-like behavior because of all the great music they've given to the world."

"C'mon." Shaggy said, wiping his eyes. "We need to set up the merch' table now."

Each city on a tour is unique unto itself. One city performance can go easily and smoothly and the next amount to a hundred-car pile-up. Moving from city to city every two days can have a blurring effect from one stage to the next on everything you do and everyone you meet. Places blur. Faces blur. Moments blur. Feelings blur. Words blur. The Tour blurs. And there are no corrective lenses for the astigmatism touring causes. -At least not yet.

Atlanta had its share of memorable moments and its own special set of challenges. Half the equipment didn't show up. RoyBob had to borrow a drum kit from The Belch. This time at Sound Check, Randy spent thirty minutes just making Scruffy readjust everything so his playback speaker was louder than everyone else's because he couldn't hear himself. "If I tell you I can't hear myself, IT MEANS I CAN'T HEAR MYSELF! UP MY DAMN PLAYBACK VOLUME!"

Scruffy, realizing Randy's playback was already as loud as it would go, shouted, "OK, double-R, I've turned it up to eleven! How's that?"

"Hmmm. Better. Just keep it at that level. Don't touch it now. It's perfect."

The show flew by in a perfect blur. For them though, in their traditional critique that religiously followed afterward, somebody always screwed the pooch, usually Luke Wharm. Though nobody was above getting called out for fucking up on stage no matter how slight the mistake.

"Randy, you sang 'a zoo,' instead of 'the zoo' in We're All Gods.

"Yeah? Well you sang *'Magdalena's Puddy,'* not *'Goody'* in *Woody*."

Sitting in the green room in Atlanta, Mindy was searching the catering table holding a cup of coffee in one hand and a spoon in the other.

"Hey has anybody seen the milk?"

RoyBob pointed to fridge on the right. "All dairy stuff is in there Min'. Man...-*Milk.* You know I once had to get a live Guernsey cow up to the hotel penthouse suite for fresh milk for Madonna?"

Truck, not known for laughing, laughed a deep guttural guffaw. "Man, ever hear about Whitney Houston keeping live lobsters in her hotel bathtub?"

"That's a classic. Speaking of matriarchies," Philly Phingers piped up, after a long swig on a beer bottle.

"That Paulette Matthews who runs Randy's Horn O Plenty office? She stood there with her hands on her hips trying to boss me and Utz around, telling me to take the trash out and move all these company file boxes from her office to the storage area right in the bleedin' middle of us packin' the lorry. Now I didn't want to make a big thing of it there, but I'll tell you, that Paulette did everything to make the move harder. Honestly, the woman thinks she's a bronze Goddess!"

Scruffy chuckled and rolled his eyes at Philly. "Yeah, well don't tell me you wouldn't want to polish her patina."

"Now that's a different story altogether, Mate."

Changing the subject as they all laughed, RoyBob shrugged. "Yup. Touring has changed even since the last tour we all did together in Japan. That's for sure. No more cash flying around. Remember when I'd have to give each of you nine grand so I wouldn't have to declare an eighth of a mil or more? Those days are long gone."

"We never got to keep the money, anyway, RoyBob." Scruffy said with a wink.

The Atlanta Show was vibrant. Their performance in Piedmont Park was inspired. They were enjoying themselves. Even Larry looked happy, sort of. Especially after the show when two fans climbed up on stage, running for two MegaHorns someone had thrown onstage near Larry. She swung her guitar less than an inch from one of their heads. "Get the fuck away from those," she barked, wearing an evil grimace.

"But they're ours." They whimpered. "We threw them on stage just so we could say hi to you, Larry. Would you sign-"

"Hi. Bye. Take your SmegmaHorns and fuck off!" Larry said with a sneering smile. The two fans stood frozen, staring at Larry.

Joey Jabonno saw what was going on as she directed Utz and Philly to start packing. She smiled, picked up the Horns and handed them to the fans. "Now you guys have a cool Larry Root story you can tell your grandchildren." They handed her a sharpie and Joey signed their 'horns. "Thanks, Joey!" they shouted as they stumbled off the stage and left, looking furtively over their shoulders at Larry. And Dille had filmed it all.

Joey was considered good-natured and always real. "The nice one of the Band" was what most people called her. Larry Root was not. Randy's nickname for Larry was "The Trickster" and it wasn't meant affectionately. In her youth before she came out, Larry would trick guys into seduction games while out on dates and then unprovoked literally beat the shit out of her unsuspecting date. Once even sodomizing her victim with a strap-on. Then as the guy sat there in a daze, she'd tell the poor idiot with a smile on her face how if he said a word-she'd tell everyone he'd tried to rape her. She was fun like that.

In her teens, Larry was always looking for a fight and her parents felt sorry for any boy who tried to date her. Even Randy had once described her as "A great guitarist and a total psycho." She once burned down her own house claiming, "It was time to move."

In the morning after the show, RoyBob was sitting in the Atlanta Hilton lobby, ready to assemble everyone to move on to New York City. He'd already dealt with check-out and was just waiting for everyone to come down from their rooms when Larry walked up to him and sat down right next to him.

For one of the few times ever in her life she started talking conversationally to a surprised RoyBob, while dragging on a cigarette in a no smoking area.

"You know, puff. Atlanta, this hotel...Puff. -Really brings back memories. Puff. The last time I played Atlanta this couple approached me after the Show. Puff. The husband willingly offered his wife to me. I could tell they both thought I was a guy! Puff. So I took her back to my room and I decided to fist her. And in the middle of me plunging into her almost up to my elbow over and over, I realize she's on the phone giving a play by play of our sex. Puff. Literally moaning she goes, *'Ahhh! He's fisting me! Oh his fist is so big!'*" Larry laughed at her own story and took another puff on her cigarette, completely ignoring the no smoking signs everywhere in the lobby.

RoyBob, happy that Dille and his camera were nowhere to be seen, replied "Wow, Larry. Quite a story."

"Yeah..." Larry smiled for a long nanosecond. Taking another puff on her cigarette, she stood up and exhaled saying, "Those were the days..." Then she walked away.

A blur of hotel desks and bell hops and suitcases, taxis, chartered buses, planes and shuttles, checkpoints and security, flight attendants and passengers and production assistants and tour coordinators and random fans blurring from city to city to city.

New York City meant a lot to the Band. It's where they got their first big break and things started to move forward for them. After they arrived and checked into the Plaza, the second thing they did was visit the site of CBGB.

"It's an over-priced clothing store." Jeffy moaned.

"No punk shit, either." Grunted Larry.

"Nothing in my size." Joey pretended to pout.

"I played there once in '06, right before it closed." Luke said, peering in the window.

"Well I'm gonna check it out, just for fun." Randy said with a smile.

The rest of them looked at each other. They all wanted to leave.

"I think we'll all just meet back up at the hotel." Jeffy said as he hailed a cab, jumped in and took off by himself. Joey, Larry and Luke looked at one another and shrugged.

"Let's go to China Town." Joey suggested. "I know a great place on Elizabeth Street and then we can go across Canal Street to Ferrara's Bakery for cannolis, in what's left of Little Italy..."

Whatever town Joey was in, she knew some of the finest eateries around. While Jeffy would religiously rely on the Zagat guide to fine dining anywhere in the world, Joey was her own Zagat guide. -Anywhere in the world. In Miami, she had dragged the roadies and Larry and RoyBob to a Cuban hole-in-the-wall on South Beach called Porto Sagua for boliche. In Atlanta it was Pittypat's Porch, for the mushroom polenta.

The restaurant she knew in New York's China Town was Lin's Garden. Joey led her companions through herds of people crowding the streets as if they had AAA passes. Past all the sales-stalls on the south side of Canal Street offering perfume, clothing, imitation pocket books and cheap Chinatown tchotchkes. Past the fish markets alive with the smell of fresh seafood displayed on beds of crushed ice. Past the exotic produce peddlers hawking lychee nuts, dragon fruit, mangosteen, Chinese broccoli, bok choy and more, all hugging the gutter and curbside, yelling their deals in Cantonese. After a quick right on Elizabeth Street and a quick left on Bayard Street, they feasted on everything from orange ginger sesame garlic chicken to giant tender sweet prawns with special noodles in lobster chunk sauce. Having left some room for dessert, Joey led Larry and Luke across Canal Street to get cannolis at the oldest Italian Bakery in Manhattan: Ferrara's.

Walking out eating her third cannoli, Joey looked at her companions and laughed. "The oldest Italian Bakery in Manhattan and all I saw in there were Asians, which is cool, as long as they get the recipes right." She almost choked laughing.

Since the late 80s, Chinatown had experienced a sudden growth spurt, jumping over Canal Street into what used to be strictly Little Italy. Streets that once featured all The Christopher Columbus Societies and Enrico Caruso Opera Appreciation Groups and Italian Brotherhood Clubs with all the old men sipping their espresso and playing Bocce ball in front had over time transformed into Cho's Noodle Factory, Tiny Shanghai, The Tai Pan Bakery, amid various shops and tourist stores all named and run by hardworking and industrious Chinese and Koreans and Vietnamese, among other assorted Asians.The once legendary paisano community was reduced to virtually Mulberry Street, which basically catered to foot traffic with outdoor tented-markets selling t-shirts and featured just a handful of Italian restaurants and cafes. Umberto's Clam House where Joey Gallo was gunned down was as gone as he was.

Shoving the last bit of cannoli into her mouth, Joey headed towards Mulberry.

"Hey, before we go back, let's get some Little Italy t-shirts over there. Who knows how long even that'll be around...Ooo-and we gotta go by Lombardi's Pizza. You gotta try a slice of their clam pie!"

Sometimes on Tour all the events that surround the Show in a city dominate memories of the Tour more than the performance itself. -Especially if the performance is flawless and goes off without one bitch. That great dinner you had. That great party you went to. That great groupie you met. New York was usually one of those towns. Usually.

Now sitting in their trailer behind the stage in Central Park at the old Wollman Skating Rink, everybody was staring into space when Ricky Rudolph walked in.

"Hey guys, Ricky Rudolph, New York Times. Remember me? Great to see you all again!"

Randy walked up to Ricky and shook his hand. "Great to see you again, Rick. Glad you could make it."

Jeffy smiled at Ricky. "Have a seat. Feel free to take a beer or whatever. Our dressing trailer is your dressing trailer."

"Great to see you all again. I'm going to follow you guys now for the rest of the Tour. I'm doing an interview with Dexter Dille in just a few minutes on his filming the Tour. This is historic." Unlike, Los Angeles, Ricky was now dressed in slacks, an Izod casual shirt and a solid black sports coat. In the right lapel of that jacket was a microphone attached to his handheld tape recorder, nestled in his pocket and recording.

Utz looked at Scruffy who looked at Truck who stared sullenly into space. "Yeah, historic." Truck deadpanned. "Never heard that before in Rock n Roll." Everybody laughed, including Ricky.

"So where's Tina?" He asked, looking around. Mindy here? They around? I'd love to say hey."

"Tina had to go back to LA for business. She'll meet up with us in San Francisco." Randy answered.

"Yeah," Jeffy added. "Mindy's coming with her. I needed her to take care of some business for me, back home." Randy flashed a puzzled look at Jeffy for a second. Mindy had left the Tour abruptly without any explanation to anyone. Jeffy saying she was coming back with Tina was more of a wish than a probability.

"Hey!" piped up Philly. "You blokes hear bout Axe Stickette from the Den of Thieves gettin' arrested for hanging out on Epstein's Island?" He giggled like a schoolboy. The others looked around the room acting like they hadn't heard him. Ricky winced as if the words themselves were painful.

Randy walked up close to Philly and whispered in his ear. "Keep that shit on the down low. That's not what we want in Dille's film. And the guy in the jacket is from the Times. Let's try to control the narrative some, Philly." Philly's eyes got wide as Randy spoke. He just nodded. Then he looked at Randy and winked.

The New York show itself was spectacular. No one who had ever seen the Orifice of the Oracle would deny that they knew how to put on a great show. It was actually more than just a great show. It turned out to be a great deal of showing. More showing than should have ever showed in any show.

As the Band launched into *Flip It Off!* Jeffy, in almost Houdini-like fashion somehow managed to flip off his pants and played the rest of the set in a string jock strap, which then also malfunctioned. When Randy and the others stared at him after the show he looked back at them incredulously, throwing up his hands, exclaiming, "What? What's the big deal? Sometimes I need to breath free on stage. You all know that!"

Larry whispered to Joey, "He's right. It AIN'T a big deal..." Joey who guffawed more than laughed, added. "So who cares?" Then she shouted to Jeffy. "Breath free, brother! In front of ten thousand people, breath free!" Then she whispered back to Larry. "I guess he didn't notice they were laughing and pointing at his *breathing.*"

Unbeknownst to any of them, from the side of stage right, Dille had filmed Jeffy's entire performance.

Shuttles, security checkpoints, boarding passes, planes, flight attendants and passengers, spinning baggage carousels, shuttles, taxis, chartered buses, bell hops, luggage, desk clerks and elevators, random fans, sharpies, autographs and production assistants and tour coordinators and caterers and chauffeurs all blurred from city to city to city.

Chicago was always a fun town for the Band. They had played everywhere from the old Comiskey Park back in the day to the venerable Riviera Theatre in Cicero and were now playing the Pritzker Music Pavilion in Millennium Park. Their dressing rooms were in the Harris Theatre for Music and Dance, which the Pavilion was partially built on top of. The scene outside the rear entrance to the facilities was what the Band had been hoping for. They hadn't said anything in Miami or Atlanta or even New York, but being Midwesterners, Chicago was a homey place for them. As the Band rolled up to the Harris theatre, a small crowd of fans rushed the van. Excited at first, Jeffy looked at them in disgust. "Guys, nothing but guys!"

He spat out the words like a curse. Both Larry and Joey echoed his dismay looking at the mostly middle-aged men wearing imitation gold space suits and MegaHorns.

"Goddamn Sausage Fest..." Joey said woefully shaking her head.

"Fuckin' nerds, Man." Larry snarled.

"We do attract some real winners." Randy agreed.

To Randy and to Jeffy too, though he needed them more, all their fans were losers. All the Band cared about fan-wise were the hot groupies who were not just an endangered species at this point, but entirely extinct. But you would never know any of that as Randy and the rest all waved and smiled and winked and thanked their fans for coming, as they escaped them into the theatre and into their dressing room.

"Definitely not like it used to be." Randy summed their fans up, falling backwards into a purple velvet easy chair. Luke plopped down next to him.

"I've played here before." Wharm said, twirling a drumstick in his right hand. "With none other than Erdman Von Hurlin. Yeah, their drummer had been busted smuggling royal bee jelly or something like that across some border in Thailand. So Erdie called me up. Told me he heard me play with the Pillagers. Asked if I'd step in. Now he is an incredible shredder-but one crazy dude. Had a skateboard race down Michigan Avenue at three in the morning. Cops chased him for eight blocks. Bail was a bitch."

Scruffy leaned into Truck and whispered. "Ever notice how Wharm talks about being in all these bands? Fucker can't hold down a job." Then he raised his voice so everyone could hear him. "You know what I heard? I heard Band of Pigeons insists on wearing parachutes on commercial flights! I'd love to see the pilot's reaction to that."

"They allow that?" Utz asked, which made everyone turn and look at him since he rarely said anything.

"Oh yeah." Scruffy said with a laugh. "And what's their answer as to why? -Buddy Holly, Otis Redding and especially Lynyrd Skynyrd!"

The room had a variety of people in it right before the guys went on. Members of other bands on the Tour would stop in for a brief visit from time to time with their compact discs and posters as gifts, as well as cd's and posters of The Oracle for the guys to autograph.

Rock Stars as fans and fans as rock stars was a fun sight for Ricky to witness and note. He also noted that a band would choose one city to do that in, get it over with and be done with it. Since The Band of Pigeons had already come for a visit to the Oracle's trailer back in Atlanta, Scruffy knew whose backs he could safely and harmlessly talk behind. Most of the acts preferred to stay within their own circles.

Tour assistants of Andromeeka followed her in and out after talking to RoyBob about the changes in the stage time three different times. Some of Jeffy and Joey's cousins had driven all the way from Flint to see the Show. After driving for five hours and then standing around a bunch of rock stars while they sipped beer and wine, they were more than dazzled. They were intimidated by the ambience. And in those rooms when more than two people laughed, everybody in the room laughed, including the Jabonno's small-town cousins without knowing what they were laughing about. They just wanted to be in with the in-crowd.

By the time the Show went on, things were running smoothly and all the previous sound check drama, this time about how Jeffy's treble was too high which he screamed about for five minutes, had all been forgotten. The Show was flawless. The place was packed. The entire concert was one long running standing ovation - as all rock shows at their best should be. Afterwards, back in the green room, Randy turned to Jeffy. "Cool show tonight. No mistakes at all. But is it my imagination, or when we do the encore, it sounds like you're singing with an English accent."

Larry walked by and nodded at Jeffy. "Yeah. Heard that."

"I noticed, too." Joey came up from behind him.

"Kinda like John Lennon. Yeah, what's up with that?" Luke Wharm came up shaking his MegaHorned head.

"Lennon?" Randy frowned. Doing Peter Townshend or Roger Daltry that would make sense. It's a *Who* song."

"Fuck you all. I'm not doing that at all." Jeffy bristled. "Pack my bass!" He yelled at Philly.

"Maybe not consciously..." Joey said with a raised eyebrow and a wry smile.

"OK, even if I did, what? Fuckin' Lennon didn't do covers?"

"Now you're talkin' Jeffy-Luv." John whispered in his ear.

"That reminds, me." Randy said more to himself than anyone there, as he walked toward the green room door. "I got to find Dille and tell him about the time I ran into Keith Moon at an exclusive bordello in Paris!"

"As for us," Jeffy said, as Joey hooked arms with her awestruck cousins. "We're gonna treat ourselves and our cousins to a visit to Berghoff's at State and Adams. Best wiener schnitzel in the Midwest."

"Plus-" Joey added, brushing a few crumbs of old pizza crust off her Pixies t-shirt, "they got their own microbrew on the saloon side. And dig this: They got the first liquor license handed out to a Chicago bar after Prohibition. It literally says number 000001!" Joey was practically drooling. A bit of white powder lingered under her nose.

"What about Twin Anchors?" Randy asked. Thought you loved that place. They say Sinatra flew in their baby back ribs and coleslaw to a performance in Saudi Arabia once!"

"That is a superb place." Jeffy agreed. "But we're all in the mood for wiener schnitzel."

"Plus, their potatoes au gratin are out of the world." Joey added, her eyes dilating.

More shuttles, more security checkpoints, boarding passes, planes, flight attendants, drinks, pills, noisy passengers, spinning carousels, falling luggage, loud taxis drivers, random fans, autographs, finger cramps, hand cramps, wrist cramps, bell hops, desk clerks and elevators, card-keys and room service and catering trucks and cafeterias and cantinas and waiters and busboys and celebrity chefs all blurred from city to city to city.

Every bit of it, every movement was orchestrated over and over again by RoyBob Fratello. RoyBob had mastered the blur of touring and rode it like a champion surfer perched high above the Great Barrier Reef.

Scruffy and Truck, along with the rest of the Oracle road crew were sitting in the Orifice of the Oracle's executive dressing-suite in T Mobile Park, the home of Seattle's American League Baseball franchise, the Mariners. Truck and Scruffy and the rest of the Oracle road crew were having an ages-old discussion of great, profound, and sometimes even heated debate within the Rock world.

"Man, I'm sicka that fuckin' bullshit, man!" The guys had found the one thing that could rile up Truck and they devilishly enjoyed watching him get bent out of shape over impugning the live performances of the Beatles.

"Fuck that shit man! I'm sick of hearing morons who don't know what the fuck they're talking about bad-mouthin' the Beatles: *The Beatles couldn't play live. The Beatles were suck-ass musicians.*" Truck mocked his invisible Beatle critics with a falsetto that had Philly holding his stomach as he laughed he inhaled and made a whining sound.

"Only someone who didn't know shit about the business would say somethin' stupid like that and I still hear morons say stupid crap like that to their girlfriends, tryin' to impress them. Makes me sick. -I'm out there in the crowd hearing dumb-ass shit like that all the fuckin' time. I once grabbed this one fucker talking shit about the Beatles right by my soundboard. Almost knocked over my beer. So, I grabbed him by the shirt collar-"

"My kind of guy." Remarked Larry. "If I was into guys."

"-And I said to the fuckhead, pointing at my board: Do you see this? The Beatles didn't have this. This is a soundboard. They didn't have soundboards or mixers or serious playback speakers back then, so they couldn't fuckin' hear themselves at all. Let's hear you hear yourself just think when all these people start screaming, and if I'm not working this right, you won't hear it right either, dipshit."

"I was once working with the Stones." Philly shared. "I swear no one could follow what the 'ell Richards was playin'. It's so bad - it's legendary. Been a very popular bootleg for years now: *Keith Richards Too Wasted To Play*-look it up on YouTube."

Seattle had another significance to the Orifice of the Oracle. It's where Skippy was born.

"I thought this would be an appropriate place to ask you some questions about Skippy Watts." Ricky took out a pad and his pen, even though his tape recorder was recording.

"Randy thought for a moment. "I suppose it makes sense to tell it here. Seeing this is where he came from. Like Jimi Hendrix or Kurt Cobain."

"And as you probably know," Jeffy took over. "-Skippy became the fifth and most famous of all electrocuted Darwin Award Winners."

"Quite a distinction in the annals of rock." Ricky quipped.

"I think it's all pretty anal if you ask me..." Larry muttered, unasked, giving Ricky a long, serious and very uncomfortable look.

"Anyway..." Randy picked up," glancing sideways at Larry. "By the mid-Eighties Skippy had had enough of being the 5th wheel -as he often felt- especially when silenced by Jeffy on talk shows."

"That's not exactly accurate." Jeffy countered, fighting back a scowl taking over his face.

114

"Ok," Randy said, going on with his story. "Skippy was taking time off from the Band. He was able to afford a nice home in the Hills. And he builds himself the most amazing pool with the most powerful and amazing underwater sound system ever created up to that time.

"He had giant concert-sized speakers with woofers installed that when he cranked the bass - made the water dance. Well one day, he goes to his pool and the Aqua-Hearing System he's paid hundreds of thousands of dollars for isn't working. So always being a bit of a DIY guy, Skippy decided he would fix it himself. He gets a screwdriver, goes into the pool with the system still on because he wanted to be able to hear when he fixed it. Skippy swam over to the water-proof cable box and began prying open the panel. The last thing his girlfriend heard him say was: "-Is red positive and black negative?" Currents of electricity ten times more powerful than an electric chair coursed through Skippy, instantly exploding his heart and leaving a large strawberry welt from his back up to his neck. That was the last solo by the Immaculate Percussionist."

"A great drummer." Jeffy said sadly.

"Better than he was an underwater electrician." Added Randy.

Ricky tried to swallow his giggle as he made a few notes.

"Got some of the freshest Scungilli I've ever had at Pikes Market thanks to Skippy." Joey said with a soft sigh.

The Seattle Show had a special spirit to it as the guys all thought of Skippy, especially Luke. Wharm was forever trying to prove he was not just as good as Skippy but better than him, though no one seemed to notice that.

Once the show was over and they had signed enough horns and posters and cd's, the guys stayed at the after-party as they did in every city, just as long as they thought required and not a second longer. The moment they figured they had paid their respects and had been social enough they bugged out back to their rooms as fast as they could. As much as it made him feel like he was back in the 80s again

Jeffy would admit to himself, staring in the hotel bathroom mirror that touring at the age of 65 was not like touring at the age of 25.

Dexter Dille had been focusing in general on one Band per city though he did take special care to film as much of The Oracle when they didn't know they were being filmed, especially Jeffy. And in each city, Randy had taken to inviting Dexter to dinner at the most expensive place in town - which Dille would politely deflect, asking for rain checks when they got back to Los Angeles. "Believe me, I'll cash them." He told Randy with a wry look on his face.

In each city, after every performance, Dille had been trying to figure out a narrative to the film. He stood before his own camera making commentary on his own film, but he was never satisfied with what he came up with, until Seattle.

"Ok, roll... -For me, this Tour is a trip back in time. The camera is our Time Machine. Each of these eight bands opens a window into a world now gone. Windows that gives us glimpses into the mindset of a generation...the mindset of a society - I like that better - in a specific point in time. From their names to their song topics to their signature sounds to their unique stage presentations, each of these eight Bands from the 80s encase a point in time which makes them like Flies In Amber, which is the name of this sonic documentary: *Flies In Amber: The Titans Of Yore Time Twist Tour. -An Autopsy*. Ok, cut. That's enough for now."

More shuttles, more checkpoints, more boarding passes and planes and sassy flight attendants and surly passengers, more pills, more drinks, sleep masks and spinning carousels, more baggage tickets and more baggage claims and more annoying taxis drivers and door men and desk clerks and random fans and hand cramps and bell hops and suitcases and elevators and room service and muscle spasms and hot showers and concierges and pay-tv and house maids and busboys and bartenders all blurred from city to city to city.

When the Orifice of the Oracle was planning its move to California in those exciting early breakthrough days, there was a brief consideration of basing themselves in San Francisco. Both Randy and Jeffy, like many of their generation were attracted to the Haight-Ashbury mystique and its bohemian allure, but in the end, they gave in to proximity to all the recording and film production in Los Angeles.

After walking from the North Beach area, where Randy bought several books of Ginsberg and Ferlinghetti poetry at the old beatnik temple to words, City Lights, he and Tina decided to walk down to Fisherman's Wharf and look at some art in a gallery across from where the ferries to Alcatraz docked. While he looked at some Salvador Dali prints, Tina came up to him with a tall slender, olive-skinned fellow on her arm.

"Look who I ran into, honey!" Tina hung a little too close to Bela, who extended his hand.

"Randy, what a surprise to find you guys here! I'd totally forgotten that you guys were playing with your old band tonight."

"Bela. What a wonderfully unexpected surprise. How great to see you again, old friend. We were just on our way to the hotel. We've got to get ready for the sound check. We go on early tonight. Hey why don't you swing by? It's at Golden Gate Park. I'll leave your name on the Pass List at the Will Call box office. We'll see you then." With that he left Bela standing there as he gently led by the hand a frowning Tina out to the street.

"Quite a coincidence Tina."

"Never drag me out of anywhere! Don't ever touch me like that again!" She hissed, spraying his face. Her eyes flashed a tinge of sharp yellow.

"C'mon, Tina, let's put this on hold and talk about it when we get home. It's bad enough how Jabonno is acting and then that pain in the ass writer and on top of that, here I am trying to court Dille, trying to make the Band not look like a bunch of out of touch old farts who don't know when its time to hang it up. So please."

She looked at him for a minute, thinking. Business always came first with her. "You're right. I'm sorry. I don't know what came over me. We're both stressed-out over things. And Bela's just a friend. I've told you till I'm blue in the face. You're being paranoid. C'mon let's get you ready for sound check."

Mindy had also arrived in San Francisco, much to the surprise of Jeffy. She walked into the Band's trailer dressed in her best Rodeo Drive ensemble, but kept her blue bug-eyed sunglasses on as she sat down in a director's chair with Jeffy's name on it. Next to her, Scruffy and Philly had been discussing some of the grand old Oracle shows back in the mid-80s.

"I do miss the old days." Philly pined. "Remember that show where they had a dozen girls dressed as sprites flyin' every which way sixty feet in the air on velvet swings wearing no panties. I can still see them swinging up there." Philly stared longingly into the air, licking his lips.

Looking at Mindy, Scruffy whispered, "She looks like one of them, Phingers. Look."

Eyeing Mindy like he was grading a royal poodle prancing at the Westminster Dog Show, Philly replied. "Well mate, maybe her grammie wuz. Right. Probably her grammie wuz."

Feeling back on their home ground, the San Francisco performance took on the spirit of a welcome home show. And again, their performance was still stunning. But to himself, Jeffy could feel that excitement, that energy that made him most feel alive, starting to wane.

Back in the hotel, Mindy once again tried to talk to Jeffy. "We still need to clear the air, Jeff."

"You want to do this now with all the things I have swirling around me?"

"There's always something swirling around you."

"Look if you're still upset about that stupid poster-"

It's what it symbolizes, Jeffy and I can't get out of my mind you saying you'd rather be with a boy than a girl who won't go anal."

118

"Listen I know this really awesome place, oldest place in the city, Tadich Grill. Joey practically lives there when we're in Town. It's in the Financial District just a few blocks from the Ferry building. Best seafood. The Zagat rating is five stars. I'm starving. We can finish our conversation there."

"I don't know Jeffy. I'm not sure anal sex and lobster tails mix."

They never found out. In the Lobby, they ran into Randy and the rest and got talked into going with them to a popular Italian Restaurant on Grant Avenue.

More shuttles and more checkpoints and more boarding passes and more planes and more pills and more drinks and more random fans and more cramps and more crowds and more rushing and more pushing and more bartenders and more busboys and more waiters and more house maids and more pay-tv and more room service and more card keys and more elevators and more muscle spasms and more hot showers and more uncomfortable beds all blurred from city to city to city.

This time the city was San Diego. They were staying at the Grant Hotel in the Gas Lamp Quarter, near the Horton Plaza, downtown and within walking distance of Petco Park, where the Titans Of Yore Time Twist Tour was playing. Petco   Park was the home field of the city's national league baseball team, the Padres. Much like T-Mobile or the Hard Rock Stadium in Miami, the facilities were executive-suite fine. The guys decided to walk from the hotel to the Park straight down 5th Avenue. When they got to 802 5th Avenue, they stopped for a moment.

Randy turned to Jeffy. "This used to be Croce's Restaurant and Jazz Bar. -Jim Croce's widow's homage to her late singer-songwriter. Man had a bunch a hits."

"Well, Shrugged Randy. "Now it's Café 21, Gas Lamp. So much for memories."

"I remember Ingrid Croce. Cute Lady." Larry said. "Liked her. She wasn't into it. Shame."

"Cool place. Good beer." Joey sighed "Believe it or not, really good Scungilli there."

"Shit, this is like mourning over CBGB's again... Let's go." Luke shook his head.

"Yeah, if I could save time in a bottle..." snickered Randy.

"Very funny." Jeffy rolled his eyes. "C'mon. We got a show to do. Let's get to our room and the sound check."

Once the sound check was done and at this point the guys had that down to a science, everyone was sitting around in their executive dressing suite, Philly and Scruffy began talking about some of the young women they'd seen over the course of the tour.

"She couldn't have been more than fifteen." Philly said.

"Well she looked twenty-one." Scruffy said.

From there the topic of the age of consent just naturally took flight.

"Hawaii was the youngest I'd ever seen. Fourteen. Can you believe that?"

"Yeah I heard they changed that Law to sweet sixteen."

"That's like Alaska, Alabama, Georgia, the Carolinas-"

"Nevada, Arizona-"

Randy walked up to them. "Are you guys teaching a class? Will you two cool it? Dille could burst in here at any moment."

"Randy, Dille's hardly been here at all."

"God Fuck It!" Randy yelled as he left the room slamming the door. Then he immediately returned. A tactic he used like wiping a blackboard clean.

"Hey, you guys remember G.G. Gweeko? Our manager in the mid-Eighties?"

"Yeah, our manager for about five minutes." Jeffy scoffed.

120

"Long enough to fuck us if you recall. He's here. I saw him outside hanging with the Rectal Thermometers. He came up to me and hugged me like an old pal and all I could think of as I smiled and hugged him back was how at that Party we did at Warhol's place, he got so drunk he was actually boasting to me about ripping us off for seventy-five grand...Man...what a fucker. That's how I feel now. Like I'm being face-fucked by a smile."

All that could have ended there in that San Diego dressing room. But it didn't. The Show was great, as usual. But it was starting to wear. Repeating perfection has a way of making itself bland and numbing. The guys left the stage satisfied but with a feeling of wanting, and fatigue. Back at the Hotel, they had agreed with Ricky and RoyBob to grab a midnight dinner. They had all agreed to meet up at Randy's room. When Ricky and RoyBob showed up at Root's room, Jeffy and Randy were already getting into it.

"How many of our performances has Dille shot? Two? Three? We've done Seven Shows already."

"Hey man, I've wanted him to do more performance footage of us. You're the one chasing him all over the place, inviting him to lunches and parties and whatever when all this is done. Why don't you ask him if he plans to shoot us back in LA?"

Sure. But it's bullshit that I have to do any of this just to get a good project from him. Fuck, he hates me for something I didn't even do."

"Oh yeah." Jeffy laughed. "I was making all those gay jokes by myself to myself and you were laughing at something else entirely. The innocent bystander, huh?"

"You think it's because of a few fucking fag jokes?" Randy had had it. And when he'd had it, he always began the same way. "You know what? This whole thing is one inch away from turning into total shit. This is a parody of a has-been tour, Jeffy. If it weren't for Dille-I would have never done this!

Jeffy let his frustration show on his face. "Has-Been, huh? I'm getting sick of you saying that phrase considering how you parley the Band's name into other jobs every chance you get so fuck that Has-Been shit, Randy. It's getting older than we are! The goddamn Tour is sold out in every city, man. C'mon, Randy. Whether it's three shows or eight, it's us he's filming on Tour. Not The Lip Readers. Not Derek Scorch! OK, yeah, he could be filming us more, but it's not Derek Scorch, Randy."

Randy rolled his eyes. "Of course not. Scorch doesn't need this shit. He wouldn't be caught dead at one of these Funeral Parades!"

Jeffy threw up his arms and began walking away. "Oh man, see if saying that shit helps you get what you want out of Dexter...Or, maybe if you blow him..."

"Oh, and by the way." Randy shouted after Jeffy, "Forget me going to the Divine Intervention! Like I want to be adored by a bunch of mongoloids? Fuck those blockheads and that idiot you introduced me to you said runs the thing: *Divining Rod*. -Fuck that noise!"

As all this played out Ricky and RoyBob stood there frozen, hoping their presence wasn't noticed by the two legends lashing out at each other. Quietly Ricky turned to RoyBob, shaking his head: "You know, all bands have sibling rivalries, from Lennon & McCartney to Jagger and Richards, but *this* is really out there."

RoyBob nodded. "I've had to deal with a lot of shit like this over the years. This one's def in the top ten."

Suddenly both Randy and Jeffy realized Ricky and RoyBob were there and turned to look at them.

"So!" Randy said, clapping his hands. "Who's hungry for what?"

At the San Diego Airport, back to LA Jeffy made one last attempt to get Randy to come with him to the Divine Intervention.

"C'mon Randy. Just this once, please. I even came up with a trippy story for you to tell. The Acolytes will freak."

"Look, if you didn't notice from me on the phone in every dressing room in every city - I've got a business to run. I've got TV themes and film cues due. I got clients breathing down my neck. I got composers I don't know what they're doin'. I've had enough of running Horn O Plenty productions from the road. You freak those loser freaks out, yourself, JJ. For the last fucking time: NO!"

The room service, the house maids, the bell hops, the desk clerks, the shuttles, the checkpoints, the boarding, the seating, the flight attendants, the passengers, the pills, the liquor, the luggage, the spinning, the fans, the handshakes, the hand cramps, the crowds, lines, buses, taxis, limos and hands out for tips all blurred into the singular image of the front door opening to home.

Once they were back in Los Angeles, though they still had one last show at The Greek Amphitheatre in Griffith Park, the Tour was over. Randy and Jeffy were barely talking. Jeffy had severe back pain and Randy was having hearing issues. Dille was just about done with filming. Tina had a fit when she heard that Lacie, Randy's first wife, had visited everyone in the Greek green room while she was involved in an incident with Solita at the house. Then when Tina learned Randy had invited her, it got much worse. Hardly anyone even brought up how Larry had set a neighbor's hair on fire "accidentally" with one of her fireworks the first night she got back home.

The last sound check inspired a free-for-all of "can-you-top-this?" anecdotes about the most notorious sound check habits known to Humankind, once the crew was back in the dressing room. The claims flew fast and feverish.

"Listen man, Whitney Houston taught ME words I'd never heard."

"Hey, Neil Diamond wouldn't let anyone in the place. Even the venue staff had to leave the theatre. Including the manager."

"That's nothing. I saw Sinatra take shots of air from a tank in between lamb blood injections while doing a mic check."

"Oh yeah? Well, I heard Aretha Franklin once insisted on having a Shetland pony at her check."

"You heard. -Bullshit."

"I ever tell ya 'bout the time I told Johnny Rotten the only person who could call me a stupid cunt pussy asshole fuckhead wuz me mum?"

"Bullshite,"

"Pureshyte."

Ricky had been recording this kind of conversation since New York. He smiled politely and feigned faint laughter as the guys bandied on. But since witnessing the fight in Randy's room in San Diego, he grappled with the realization of seeing rock stars he loved and looked up to not just as ordinary people struggling to survive the dog eat dog arena called the Hollywood basin but as pretend revolutionaries who had truly sold out on every level.

"Hey anybody seen RoyBob?" Randy suddenly walked into the Greek dressing room. It was a comfortable, big room. It had the look and feel of a wood paneled rec room from the 1960s. It was filled with Ansel Adams-quality black and white photos showing the legendary venue when The Greek was first built. They gave proper perspective to the dressing room's age. Straightening one of the photos near him, Randy explained. "Jason Barter and his wife need a pass...Man this room hasn't changed in years..."

"Fratello's being interviewed by Dille." Larry offered, popping off a beer cap with her thumb.

"Yeah," RoyBob took a long breath putting on a thoughtful face as he summed up tour managing the Band. "I have tour managed for a variety of Bands across the music spectrum and I'm proud of every one. But touring for the Orifice was always a lifelong dream since I was a kid. And now here I am - Livin' The Dream."

"Thanks, RoyBob. That's fine. That'll do it." Dexter winked at him. Howell nodded his approval, dropping the camera from his shoulder.

"So what's next, Dex?" RoyBob had people-skills that worked with 99.9% of those he came into contact with. Dexter was no different. RoyBob was too likeable.

"I'm going to film the Orifice of the Oracle in their final performance in its entirety. Then I'm going to cash in some of Mr. Root's rain checks and see if there isn't something for me to give him in return."

As for Jeffy, after realizing he couldn't stop singing *Who Are You* with an English accent for the encore even if he wanted to, he wondered, as he was thinking about what he was going to do at the Divine Intervention, if hearing voices in his head was due to all those drugs in the 70s and 80s, let alone the drugs he still did. So as Mindy once again tried talking to him there in the dressing room, he was engaged in another conversation altogether.

"Are you listening to me at all? Jeffy?"

He wasn't. He didn't hear her at all. He was obsessed with what he'd been hearing on and off now for weeks. "Is this from all those years of doing shit? Is that why? It was only cocaine. Some weed. Some hashish. No more than I do now. I haven't done acid in years. Ok, I did go through a mushroom phase. But not long. - So why this? Why now?"

"I'm not sure I know who you are anymore, Jeffy. -Jeffy!"

"But...I mean... They're still *my* thoughts, only I'm putting John Lennon's voice on them. That explains it."

"Yeah." John Lennon chuckled softly. "Keep telling yourself that, dearie. After all, Jeffrey Brutus Jabonno, I *do* know who *you* are."

CHAPTER 6

The auditorium was dark and hushed amid fast breathing, excited whispers and shushes. Then the voice of Samuel L. Jackson as Jules Winnfield in Pulp Fiction thundered through the room.

"You know what Divine Intervention is?"

A roar grew from the crowd.

"Divine Intervention, my friend. Divine Intervention, my friend. Divine Intervention, my friend-" Jackson's line had been looped into a chant that the crowd now yelled back.

"DIVINE INTERVENTION! DIVINE INTERVENTION! DIVINE INTERVENTION!"

Shaggy, who at his own expense had accompanied Jeffy to the last ten Interventions, turned up the volume on the Jackson tape loop. Standing off to the side of stage left, he shot a thumbs-up at a shrouded figure perched by the edge of stage right. A film screen set in the back of the stage suddenly lit up with a giant image of the Band from the *We're All Gods* album. The acolytes gazed up at the screen, exhaling altogether in one long awed "AHHHHHHHHHHHHHHHHHHHHHH!

Out of the shadows walked the figure from stage right. He was dressed in a sparkling purple minister's robe and crowned with a gleaming gold MegaHorn. A spotlight hit the thin, pale six-foot figure. He lowered his head to the mic held in his left hand. He spoke softly at first, raising his voice slightly on each phrase, stairstepping all the way to the top of his lungs:

"We Are Assembled Here To Celebrate Our Own Divine Natures, To Rock Out To The Realization Of Our True Godly Selves, To Give Thanks To Our Guides To Our Godliness, To Bear Witness To Their Greatness. Ladies And Gentlemen And Everyone In Between - I Am Your Minister Of Ceremonies: Divining Rod! Welcoming You To The Nineteenth Annual Divine Intervention! Our Convention Celebrating The Orifice Of The Oracle And Their Eternal Musical Gospel! FELLOW ACOLYTES, LET US BEGIN!!!!"

Five hundred ultra-fans went insane like an imaginary "Go Insane" light had been turned on in front of them. *We're All Gods* started playing in the background. The high priest of the gathering, "Divining" Rodney Rosenberg waved his arms over the crowd as if conducting an orchestra. His solid gold MegaHorn shifted left and right on his head. As he stood before the *We're All Gods* album, the audience was a seething jungle, a sweaty mish-mash of sparkling gold space suits, MegaHorns, Mylar togas and costumes of every deity ever imagined and some never imagined.

The annual convention held in Flint, Michigan was in a large, modern theatrical prayer hall next to an old non-denominational church, Our Lady Of The Blessed Crossed Fingers. Every year fans congregated there to celebrate the Orifice of the Oracle dressed in costumes inspired by the Band with inventive interpretations worthy of a comic-con. Divine Intervention attendees came as their favorite gods from every religion past, present and perhaps in some cases future-from Roman gods to Greek gods, Phoenician gods, Egyptian gods, Chinese gods, Hittite gods, Mayan gods, Zulu gods, Indian gods, Native American gods, fictional gods out of epic fantasies and gods out of their own acolyte minds made in their own acolyte images.

Shaggy turned the house lights up slightly as he winked at Jeffy. Jeffy stood off stage left, right next to Shaggy, waiting to go on. "Not a bad crowd, huh?" Shaggy whispered. "Looks like five hundred people out there, huh?" Shaggy nodded at Jeffy looking for agreement.

Jeffy shrugged dismissively. "Yeah. Not bad. But I remember when a thousand would show up." Still, Jeffy had to admit to himself he found the sound of hundreds of MegaHorns all being blown at once the best drug he had done in a very long time.

Divining Rod put his MegaHorn to his lips and blew it with all the passionate force he had. Then he announced: "AND NOW, LIKE GEE-ZAHZ HIMSELF," Rod boomed like a circus ringmaster. "HERE IS YOUR ORIFICE OF THE ORACLE: JEFFY JABONNO!"

Jeffy walked out with his right arm outstretched, his fingers spread wide. As blasts on MegaHorns heralded his approach to center stage, he smiled and waved the audience calm. He adjusted the microphone stand and tapped on the mic.

"You know we did several Jesus songs in the day, to a bit of criticism and a lot of stage attacks." Laughter crested through the audience. "But we were raised on Jesus. We grazed on Jesus. And we got braised on Jesus. So it's important to face Jesus head-on!"

Shaggy started the karaoke tape from the wings. The intro went two bars and then Jeffy began singing.

"JESUS WHAT'S YOUR HANGUP?!

THIS BULLSHIT AIN'T YOUR FATE!

GET UP OFF OF THAT FUCKIN' CROSS

BEFORE IT'S TOO DAMNED LATE!

YOU LOOK ALL KINDA BANGED UP

YOU LET THE MONSTERS GANG UP

IT'S TIME TO GET THAT DICK UP

FUCKIN' ACT LIKE YOU'RE A GOD!

IT AIN'T A DREAM YOU'RE SEEING!

YOU ARE A SUPREME BEING!

YOU LIKE SUFFERING THAT MUCH?

THAT FUCKIN' CROSS IS JUST A CRUTCH!

JESUS WHAT'S YOUR HANG UP?

I MEAN, JESUS WHAT'S YOUR HANG UP?

HEY NOW, JESUS WHAT'S YOUR HANG UP?

GET UP OFF OF THAT CROSS! HEY!

GET UP OFF OF THAT CROSS! HEY!

GET UP OFF OF THAT CROSS! HEY!"

At song's end Jeffy did what he always did. He imitated James Brown's vocals in *Get Up Offa That Thing!* He danced around with his arms out as if on a cross and then resembled the scarecrow in the Wizard of Oz jumping free from his pole.

"GET UP OFF OF THAT CROSS! HEY!

GET UP OFF OF THAT CROSS! HO!

GET UP OFF OF THAT CROSS! HA!"

He pulled the muscles in his back all over again fresh from the Tour, but in the finest tradition of showbiz, Jeffy gave it his all. The place went berserk. What flashed through Jeffy's head as his lower back began twitching and throbbing was how when the Godfather Of Soul first learned that the Band was doing a cover of his song, James Brown toyed with the idea of touring with the Orifice Of The Oracle. Then he heard the full lyrics. *"Heeeeeey-No!"* was all he reportedly said.

Once the crowd had calmed down, Jeffy took the mic off the stand and addressed the one crowd he was certain knew who he was.

"You know, fellow GodHeads, it occurred to me, thinking of this song, which invites all of us to get up off our own crosses - If the theory of the multiverse is true, that there are infinite versions of Earth and of me and you and all of us, then dig this:

"That would mean on one version of Earth, Jesus was not crucified. It would mean Jesus established his kingdom of Heaven on Earth. And that means somewhere out there in the multiverse is not only Jesus but also Heaven on Earth! And all those versions of you and I on that Earth are God-like. Just like Jesus told us we could be. Which means, if we're all Gods *there* - we're all Gods *here, too!* Just like the Orifice of the Oracle has been saying all along in our songs: Wake Up To Your Own GodHead! That's what the Divine Intervention is for: WAKE THE FUCK UP! YOU'RE A GOD!" Jeffy dropped the mic, letting it fall to the stage floor and walked off.

That was Shaggy's cue to play *Divine Intervention* over the house speakers. The crowd resembled the roiled red spot on Jupiter as Divining Rod came running back onstage blowing his MegaHorn and screaming.

"YOU'VE HEARD THE REVELATION! YOU'VE HEARD IT FROM THE ORIFICE OF THE ORACLE HIMSELF! NEXT, WE'LL HAVE OUR AUTOGRAPH SESSION, THE RAFFLE FOR AN AUTOGRAPHED SOLID GOLD PLATED MEGAHORN, THERE'LL BE FREE COPIES OF JEFFY'S SOLO ALBUM, FOLLOWED BY OUR TRADITIONAL INVOCATION OF THE GODSELF, OUR INVOCATION OF DIVINE IDENTITY, OUR INVOCATION OF THE DIVINE BELOVED AND, OF COURSE, OUR ANNUAL LAST SUPPER!"

As they walked backstage heading to the green room, which was actually green with a matching green door, Rod turned to Jeffy quizzically. "Was that a Randy story? Sounds like a Root story all the way. That guy is brilliant. Inventing the MegaHorn n' all. Please tell him for me! That was really cool, Jeffy."

"Sure Rod." Jeffy answered through clenched teeth. "But let me ask you something. When you were born, did the doctor come up to your Dad and tell him to congratulate your real father?"

"Huh?" Rod looked like a dog that was trying to understand why it was just kicked by its master. He raised his thick black bushy eyebrows, lowered his slightly hooked nose and tilted his head sideways, scrunching his thin lips.

"You know," Jeffy said nodding his head now, "for someone who's supposed to be the high priest here, saying stupid things like Root must've come up with that story and he designed the MegaHorn all by himself tells me you know shit about me, the Band or any fucking thing we do."

Rodney's eyes widened as he tried to explain. "I just figured it was Randy's story 'cause of what I heard him say about the MegaHorn and everything else."

"What did he say about the MegaHorn?"

"I-I-I always thought it was the both of you, Jeffy. But I saw this interview Randy just did for this show for that energy drink and he says he did the 'Horn all by himself...actually he says that pretty much about everything... You didn't know? I wondered why you weren't in it and why he never mentioned you once."

Rather than make a bad situation worse, Jeffy was able to focus on the real subject he wanted literally at hand.

"Fuck that. What was the gate, Rosenberg?"

"Five hundred and twenty-seven guests.

"Fifty-two grand, seven hundred. Not bad."

"That's before some additional expenses and my commission, Jeffy."

"I remember when you did this just for the honor of doing it. -Look, Rosenberg, my back is in knots. I've had enough of you to last another year. If the head-count is five hundred and twenty-seven, I expect fifty-two grand and seven hundred without any bullshit."

Shaggy tried to get Jeffy's attention, but couldn't.

Standing your ground with someone you idolize is hard, but Divining Rod managed to do it, replying, "We go through this every year, Jeffy. This prayer hall costs five grand to rent for the event. I put up the money myself. That's forgetting all the flyers and all the time-intensive emails and everything else just to set all this up. I belong to this church's congregation just so I can get the Goddamn twenty-five per cent discount, otherwise that rental fee would be seventy-five hundred. So on top of my ten-percent commission which you also forget every year - fifteen grand sounds right and your cut is thirty-seven grand and two hundred and seventy bucks."

"Ok, I'll take it in cash, now. And after the autograph meet and greet, I'm out of here."

"Aren't you gonna stay for the Last Supper? We're having fish tacos."

Before Jeffy left the prayer hall to go visit his parents for a few hours, he pulled Shaggy over to a corner of his dressing room. "I appreciate the job you're doing here, Shag' even though I'm disappointed by the turnout. -And that Rosenberg. I know he isn't, but he sure acts like a Jew."

"You're gonna miss our conference on getting the Oracle in the Rock n' Roll Hall of fame. Our committee thinks this is the year."

"You guys think this is the year, every year. Not that I, we, don't appreciate the effort. Hey, do you know what Rosenberg was talking about with that energy drink thing Randy did?"

Shaggy stared blank-faced at Jeffy, shaking his head.

"Never mind...I'll find out... Should've seen this coming. Now that we're in our end-days - the Orifice is subject to our own creed. We've forgotten what made us Gods in the first place. We've got amnesia and now we, me, have fallen back down to earth...hard. Now to think people see us...me as a mere mortal especially compared to Randy Root..."

"The Root of all evil, Jeffy." John Lennon said suddenly as seriously as possible. "People still see him as a God, Jeffy. Not you."

"The Root of all evil." Jeffy repeated. Then he bit his tongue.

Shaggy laughed uncomfortably, but understood Jeffy's frustration. "You going to see your folks from here? Or you going right back? I go home to Macon, mañana."

"I always see my folks when I'm in Flint, Shag."

Whenever Jeffy visited his parents, he could only bear it for a few hours. At the height of his success, Jeffy offered to buy his folks a new house in the wealthy College Cultural neighborhood of Flint. They chose to stay in the modest tract house where Jeffy and Joey had grown up in Grand Blanc. "Too many ghosts there." He had once confided in Joey. He'd bring flowers for his mother, a case of his dad's favorite imported beer and take them out to dinner. They'd offer him his old room and he'd tell them he already had a room at the Sweetwater Suites in Downtown Flint.

History repeated itself down to the sheets on his old bed. He tried not to let his mother see him cringe when she told him she changed the old sheets on his bed weekly like she always did. Then after taking his parents to dinner, he took a taxi back to the hotel.

On the way, he realized *Who Are You?* was playing on the radio. "Please turn that off or switch it to something else." Jeffy asked impatiently. The driver instantly switched it off.

"That isn't going to affect my tip, is it?" The driver turned around to give Jeffy a pitiable look but instead did a double take. "Hey, aren't you Randy Root? I went to high school with you, man!" The taxi pulled up in front of the hotel.

Jeffy was too tired to do anything but give the guy a half-smile. As he opened the car door and got out, he turned to the driver. "Great to see you again. -*Man*. And while I could and should give you a handsome tip, I'd rather you tell everyone what an asshole Randy Root was for giving you nothing."

The driver stared at Jeffy for a moment dumbfounded before breaking into a big smile. "You're right! That's a great life story much bigger than a tip! Thanks ASSHOLE!" Then he drove off, tires squealing.

Pain blasts the size of knitting needles pierced through his lower back muscles. They tore through his extensors, through his flexors and through his obliques and then repeated the cycle with each excruciating step he took into the Sweetwater Suites.Riding the elevator to his floor, the muzak warbling out sounded suspiciously enough like *Who Are You?* for Jeffy to cradle the bridge of his nose between his thumb and forefinger and then cover his eyes with his hand until the doors opened. He settled into his room for the night with a glass of pinot noir, a muscle relaxer and a heating pad applied to his back. For one brief moment he turned on the television. It was a documentary on the Who. He sighed, rolled his eyes and turned the flat screen off. His cellphone rang. It was Mindy.

"Jeffy. How are things going? How are your parents?"

"You'd know if you'd have come with me like I asked."

"I didn't feel like it."

"Didn't feel-Why? What the fuck? The Divine Intervention is where we met. My folks asked about you. They wanted to know if things were alright."

"Things aren't alright Jeffy. They haven't been all right for a while, now. And after the Tour...I've been trying to figure out how to tell you about something that happened...started in San Francisco after the concert."

"What now? -Always dramatic. -Always about you. My back is killing me. I'm trying to figure out why the guy I started all this with is trying to take the Oracle away from me-"

"Jeffy. When we had dinner in San Francisco at that Italian place, right after we ordered, I left to go to the bathroom. Randy got up at the same time, saying he had to go, too. Remember?"

"No..."

"That's right. You were talking to that Times reporter about gender fascism."

"Go on Mindy."

"The bathrooms were up these stairs. I was wearing my go-go dress. Pretending to be polite, Randy insisted I go first. He did this whole bowing thing, it was cute and I laughed and felt obligated to go. So I went first. He waited a few seconds before following me and I had the weirdest feeling he was staring up my dress the whole time. Then, as I turned toward the women's bathroom, he came up from behind, took my hand and tried to lead me into the men's room. He smiled really big and did that innocent thing I now realize he's so good at. He pulled on my arm and said with this wink: 'This place doesn't mind that, so long as we're quiet. -C'mon...' I politely pulled my hand out of his. I said 'Thanks but no thanks.' I went into the women's and waited until I figured he was back downstairs. I guess you didn't notice but I couldn't look at him the rest of the night."

Jeffy looked at himself in the mirror above the dresser and didn't recognize who he was looking at as he listened expressionless to his young wife.

"What happened in San Diego was worse, Jeffy. I went to his hotel room looking for Tina. I thought she might want to have lunch. I thought it might be cool for the two wives of the co-founders of The Orifice Of The Oracle to be friends. When I got there, Randy opened the door wearing speedos or underwear, I really couldn't tell which. He welcomed me in and jumped on this long love seat couch-thing in their suite. I asked him where Tina was and he said she was out with the girls somewhere doing something. Then he stretched his arms out beckoning me I thought at first to hug him and then I realized he was inviting me to lay down on top of him, Jeffy. I asked him what he was doing. So he sat up straddling the couch and patted the spot in front of him, inviting me to sit down facing him like I'd be sitting on his dick. I was wearing my plaid mini skirt and he kept making these obscene gestures like he was planning to hike up my dress as I sat down. Then he looks me in the eye and says: *I spent a lot of dough to adopt two young nubile Ethiopian girls. Aren't I a cool dirty old man?'* I just stood there staring at him. But the worst part was just about a minute later. Tina shows up with those girls! I mean, what did he expect to happen? He wanted to get caught in some weird scene with me. Sick Fuck. I never realized what a creep he could be. I wasn't sure if I should tell Tina. It took me this long to tell you."

Jeffy was literally staring at his phone as he listened to his wife on speaker mode.

"That FUCK!" Jeffy exploded with rage. "That absolute lying, cheating criminal FUCK!He's literally trying to take EVERYTHING. -He claims he invented the MegaHorn all by himself. The MegaHorn. MY MEGAHORN! MY CREATION! I THOUGHT OF IT! I NAMED IT! He claims he wrote all our hit songs without ME! He's claiming he did EVERYTHING without ME! He's literally erasing ME from the history of the Band I fucking named...ME! THAT OWL-FACED MOTHERFUCKER! There'd be no Orifice Of The Oracle without ME!"

"Jeffy, do you hear what I'm saying he did??"

"Of course I hear what you're saying he did! For that son of a bitch, it's just one more thing to take from ME!"

"Just one more *thing*??"

"You know what I mean, goddamn it! Don't fucking twist my words, Mindy! Don't make this all about you! I got enough bullshit to deal with!"

"Yes Jeffy." Mindy said, sounding like she had made up her mind on something. "You do."

Then she hung up.

The next morning, as Jeffy struggled to get up late out of bed with his back still throbbing and an hour to get to the Flint airport, Randy woke up in the Hollywood Hills to Tina screaming.

"SOLITA! What shit are you cooking in the kitchen now? I can smell it throughout the house! I told you I didn't like you cooking that ethnic-country crap here. No wonder you stink all the time...Where are you??"

"I'm preparing the children for summer day camp, Miss Tina."

"Did you feed the dog yet?"

"I'm preparing the girls for summer camp, Miss Tina."

"You already said that, stupid. Did you feed Nipper?"

"Right after I finish dressing the girls, Miss Tina. -There. Show your Mama how nice you both look."

Bathsheba and Khungit ran into the kitchen where Tina stood with her arms folded. They circled her running round and round giggling with their arms stretched out like wings. Tina looked at the girls and then glared at their nanny.

"Solita, you moron! These are their Friday ensembles and this is Thursday! How Goddamn stupid can you be? Now go back in and change them. And take that crap off the stove and throw it away before I throw up!"

By this time, Randy had gotten up, dressed and shuffled into the kitchen as Solita ushered the girls back into their room to redress them in their Thursday ensembles. He poured himself a cup of coffee as Tina stared at him relentlessly.

"OK," he said, not even looking at her. "You're gonna continue this *now*?"

"We never finished it Randy. Now's as good a time as any."

"Marconi shows up by coincidence in San Francisco and oh, that's no big deal. But now you're all upset because my ex-wife shows up at the Greek with another guy? The best defense, huh, Tina?"

"That guy was gay, Randy."

"How do you know that, Tina? You don't know him."

"He showed no interest in me at all."

"Fuck. My left ear is still ringing from this tour. I'm in the middle of arranging some of the most crucial professional events of my life and you want to drag me down to your manipulative jealousy about Lacie on top of waking me up practically screaming in my ear about Solita's stupid mistakes, her pig-shit cooking, dressing the girls wrong and letting the dog shit all over the place?

"I can't waste my time on that if you like how we live here, Tina. -I got art shows and a documentary series focusing on me. I got two movie projects and two TV shows to make sure get done. I don't need you dragging me into your drama and especially into Solita's dumb ass stupid crap. I'm sick of it, your bitching - *and* Her!

You don't like her? Get rid of the old bag. She moves like a lazy cow. Worse, like a stable horse. Only time I ever see her move that fat ass of hers is when she's going back home to her stable for the fucking day. I've had e-"

Randy stopped. He and Tina turned around. Solita stood there staring at the both of them with the girls by her side.

"Here they are in their Thursday clothes, Miss Tina." Solita smiled sweetly. There was a certain look in her eyes that neither Randy nor Tina caught. But it was there.

"Next time do that the first time." Tina said softly. "You look nice girls. Give me a minute and I'll take you to camp for the day. We've got to get moving soon. Mommy has a charity lunch for abused domestic women of color to attend, right after she drops you off."

"Before you go, I need to speak to you and Mr. Randy." Solita said so sweetly, acting as if she hadn't heard a word of what Randy and Tina had said right in front of her, that Tina and Randy both believed that she hadn't heard one single poisoned word they had said about her.

"What's up, Solita?" Randy even forced a smile after trying to sound conversational.

"Me Mama has passed in the night. I must return to Jamaica immediately. The ceremony lasts nine days. I will be gone two weeks-if that's ok with you two."

Tina and Randy looked at each other. Tina tried to force back a smile. She turned to Solita. Oh, Solita my condolences. -Your poor mother. What could be worse? I'm so sorry. Of course it's OK with us that you go."

"And don't worry, your job will be here when you get back." Randy said, looking Solita right in her eyes.

"Thank you Sir. I'll hold you to your words."

Randy turned to Tina, still staring at him. "I've got to get to the Horn. Dille is coming by today for lunch. I've got a lot to prepare."

Suddenly Bathsheba blurted out to Tina.

"MOMMY, WHAT'S A STUPID FAT PIG LAZY COW STABLE HORSE?"

After much wooing, Randy had finally cajoled Dille to come to the Horn and shoot his studios there. He showed him and the cameraman Haskell around. Haskell filmed most of Randy's tour of the Horn. Randy talked about the history of the Sunset Strip itself. Miraculously for Root, Tarzan remained hidden in his tree somewhere.

"The Strip was a strip of unincorporated land the City didn't control. So in its day it was a haven for con artists, crooks, cranks and gangsters. And over the years it really hasn't changed all that much, just the red double-decker tour buses rolling by. Now it's all the pay-to-play places on the Strip like the Whiskey and the Roxy."

"Pay to play, how?" Dille really knew but wanted to hear Randy's answer.

"These places either make the bands just pay for the venue, basically renting it and then they have to sell tickets to their own shows. And if they don't pay upfront and they don't meet the venue's quota, they don't get paid and they may still have to pay the club more if the crowd size and liquor sales suck. So after most of those bands pay SIR, just a bit further down on Sunset to rehearse, they then pay the Whiskey or the Roxy to play. They bring in their fifty to a hundred friends and get to tell their kids n' grandkids how they played the Whiskey or the Roxy on Sunset Boulevard. So like I said, there are still con artists, crooks, cranks and gangsters on the Sunset Strip."

"Interesting and poetic perspective, Randall." Dille turned and smiled.

Randy went on to tell Dille his typical stories about the Horn and Frank Lloyd Wright and encounters with other celebrities and noteworthy people, all without ever mentioning Jeffy once. He took Dille floor by floor from the kiddie rides and circus mirrors and weird furniture and artwork to his instrument rooms and studios.

And while he was doing it, he even went so far as to talk about what used to be on that spot before the Horn.

"I heard it was once a caballero ranch house like back in the 1800s. Then it was a flower farm. Then later it was a brothel. In a way, it's still kinda a brothel." Randy thought that would get at least a chuckle out of Dille. It didn't.

Now standing in the main studio, Dille glanced over at some books on the lady coffee table in front of the client couch. Dille raised his eyebrows.

"You do have a lot of art books with naked underage girls, don't you?"

Randy cocked his head, looking a bit sheepish. "Oh, that's just for the clients. You know what perves they are..."

"Oh Yes. Of course..." Dille said as condescendingly as possible.

"And for our last stop on this tour, I direct your attention to our dining room/conference room."

"How convenient to have both in one. I have to run from one to the other in my studios."

As Randy led Dexter Dille into the dining room, he raised his right arm in presenting a long buffet that he had arranged with Paulette.

As you know I had saved two young girls from Ethiopia and I had to spend a lot of time there and I got to know their food very well. So I thought it'd be fun to treat you to this banquet of Ethiopian cuisine including Genfu, which is this delicious barley based porridge. A feast like this is called a *Gursha*."

Haskell's camera scanned the entire table of east African delights. Everything from Injera flatbread to sautéed beef chunks called Tibs, Shino be Kibbe, a bean stew, a chicken stew called Doro Wat, among a variety of other Ethiopian delicacies. It was a beautiful, colorful display meticulously arranged.

Dille looked over it all with a faint smile and waving his right hand back replied, "Thank you, Randall, I appreciate the gesture. -Very nice. It all looks...so nice. But unfortunately, I was on a shoot in Addis Ababa not too long ago and I got the worst dysentery of my life from food just like this. So you'll forgive me if I pass."

"Oh, I understand!" Randy replied a little too ingratiating. "I'll have one of my people run out right now and get you whatever you'd like."

"What a dear. Well, the Palm is nearby on Santa Monica, and I have been craving lobster lately."

Randy turned to Paulette, gritting his teeth. "Go call the Palm and make the order. And get Joey, Barter and the rest of the crew to eat all this Ethiopian stuff."

Later, as Haskell sat in a corner dining on Tibs wrapped in Injera bread, Dille dunked a bit of lobster tail into melted butter and turned to Randy, who was pretending to slowly eat a bowl of Ethiopian porridge.   "So tell me, Mr. Root. Is it fair to say your work is highly derivative of Vivaldi, Shostakovich and especially Schubert? And I'm being nice by saying *derivative*."

For a split-second hardly noticeable to the naked eye, Randy flinched. Then he broke out into a broad smile. 'C'mon Dex. You know everything in one way or another is derivative of something else. How could something not be? Look at John Williams. Listen to his scores for all the Indiana Jones movies. It all comes from Strauss, for the most part. And didn't he say, *If you gonna steal - steal from the best*?"

"The actual quote is "Good artists copy. Great artists steal. And that was Picasso."

"Well I steal from him, too." Randy answered, his eyes twinkling.

Dille laughed. "You do have an interesting way of putting things, Randall.

"How you like your lobster, Dex?"

"Very nice. But next time, let's go to a few restaurants I know."

"Absolutely."

"You know-" Dille said with a teasing lilt in his voice, "I may have something for you, if you're interested."

"Of course."

"It's something I need done that I shot as a favor to friend of mine who owns a bunch of cement plants across the country. It's a thirty-minute industrial film for a cement convention coming up. It needs music to underline the drama and the energy in it. Are you sure you're interested?

"Of course, Dex. I love concrete."

"Great, It needs to be composed, recorded, mixed and delivered three days from now. Thanks."

It took two flights to get to Flint from Los Angeles. -One plane to Chicago. -One plane to Flint. Only two airlines flew there: Delta and American. Jeffy never cared which he took. He had taken the connection at O'Hare in Chicago to Flint and now found himself boomeranged to O'Hare waiting for his flight back to LA.He sat at his gate staring deeply into his laptop.

"And Now Golden Calf Energy Drink invites you to be a Witness To Wonder in our New Wonders Of The World series. In this episode we focus on the legendary Randy Root, founder and front man of the 80s phenomenon The Orifice Of The Oracle and beloved children's film and television composer."

There was Randy sitting on a Lucite throne that pulsed with a rainbow of colors flashing through it. He was flanked by two giant cans of the energy drink resembling pillars. Dressed in his gold Oracle space suit, he cradled a MegaHorn in his lap.

"I came up with the MegaHorn the same way I came up with our outfits or even the name of the Band: Hunger. Ha.No really, it was inspiration that I derive from many different sources. Others can claim they had a hand in putting all this together, but when it came to presenting it out there on the stage for the world to

see, you all saw who was doing it first and foremost. So naturally I'll be displaying Oracle artifacts at my new art show in Santa Fe this coming seventeenth."

Jeffy couldn't take it one more second. He jumped up, slamming the laptop down on his luggage while it was still playing. He walked off as he heard Randy going on about everything he had done all by himself.

"-The album artwork. -The choreography. -The stage design. I'm an artist."

Jeffy stumbled around barely able to see through the lightening storm striking everywhere in his head at once. He took out his phone feeling dizzy having nothing to hit or yell at. He called Randy. It went right to voice mail. He hung up and called again. It went right to voicemail again. He hung up and called again. It went right to voicemail again. No matter how many times Jeffy called it went right to voicemail again. After two, maybe three-dozen attempts, Jeffy finally left one short message.

"YOU MOTHERFUCKER!"

People close by in the terminal turned around to see who was cursing. As Jeffy put the phone away and walked back to the seat his eyes popped wide. His laptop was gone.

He stood frozen for a second, paralyzed by the realization that it wasn't just the laptop that was gone. He took a deep breath and walked over to the airline agent standing at the gate counter. Realizing his hair was all out of place with his bald spot showing and his hair plugs in front exposed, he tried to flatten it all down on his head as he got the agent's attention.

"My computer's been stolen. Can you contact security?"

"Are you sure it was stolen, Sir?"

"Sure it was stolen? I came back and it was gone. What else would you call it?"

"You mean you left it unattended?"

"I walked away from it a second. A split second."

"That's all it takes, Sir."

"Thanks for the expert advice."

"There's no reason to get snippy, Sir."

"Snippy? I just had a five thousand dollar laptop stolen from your gate!"

"Sir, please keep your voice down. Informing whoever took it of its value can't be a good argument for their returning it. I'll call security."

"Nobody's gonna fucking return it. Unless you guys took it."

"Sir, we'd only take it if we suspected it to be of a dangerous and threatening nature. Was it?"

"Only to me..."

Two airlines security agents came quickly.

"What seems to be the trouble, Mister-?"

"Don't you know who I am?"

"Would I ask who you are if I knew who you were?

"Unfuckingbelievable-"

"Please, your language, Mister-?"

"Jeffy Jabonno of the Orifice of the Oracle."

"Never heard of it, Mr. Oracle. How can I help you?"

"How can you help me... My laptop was stolen."

"Do you have any insurance for the device?"

"Don't you guys cover it?"

"I'll get you a form to fill out. An investigator will look over your case. If you didn't just leave your computer out for anyone to take - the airline will cover the cost of a replacement a hundred percent."

Jeffy stood by his luggage protectively, consumed by what was happening to him. Consumed by feeling like a mortal victim. There was still fifteen minutes before boarding. John Lennon suddenly started talking.

"Don't let that Root Of All Evil get away with this Jeffy."

"Wha-what?"

"Don't let that Randy Root Of All Evil get away with this."

"Not now, please...Please."

"Now is the time, Jeffy. *Now*. Say it with me: Randy is the Root of all evil. -Root Of all evil. -Root Of All evil. -Root Of All Evil. -ROOT OF ALL EVIL."

The chant became a mantra. The mantra became a chorus. The chorus became a howling hurricane inside Jeffy Jabonno. John wasn't through.

"C'mon Jeffy. Don't you know who *I* am? I'm *your* Oracle, Jeffy-poo. Kotex on me head n' all, dearie."

With a sigh, Jeffy didn't know what to do anymore but accept it. Ignoring it hadn't worked. Pretending he controlled it hadn't work. Reasoning with it hadn't work. Pleading with it to leave him alone hadn't worked.

"You know John, you're right. He is the Root Of All Evil. I've said it before, myself. And you know what really hurts the most? I got that traitor a rare, bone china classic antique Adolph Hitler Head Tea Pot and Cup set. That fucking Root Of All Evil."

"Ah, Jeffy. Nothing says love like a teapot made in the image of Adolph Hitler. That Root Of All Evil doesn't deserve it."

"No, he doesn't, John."

Tina was on the phone in her car, sitting outside the La Fonda restaurant in the heart of the mid-Wilshire district. She had just finished attending her luncheon there. La Fonda with its Spanish and Moorish interior and Mariachi entertainment was the last of its breed of fine eateries, harkening back to the themed supper clubs of the 1920s and 30s. The moment she got in her new Mercedes, Bela called.

"Hi Baby. No. I don't know about that project yet. I'm up to my ears in Randy's bullshit at the Horn. Like what? Paulette Matthews has got to go. She acts like she's queen bee of the Horn. Keeps her own hours. Comes in when she pleases. Leaves when she pleases. I don't know why he keeps her. She must have something on him. Photos of him with farm animals, something. She doesn't answer to anyone.

"And talking about answering, that Mei Ling talks on the phone more than she answers it. And lately I've seen that RoyBob fellow with her a lot. I don't trust him. He's got too much of Randy's ear. I'll put a stop to that and all the other shit, too. The place needs a firm hand. And for all I know, Randy's fucking Lacie again... Why do I care? I'm not quite ready to leave yet, Bela. Soon. -But not quite yet. I swear if I ran this place, it would make twice as much. That reminds me. I'm going to get Randy to give me a hundred grand to kick-start my new company you and I were brainstorming about. Remember? -The Garden Of Eat'n? Edible condoms in gourmet meat flavors: Corned beef, bacon, pastrami, and smoked salmon. I've been thinking about it. We'll give ten percent of the profits to the National Veal Boycott. I bet that would get national coverage! No, really."

Listening in on his laptop, Randy had to cover his mouth from not laughing at Tina's latest business idea. Though in the back of his head something told him if he was really honest with himself - he'd give her the money.

Now that the Tour was done, RoyBob with one foot still in advertising had gotten a call from an old producer buddy who wanted to use *Blow It Out* in a commercial. He'd already made decent money for the Band by getting them to do re-records of all their hits. That way they'd make the money instead of the label by offering the advertisers a better quality recording of the song, identical to the original at a slight discount rather than let the record label license the original master they own of the song, leaving the Band basically nothing. Jeffy was relieved when he heard. RoyBob was well known for his management skills of diplomacy, negotiation and pouring on the charm at the right moment.

Randy couldn't be bothered. He was preoccupied by assembling, cataloguing and pricing literally thousands of ceramic Rosebud sculptures for exhibition and had agreed to the *Blow it Out* deal just to get it out of his hair. He also had all those other sculptures that were entertainingly twisted reminders (the critics said rip-offs) of 60s Robert Crumb underground comics and Big Daddy Roth's Kustom Kulture.

Solita returned home to Jamaica as quick as she could. She had to. Once her mother died she was running against a cultural clock to return to her old hometown neighborhood before more than a day had gone by since her Mama Sally-Virginia had passed. It had been awhile since she had been in Trenchtown. It was hot and muggy. This legendary part of Saint Andrews Parish looked mostly the same to her. It sprawled around three-quarters of the city of Kingston with the Blue Mountains on the horizon. There was still music in the streets where Rocksteady and Reggae had been born. She recalled seeing Bob Marley back then all the time, along with Peter Tosh and Toots Hibbert and many others just bouncing down those lively streets. She could hear *Jammin* thumping from somewhere, gently bumping through the air.

When Solita was a girl, Trenchtown was known as the Hollywood of Jamaica. It still felt that way to her, though all the earthy old clubs and the raw vibrancy she had once known there had been replaced by bar & grill and restaurant chains owned by foreign corporations. The Trenchtown Culture Yard Museum, a National Heritage Site was much like an above ground burial mound to her as she drove past it on the way to her mother's house. She couldn't help but think that way. She now had to carry out the Nine Night Ritual for her mother. The simple tin-roofed two-bedroom blue house where Solita grew up in would soon rock and shake with laughter, sobbing, singing and wailing for nine nights straight.

Nine nights of making sure her mother's spirit or *duppy* in Jamaican *patroi,* would truly rest in peace. According to Jamaican tradition, after dying of a sudden heart attack at the age of 90, Mama Sally Virginia required more than just a funeral service and burial. That was only the start. On Days One and Two, Mama Sally-V lay in state at the Parlor while Solita got the minister and arranged for the bible readings and her cousins to sing the hymns with her and keep the candles lit throughout all nine days. On Day Three, Sally-V was buried.   Solita lit "the rising light" candle, symbolizing the resurrection of Christ on the Third Day and invited her mother to do the same, praying and singing day and night for Days Four and Five.   On Day Six, a triple tier of black and white candles was built and lit in her bedroom, where she had died in her sleep. Two large glasses of water flanked the bedroom altar with a vase filled with Lignum vitae, Jamaica's national flower. A framed 8x10 glossy photo of modest-faced Mama Sally Virginia rested against the vase.

Not a single second was supposed to be about mourning. Each day Solita reminded herself and guests that this was a celebration of her mother's life. Stories of her fabled cooking, funny incidences and her nurturing, loving soul were told by scores of people who came by to join in for some if not all of the nine days.

On Day Nine, the old shanty house was packed with people. Solita's cousins had brought food for everyone. There was 150-proof rum. There was fried fish and of course, *bammy,* the traditional bread made from a cassava flour recipe passed down from the long-gone Arawak tribe. People were playing dominoes as more hymns were sung and more rum was drunk.

After enough rum, Solita was the first to experience what Jamaicans call *The Seeing*. This crucial part of the Nine Nights ceremony was something Solita wasn't sure she'd be able to honestly do. But when Solita looked at the doorway and through tears welling up in her eyes saw her mother's face there - she exclaimed, "I SEE MAMA SALLY-V!" And then everyone else, especially those enjoying all the rum, saw Mama Sally-V, too.

"WELCOME MAMA!" Solita greeted her mother's spirit in the same way her mother had greeted her mother's spirit and her mother before her. A table had been set outside under a tent with the finest delicacies one could imagine. But no one could take one bite before midnight, which was when Mama Sally-V's spirit was scheduled to leave the house and peacefully rest in her grave. That food was for Mama Sally to take with her to her final resting place, should she get the munchies.

After that, the Night Song was played for Mama Sally as more stories about her were told. Her bed and mattress were turned up against the wall to encourage her spirit to leave the house. The minister drew a cross in white chalk over the door leading out in the direction of her grave. Everyone said they felt Mama Sally leave, testifying by dancing and raising their arms in praise that she was now resting peacefully and would never return an unsettled and unhappy spirit haunting her descendants. Many Jamaicans believe a duppy not at rest can cause endless grief for their living relatives just as many do in life. Solita did everything in her power to make sure Mama Sally Virginia was resting as peacefully as possible.

She wished she could stay longer. Her friends and cousins tried hard to get her to. But she thought she needed to get back. Not for Randy and Tina, but for those girls. So totally exhausted and sleep-deprived, Solita rushed back to LA to make sure the girls were being properly cared for. She took a shuttle straight from the airport to Mount Olympus.

She hadn't been in the Root's house thirty seconds when Randy came up to her.

"Welcome Back, Solita! Didn't know you were returning today. -Tina's at the Horn, handling some business. Hey...uh...we had to get someone else while you were away and because of that, we're going to have to reduce your work hours down to five a week. I hope that's not inconvenient. Anyway, let me introduce you to Rex. The girls really like him! Tina hired him, herself."

Solita smiled and nodded at the chiseled chested young man with blonde hair and hazel eyes, smiling one of those smiles that actually glint in the sun.

"But, as I promised-" Randy said, looking like he was doing her the greatest favor of her life, "-You *still* have your job. And if that doesn't work for you, you're free to leave at any time."

Solita simply smiled, said, "Five hours a week. How very generous, Mista Randy. Thank you very much, Mista Randy. But I'll just say goodbye to the girls and leave." She turned around briefly giving Randy a look. "I'll always be there for those girls if they need me."

Feeling triumphant after watching Solita leave, Randy's cell phone began ringing. Expecting it to be Paulette or Tina at the Horn, he answered without looking at the phone to see who was calling.

"Hey there Mister RandyMan." A female voice said.

"Have a good tour?" A second female voice asked.

"Have a good time?"

"Ya make more little girls *happy*?"

The two female voices started singing together in harmony to the tune of *The Candy Man.*

"The Randyman can 'cause he mixes it with love and makes the world taste good! Hey, RandyMan! Wanna play some of the old games? Or, are we too old for you now?"

The two female voices now made grunting sex sounds. "Oh yeah, Randyman, yeah!" And then they hung up.

"Wha-what was that? Hello?" Randy suddenly acted like he was a Civil War veteran in need of a brass hearing horn, talking to a dial tone. "I couldn't hear a word you two girls sung, uh, said. This has got to stop. -Hello? -HELLO??"

CHAPTER 7

*

The commercial opens deep in space on a medium shot of the asteroid belt between Jupiter and Mars panning over hundreds upon hundreds of asteroids all locked tightly into place. They bump up against one another with nowhere to go as the camera moves in closer, dramatizing the tension.

A deep echoing, cosmic voice-over fades up asking:

"FEELING BLOCKED?

CRAMPED?

LOCKED IN?

-PREPARE TO BLAST OFF-

AND

BLOW IT OUT

WITH GASTRO-FIZZIX!"

The scene cuts to a green rocket-shaped tablet dropped into a glass of water in slow motion. As the tablet hits the H_2O with a 3-2-1-like countdown followed by a rhythmic ballet of splash, the Orifice Of The Oracle's song, *Blow It Out* blasts its melody underlining a chorus line of supernovas exploding one after the other like cosmic cannons going off as the vocals erupt:

"Blow It Up/ Blow It Out/Clear The Air/Twist & Shout!

The voice-over comes in:

"GASTRO-FIZZIX!

SCIENTIFICALLY FORMULATED TO FREE YOU UP

AT THE SPEED OF LIGHT

DON'T GET LOCKED IN SPACE!

BLOW IT OUT WITH

GASTRO-FIZZIX!"

A group of loosened asteroids begin a synchronized dance spelling out the product name as the song continues.

"Don't Just Pout/There's No Doubt/Clear The Air-"

The song goes into its drum roll. The camera pulls back, showing the asteroid belt taking the basic shape of an intestinal tract. The asteroids swirl down faster and faster disappearing into the middle of a giant spiral galaxy. The camera pulls back further to reveal that spiral galaxy is the product logo on its rocket-shaped box. Next to that stands another glass of water with a rocket-shaped tablet dropped into it, bubbling and fizzing in effervescent slow motion.

"BLAST OFF WITH

GASTRO-FIZZIX

AND-"

"-Blow It Out!!!!!"

The voiceover comes on once more, sped up, reading a subtitle at the bottom of the screen:

A JONESON & JONESON

REGULARITY PRODUCT"

The screen fades to black. A production slate fades up in white type:

Post: Cut Throat Productions

Spot: Gastro-Fizzix-Loosen That Asteroid Belt

TV: 30

Agency: Flyby/Knight Advertising

Client: Joneson & Joneson Industries

*

RoyBob clicked off the set with the remote. "So, whadya think?" He asked Jeffy and Joey who stood in the reviewing room at the Cut Throat post-production house with their arms folded.

"I still think 'Uranus Will Thank You' would've been a better ending." Joey laughed, looking at Jeffy.

"So did the copywriter. The client, not so much." RoyBob explained, laughing as well. He turned to Jeffy, waiting to hear his opinion.

"I think I just wanna know when we get the check for this. That's the best I can say. Not exactly Stanley Kubrick."

"It's supposed to be the strongest gas reliever laxative on the planet, Jeffy."

"And that has me blushing with pride, RoyBob. Don't get me wrong. You did a good deal. But to have an Oracle song forever tied to it..."

"But it's not, Jeffy. No one will remember this in the long run. They can only rent the song. They can never own it - ever. The song is the song and stays that way. The Song Remains The Same, Jeffy."

"You are a good bullshitter, Fratello."

"Thanks, Jeffy. But like I said. All any of these companies do, is rent it. They can't ever own any song they license. And the more it's been licensed - the more it can't be tied to any one product and stays always tied to you. So the song maintains its integrity, whoever uses it because it's always a *cool-by-association* tie-in and nothing more."

"You say tie-in." Joey countered.

"Others say sell-out." Jeffy challenged.

"Well a sell-out that gets back at the record label that ripped them off by using corporate America to do it, sounds pretty rock n roll to me, gentlemen." RoyBob said with a big confident grin.

"That, I can agree with." Jeffy said, conceding RoyBob's point. "The way things have been going we need more opportunities to sell out."

Joey laughed at that. Then a serious look grew on her face. "That was all CGI, except for the product shot. That must have cost."

"As computer generated imagery advances - so do the fees." RoyBob answered. "You are good at this." Joey said, impressed.

"The production on that side was over two hundred grand alone. The music was another two hundred grand. -A hundred and ten thou' for the publishing and ninety grand for our re-record of *Blow It Out*. It's a one-year run on TV, radio and internet in the US, its territories, possessions and commonwealths, including Puerto Rico and Canada with a ten-percent increase in the fee for a second year. We get the ninety-K, though you'll see some of the publishing money through the writer's credits."

"Very little." Jeffy sighed.

"IME controls the publishing." Joey sighed.

"Yeah, but they work with us on these re-records when they come up."

"Too bad they don't come up more often. Used to be all the time..."

"Everything changes, Jeffy. The creatives who used to use your songs have all retired. These guys heard the song on some old time radio show and thought it'd be a gas, no pun intended, to use it on their spot. We were lucky. Haven't had a call in months and months."

"Like, I've been sayin' for a while now - we make just enough for laundry money." Joey said, shaking her head.

"Things are tougher nowadays. Everybody's jumping through hoops on fire. The copywriter on this was forced to write scene objectives."

"Scene-whats?"

"You gotta write out an explanation of every scene, scene by scene, frame by frame to prove how it helps sell the client's product-or to be totally honest, to justify why their thirty second spot costs over ten-K a second."

"For this shit?"

"For this shit."

"Vestal Records gets nothing after years of giving us nothing. That's the part that I like." Joey said smiling.

"Yeah." Jeffy agreed. "But we used to make a mill a year on licensing these re-records."

"*Used-to* are the operative words alright." Joey said looking at Jeffy. "Nothing stays the same forever, brother. Let's face it. We're lucky we got this."

"Hey, I'm grateful we got this too, you guys." RoyBob always had the positive spin on things. The business is always changing."

"You mentioned Vestal before. You hear that Airship thing of Grahamstone is really taking off?" Joey asked with an air of surprise in her voice.

"Taking off. Ha. Good one, Jo. You know, the way things are going, maybe I could play the lounge up there." Jeffy muttered. "Has the Root Of All Evil seen this?"

RoyBob nodded remembering Jeffy's new nickname for Randy. "He glanced at it. Said yes. Asked when the check would be in. Then he had an interview to go to."

"I bet he did. The motherfucker." Jeffy's eyes squinted on his last lingering word as it hung in the air.

"The Root Of All Evil, Jeffy." John said in his head.

"The Root Of All Evil, John." Jeffy said in his head.

While Jeffy was on his way back to Venice, Tina was on her way to getting Randy to get rid of Joey. They were both home on Mount Olympus having an early dinner. Tina had been working on Randy to fire Joey ever since they'd returned from the Tour.

"Every day you let it go is another day you let money go. You let equity go. You let your reputation go. You're letting the Horn go to Hell."

"Ok-OK! Give it a rest, Tina. I've got multiple projects she needs to finish. I'll tell Joey next week on Monday she's got two more weeks. I'm not gonna throw her out on the street."

"I think it's better to fire an employee on Fridays. But nobody's saying be heartless, Randy. Just business-smart. I mean the same thing applies to Mei Ling. Look at my assistant. Noel Bamberger is buttoned up."

"You can say that again, but please don't, Tina. That's *enough* for now."

Jeffy returned from the edit house still thinking about dancing astro-turds in space all done to music he once thought would change the world. Then he had a conversation with John Lennon about what a scumbag Randy was - and when and where to confront him. That lasted until he got in the door and saw two suitcases in the living room. They were Mindy's.

"All this time and you still haven't unpacked?" Jeffy said to the air.

"Oh, I had unpacked, Jeffy." Mindy came out of the bedroom with another bag slung over her shoulder. "Then I realized I needed to pack again. I'm glad to see you before I go. You know, from what I heard, the entire city of New York has seen more of you recently than I have. But that doesn't matter anymore. I think you get your jollies off like that and where am I in all that? -Nowhere.

"Now you go on about how Randy's stealing everything and that matters more than him trying to fuck me? You haven't shown me attention in months. I get the feeling people are laughing at me behind my back. I went along with all the things you wanted to do at our wedding 'cause you're the artist, you're the rock star. I looked up to you and trusted you.

"And what did it get me? -Ridiculed. -Humiliated. -A wedding photo album from Hell. I was even willing to put up with that, with you ignoring me, treating me like a prop and an afterthought. Even the weird things I was finding about you like that gay Batman poster or your bondage video collection in the back of the closet. But it just gets weirder and weirder. You talk to yourself more than you talk to me. I can't do this anymore. I don't know who you are anymore. Goodbye, Jeffy." She picked up her luggage and left.

Jeffy stood there as he heard her drive off. "I wouldn't let it get me down, Jeffy." John said, trying to console him. "She was no Yoko Ono."

The next morning, Randy came in early to the Horn and went right to Jason Barter's small composing room.

"How's that Concrete Poetry In Motion track going? Dille's people are gonna wanna hear that tomorrow."

"I got it right here."

"Play it for me."

Barter clicked on a computer file and the music started. Five seconds in, Randy jumped up. "Stop! I said energy! This is cement! When it pours out I want the sound of a cascading waterfall, but with irony, man! Something like Piazolla's *Primavera Portena*. I told you before!"

"But I did..."

"Yeah, but this something isn't the something I was hearing in my head. Now go back and do it again until it sounds like the something I was hearing in my head and not like the something I wasn't!"

"Ok, I know you've told me what it sounds like in your head and I'll try to hear it like that in mine. Anything else you want me to do to it?"

"No. Just have it ready for me to hear again tomorrow. I'm going down the street a ways for lunch with Tina. I'm not sure when I'll be back. Just do what I asked you to do without making me do it myself. Dille will be here tomorrow so we'll be cutting it close. Just make it work."

Even over a five star meal, Tina would not let up on Randy. He could tell her enough is enough all he liked. It wasn't enough for Tina. She had an agenda and nothing was going to stop her.

Tina decided it was Paulette's turn. "She's been taking advantage of you for years, Randy. It's virtually abuse to you! How long have you given her everything she wants? She acts like it's her place, not yours. She has no concern for you and doesn't appreciate what a privilege it is to work for you. If she did, she wouldn't have made the demands you so sweetly and easily gave into. You're such a pushover. Same thing with Mei Ling. She's another one."

"OK. But I don't like discussing it here at an open street-side café a half a block from the Horn. You never know who's listening."

"I just want to make sure you're lis-"

"Excuse me, are you Randy Root??" A middle-aged guy looking like a typical Oracle fan was walking by and gaped at Randy like he had discovered gold.

"Yes."

"And this is your amazing wife, Tina?"

Tina's eyes grew wide at the thought that she was actually recognized by a fan.

"Why yes." She said, sounding a little too much like Blanche Dubois in *Street Car Named Desire*. "I am."

"You want my autograph, right? Got a pen?" Randy was used to this.

"Nope." The fellow said slapping down a large manila envelope. "I just wanted you to have *this*. You've both been served."

As the process server skipped off to his next happy delivery, Randy nervously ripped open the envelope.

"What the fuck is that?" Tina asked. Her face muscles twisted despite her Botox. "We've *both* been served?"

"Solita is suing us." Randy said, frowning as he read the top page of the lawsuit.

"For what? Why, that ungrateful, stupid pig! We were really good to her!"

"We'll deal with this later, Tina. I have to get back and deal with a bunch of other mind-fucking shit."

"I have a meeting myself." Tina replied coyly. "I'll be home around six."

The phone at the Horn rarely ever stopped ringing.

"-Horn O Plenty Productions! How may I help you?" Mei Ling Wang had one of those endearing little-girl voices people enjoyed hearing when they called the Horn. It lent to the feeling of the place being fun, special and definitely a music house for children's productions. Of course Joey joked Randy hired her the moment he heard her speak. All 5'3" of her radiated this infectious spitfire smiling energy that could literally be heard over the phone and never failed to charm the caller. Her demeanor made it very hard for those calling with not-so-friendly intentions, which happened occasionally like it happens anywhere else. She had been the voice of the Horn for over 10 years.

"Hey Baby, I just wanted you to know I'm on my way over. I'm bringing Randy a bunch of *Titans Of Yore* tour t-shirts he asked for."

"Great Royal-Bee! See you soon, honey."

The first time RoyBob heard Mei Ling's voice it felt like candy in his ear. It took him several seconds to remember he was calling to speak with Randy. The first time he saw Mei Ling he was asking her out before he knew what he was doing. Joey had to lead him into the conference room/dining room for a meeting to discuss the first tour he ever did with the Band. RoyBob and Mei Ling began quietly dating soon after. They possessed energies that dovetailed with each other. But they kept it completely out of the Horn so only Paulette, Joey and Larry knew they were making plans to get married by the Holidays.

While Tina had her office on the third floor, it was not part of Horn O' Plenty Productions. Tina's assistant Noel Bamberger, fielded calls for Tina about jobs for Bela or one of her other three clients, including Randy - in between filing his nails and peering over websites dedicated to international cuisine.

Noel Bamberger was a textbook example of an early 21st century metrosexual: Completely manscaped, clipped and shaved and buffed and polished and pedicured and manicured once a week, impeccable, obsessive taste in the finest fashions on sale at Barneys on Wilshire and a discriminating palate for the trendiest foods at the trendiest spots with the trendiest people. All Noel thought of outside of work was what he called *food mash-ups*: combining two very different types of cuisine to create new tastes, like a Tandoori Chicken, Peanut Butter and Jelly Sandwich. -Or a Sushi Burrito. -Or a Donut Burger.

Noel was extremely loyal to Tina. She paid him princely (thanks to Randy) and used him as a well-groomed guard dog to her business. And he did not disappoint. He was friendly with the Horn personnel but he didn't hang out with them. He didn't go out with them. Besides, part of being metrosexual was acting effortlessly aloof.

Despite all that, RoyBob being RoyBob, he set out to be friendly to the only other Jew in the Horn. Being from the east coast, he didn't know any west coast Jews. He'd been told there was a difference. But RoyBob always tried to find the best in everybody. So RoyBob went up to the third floor and introduced himself to Bamberger. And trying to relate to Noel, RoyBob simply asked, "Hey man, have you been to Israel yet?"

"Not yet." Noel politely answered.

"Well wait till you are there. You get this incredible feeling."

Bamberger smiled weakly and turned back to his computer screen.

"Sounds great. See you later. Oo-Lookey! They came out with the *ManMower 5.0!*"

Seeing Noel wasn't all that interested, RoyBob smiled, said, "Yeah, Later." Then he left.

Barely noticing RoyBob leave, Noel clicked on a photo of a Hot Dog Éclair. He murmured softly to himself as he clicked on a photo of Pizza-Tiramisu. "I wonder how Tina's business meeting is going."

Tina was in a motel bathroom, washing up, wondering if she needed more Botox.

"Hey-" Bela Marconi called to her from bed. He'd been flipping through channels when one caught his attention. "You better come here. I just saw a promo about something I think you need to see-"

"Fuck! About what?" She shouted, looking at herself in the mirror.

"Come see for yourself."

"Welcome to Hollywood Hear/Say! I'm your host, Hap Hazard!"

A man sitting on the side of a desk in front of a row of desks in a newsroom held a sheet of paper in his hand as he spoke: *"And Here's Your Hollywood Hear/Say For The Day! -Item One: "*

Stomping out of the bathroom with a toothbrush in her hand, Tina glared at Bela.

"OK, What's so fucking impor-" was all Tina got out, as her eyes bulged for a second now glaring at the big screen mounted above the dresser. A photo of

Randy from the 1980s took up the entire right side of the screen as Hap Hazard began his report:

"The Orifice Of The Oracle's Randy Root and his wife apparently got a little too Old Testament God-like according to their ex-nanny who claims the couple abused her verbally and financially - and then dropped her for a younger model.

Solita Vaughn, the ex-nanny, says she got canned by Randy back in July when she returned from two weeks personal leave for a family funeral in Jamaica. This according to the lawsuit she just filed in L.A.

"Hollywood Hear/Say obtained a copy of the suit, and in it Solita Vaughn says the Roots cut her hours to five per week and when she complained, Randy told her, "We understand how you feel. So if you don't like it, don't bother coming back."

"Sixty-six year old Vaughn describes Randy's wife as a real tyrant in her suit. She says Mrs. R. commonly called her a pig, an idiot, stupid and dumb right to her face. Vaughn also claims she regularly worked more than forty hours a week, but rarely got overtime.

"In the suit, she says the couple had already hired a new, younger nanny when she got back from her mother's funeral and feels cutting her hours was a ploy to force her to quit.

"Vaughn is suing for wrongful termination, age discrimination, gender discrimination, emotional distress, her unpaid overtime and for them just being very mean almost all the time.

"Looks like she's taking advice from Randy Root's old band and flipping him and the Mrs. -OFF! Next, a world famous director is found naked swimming in a pool filled with cherry Jello and vodka!"

It had taken the Hollywood Gossip media mill mere hours from the moment Solita filed her complaint downtown in court for them to find out all about it.

Tina jerked the remote out of Bela's hand. She clicked from channel to channel, looking for a more serious source of news.

"Let's see what HNN has to say. And get dressed. We're done here."

The woman on the screen was seated at a counter bearing the network name in large red letters: HOLLYWOOD NETWORK NEWS. In the most professional and British tone possible, the anchorwoman began reading from her teleprompter:

"Next up on HHN: In news that has already triggered dozens of attempts at witty quips and memes based around the 80s hit "Flip It Off," The Orifice Of The Oracle's Randy Root is being sued by his family's former nanny for wrongful termination, age discrimination, gender discrimination, emotional distress, her unpaid overtime - and extremely poor management skills.

"As tends to be the case with these sort of things, HHN has the scoop, which stems from legal proceedings filed by the former nanny in question, Solita Vaughn, this week in Los Angeles court. Vaughn accuses Root of firing her in July after she returned from two weeks of personal leave, which she'd taken in order to go to her mother's funeral in Jamaica. When she came back, she says she discovered that the family cut her hours severely, and had already hired a younger male replacement.

"The suit goes on to accuse the family of various abuses, particularly with regards to Root's wife, who's quoted as calling Vaughn "a pig, an idiot, stupid and dumb right to her face." Although Vaughn insists she regularly worked more than her allotted 40 hours a week, she claims she was rarely paid overtime, and says when she complained about having her hours cut down to five a week, Root told her, 'If you don't like it, you're welcome to not bother coming back.' Which undoubtedly has Ms. Vaughn asking, 'Jesus, What's Your Hang-Up?' Coming up *next on HNN: How a foot-long Philly Cheesesteak sandwich saved a vegan movie star's life!"*

"THAT'S PROFESSIONAL REPORTING? WHAT SHIT! WHAT TOTAL FUCKED UP HACK SHIT!" What upset Tina more than anything as she watched these reports, was not that she was described as a tyrant, or abusive or any of the rest of it.

"BASTARDS! THEY ONLY MENTIONED ME AS RANDY'S *WIFE!* HIS GODDAMNED WIFE! LIKE I'M JUST CHATTEL! NO PROFESSIONAL RECOGNITION OF MY OWN! NO MENTION OF MY BUSINESS! NOT EVEN ANY MENTION OF MY GODDAMNED NAME! NO! JUST '*ROOT'S WIFE.*' THE LEAST FUCKING IMPORTANT THING TO REPORT IN THE FUCKING WORLD!"

She punched the wall next to the TV and screamed at Bela.

"DON'T THEY KNOW WHO I AM?!"

The next day, RoyBob came by the Horn to bring back more tour t-shirts for everybody. Tina walked up to him broadly smiling, her eyes on fire.

"Can we speak privately for a minute?" She said, again smiling like she was going to ask RoyBob to the Prom.

"Sure, Tina. How can I help you?" He expected her to say something fun.

She made him walk down the hall, into an empty office and closed the door getting directly into his face. "Do me a favor and *cut the Jew Thing* you're pulling with my assistant, ok? Noel's not here to be your friend. He's here to help me make this place run more efficiently. And I notice you around Mei Ling quite a lot. No wonder she doesn't do her job properly, either."

"Well, we were going to wait to announce it. But we're engaged."

166

Tina looked at him, studiously for a moment and in a flash, changed her attitude totally. "Well, congratulations! That's wonderful! I hope we're invited to the wedding! I can't wait to tell Randy!"

Only a few offices down from them, Jason Barter had struggled all day, all night and now all morning to figure out what Randy heard in his head. He was certain Randy would be coming through his door any moment. The associate composers, Jake and Bertie, hearing what sounded like someone hitting their head against the wall that Jake shared with Jason, came into Barter's room. Barter jumped, thinking it was Randy.

"Jason, we heard what Randy said to you and thought we could help you out, man." Jake gave Barter a light, brotherly slap on the back.

"Yeah, we've been there. You know that." Bertie added. "Us Horn Dogs got to stick together."

Barter smiled gratefully. "Thanks guys. You know how he can be. And I'm no psychic."

"Here-" Jake held out a flash drive. "We did a few variations on the same thing for you, just to fill things out."

"How many tracks did you come up with, Jason?"

"Two. So far."

"Well now you got six."

"We did two each, too."

At that very moment Randy knocked once and burst through the door. With the door open, Barter could see Dexter Dille walking into Studio Zero across the hall. Bertie and Jake smiled at Randy, winked at Jason and left the room quickly.

"Ok, what you got for me, Barter? Play them now. Let's go."

Barter nervously played his first new track. Randy listened patiently to the first few bars. He looked over at Barter deadpan and then broke into a smile.

"That's enough. You nailed it on the first one! Good job. Now give me a flash drive of that tied to picture and I'll go deal with Dille."

"Got it right here-"

Randy grabbed the flash drive out of Jason's hand and went into his studio.

Dille was sitting on the client couch, examining in great detail another one of Randy's art books on the naked lady coffee table.

"My. You really do have quite a lot of these girls around."

"Let me play this for you. I think it makes a dramatic hero out of wet cement-"

Dexter laughed out loud. "Do you now? Ok, let's hear it. Tied to picture."

"It is. Listen to this. Watch what it does for the video."

The track played to picture and Dille started concentrating on it as intensely as if it was something he was going to submit to the Academy for an Oscar. His intensity actually made Randy as nervous as he usually made Jason Barter when reviewing his tracks. Randy hadn't expected him to sit through the entire piece, but he did. He sat through every single second of the 1,800 seconds that make up thirty minutes. Randy wished he had some wet clay to play with.

"Well done, Randall. This might well win some award at the Concrete Film Festival this year."

"Is there really such a thing?"

"Dexter laughed. "No, but it did sound, good didn't it? But that was fun, wasn't it? I have something else for you."

Randy got excited, thinking his time and effort had been worth taking on the cement project. "Great, Dexter!"

"The tour movie I just shot with you guys and the rest is slated for distribution later next year. And I can't get to it until I get this other project out of the way. I've been bogged down in this project with a big, difficult movie star who belongs to that religion, the Temple of Technotology. You know - the Technotologists?"

Technotology was a religion created by a Hollywood Webmaster on a dare in the 1980s. They boasted a roster of mega movie star members whom they treated much better than the ordinary supplicants.

"Yeah. Sure. You mean Tip Slyde, the action star, don't you? Who doesn't know the Technotologists? They're everywhere around here, Dex. So hey, you want *me* to work on a Tip Slyde film! That's awesome!" He sounded a little too excited when he said that - and he knew it.

Dille gave him a sly cat-like look. "Well... -In a way. You see, to get Slyde to work with me, I had to shoot a sixty-minute film about his faith and its great founder, Elroy Flotsamheimer. So I need music for this, too. And I need it in a week. -Can you do it?"

"Whatever you need, Dex."

"I'll never get tired of hearing that. Great, see you in a week, then."

Just as Randy was about to call the guys in to discuss this new project, his phone suddenly rang. He was expecting this art dealer he was negotiating with for a show at the man's gallery. He figured this was the guy.

"Hey. So let's talk about my Rosebud collection." He said, answering the phone.

"Rosebud collection? Is that what you call us now?"

Randy slammed the door to studio zero shut. "I'm getting sick of these calls, girls. I've got an NDA. I want this to stop-"

"Our mother signed that NDA, Randy. Not us. Remember?"

"We were too young."

"We were underage."

"Waaay underage."

"Minors."

"Children."

"Still little girls."

"Hey, still wanna play?

"How about Coco Puffs?

"Or How about a Jujy fruit Blow Job?"

"I know! -A double banana split? That was always your favorite!"

"With our cherries on top?"

"Don't forget the whipped cream?"

"OK. OK." Randy tried to take control. "-Melody. -Melanie. That was a long time ago. And you girls remember it differently. Just tell me what you want."

"Girls? We're still girls? Gosh, I don't know if an NDA covers child molestation?"

"What the fuck do you two want after all these years?"

"How about our lives back, Randy? Years don't matter? Just *compensation* does?"

"Call Avi. Tell him what you want. And then *this* is done, once and for fucking all."

"But it's so much more fun to talk with you about it, Randy. -Done?.."

With that, he hung up. But for once, he couldn't just shrug it off. Too many things were converging at once. He was actually feeling something he had long ignored: Pressure.

As he tried to calm down, he tried to call Avi on his private line. Avi didn't answer so he left a message. Then he gathered his composers together and told them about the project.

"So we have to score this full-hour religious drivel for Dexter. He says he's got a big project for me if we can come through on this. Ok, you all have the film. We got one week."

"A sham religion prospering in a town built on sham. Makes sense to me." Joey said. Everyone laughed. -Except Randy.

"Looks like you got a problem with the project, Joey."

"Looks like you could use some Gastro-Fizzix, Randy. And you're in luck! They just gave us a lifetime supply."

Randy wanted to say: "Hey, Joey, if it's too much for you-you can always have two weeks...and as a matter a fact, why don't you take two weeks? Consider this your notice!" Instead, he said, "Judging from your t-shirt, which is a virtual menu for that rat hole you usually hang around lunchtime, you need a box of that shit more than me."

Never one to be outgunned, Joey replied with a snort, "Randy, I need a case of that shit just for working here!" Everybody laughed at that. Randy chuckled the chuckle of someone playing poker.

With all the pressures building up on Randy, he just didn't have it in him to tell Joey to her face that he wanted her gone. Later at home, after listening to Tina go on about how the TV reports of Solita suing them had insulted her by not mentioning her professionally, he admitted to Tina he just didn't have the heart to do it.

"Oh, I've got the *heart.* Leave it to me, honey. It'll be my pleasure. -First thing in the morning. I can't wait."

That evening, home for the night, Joey had decided to treat her self to a bit of blow. -Actually, a lot more than a bit of blow. She hadn't done that in over a week. She was bored and over the objections of her newest girlfriend, didn't see why she shouldn't enjoy an evening of virtually pure, high-grade cocaine like she used to in those high-octane wild early days. She took a large snort. She always loved the numbing taste of coke. Joey rubbed another half line on her upper and lower gums and put the other half on her tongue. Enjoying that, she decided to do another large line. She inhaled Peru in one long powerful snort. She arched her back with a curious look on her face. Her eyes went wide. She spit up blood and collapsed. Joey Jabonno died without regaining consciousness on the way to the hospital.

CHAPTER 8

The screen shone with an ultraviolet video of the sun, recorded by NASA's Solar Dynamics Observatory. The convulsing ball of electro-magnetic explosions cast out endless swirling fields of plasma energy waves pulsing in figure eights of infinity.

As this view of the sun remained steadily spinning and weaving back in on itself with its golden spiraling waves, a voice-over began. The voice sounded as if it were speaking to a group of people in a hall somewhere, some time ago and carried a slight echo and dusty quality to it adding a touch more dramatic depth.

"Electrical Impulses. That's what we are. Currents all bundled up tightly into Electrical Beings. Who hasn't felt that jolt of electricity run up their spines and hit the back of their heads in a moment of excitement or danger? Who hasn't felt that in their legs? -Or their arms? -Or other places? Ha. Yes. I know. And what do we say? 'It's How We're Wired!' Think about that now. Because scientifically we know nerves carry electrical impulses throughout the body. You heard Walt Whitman's poem: I Sing The Body Electric: 'The Universe is a procession with measured and perfect motion." These things are not coincidences. When you come to realize your true Electrical Self, this is when you realize you are part of the Grid. *-The fuse box*

of everything in existence. -The circuit breaker that channels all energies. -The oscillating hard-drive to all consciousness. This is really what Tesla was talking about. The Grid - the one true God. And when you become part of the Grid - You are the Grid. You are the eternal energy source manifested through the portals of the stars just like our sun. And we, you, I, all of us as carbon-based beings are stardust. Once you grasp how you're hooked up to the Grid, you'll be able to remake your reality exactly as you want it. The life currents flowing though all our bodies is Divine Electricity. -The highest voltage transmission. Start thinking of yourself as the Grid. Not merely a part of the Grid. Each of us is the Grid.

"The sun and every star in the heavens is our portal in and out of this universe. When you hear of people going to the light, that is what they are taking about. The light generated by those portals we call stars. We are the children of those stars. We ourselves are beautiful balls of electromagnetic spiritual energy. We are electrical beings pure and simple! We worship the literal God-Electricity in ourselves coursing through our veins and every fiber of our Being.

"Here in the Temple of Technotology we simply cut to the point where we focus on our own techno-physical-electric nature. To open up and amplify our inner EMF, our electromotive force that when properly directed can generate an ocean of electrical currents to create an entirely new and positive world around you filled with prosperity and happiness of your own personal making. You see more. Hear more. Observe more. Absorb more. Understand more. Control more.

"But it takes work. And service! -Lots and lots of service to the Temple. It may take you a billion years of service. That's OK. We are all Electrical Energy. We don't ever die. We regenerate at our Grid Source and reassign ourselves as we see fit. That is how I am with you now."

The swirling ultra-violet sun suddenly opened up in its center, giving birth to the glowing image of Technotology's Founder, Elroy Flotsamheimer. His full-length 6'4" clean-shaven Santa Claus appearance shimmered and glowed as a ghostly computer generated image. He smiled, nodded and then gestured for the viewer to join him.

"So come along with me on this Amazing Journey. Join us on the greatest adventure this or any other galaxy has ever seen!" The Founder's ethereal form smiled, waved, bowed slightly and stepped back into the roiling portal as his last words echoed out. *"I will see you soon."*

The sun suddenly collapsed into itself constricting into limitless black for a nanosecond, replaced by a blinding lightning strike that produced center screen one of the brightest stars in Hollywood. Behind him flashed a panoramic montage of every blockbuster film he'd been the box office draw in for the last 25 years.

"Hello. I'm Tip Slyde and you and I just witnessed an appearance of the man who changed my life and yours and still millions and billions and trillions to come. The Founder of Technotology and the Savior of Post Modern Humanity, our Beloved Elroy Flotsamheimer."

He stood wearing the skin-tight black metallic uni-suit shimmering with flecks of copper, silver and gold from his blockbuster hit, *Collect Call From An Alternate Universe.* Slyde was blessed with handsome features. -A head of lustrous jet-black hair. -An aquiline nose. -High cheekbones. -A square jaw. -Dazzling blue eyes.

He was known principally for his action-adventure films across several genres from science fiction to political intrigue to crime drama. Tip had time traveled into the future to save alien civilizations. He had jumped across galaxies to find true love. He had uncovered and thwarted countless conspiracies to overthrow everybody, including Greenland. He had singlehandedly taken down every known drug cartel in the world, plus a few no one in the world even knew were there to take down. As such, Tip was one of the few mega-stars in the Hollywood religion's firmament that remained an A-Lister consistently through the years. He had a keen knack for picking the right script at the right time with his finger on the pulse of what the average moviegoer went to the movies for. Tip had originally *Gone Grid*, as converting to the Temple was called, after falling in love with an actress already in the Faith. When she left - he stayed.

"His inspiring appearance proves what the Founder just made abundantly clear." Tip looked seriously into the camera. *"Elroy is NOT dead. It's like he said. There is no real death. Just electrical energy transference. Elroy just dropped his body.*

He discarded it in order to move on to the next level of conductivity. There comes a time in all grid-conscious people's lives where their bodies can no longer hold the electrical energy you're now generating, especially at the higher levels of Technotology consciousness you're working toward right now.

When that happens, we oscillate until we are ready for further electrical assignment. And before you know it, I'll be doing that higher work with Elroy soon enough. Until then, just my presence in any film you see, should make you, as part of our elite vanguard, think of the words of our beloved Founder about how our electrical consciousness will save the world. Electrical impulses are-"

"Ok. Stop it here for a second." Jake said to Bertie. "I think we can add a cue right there."

"Bertie, let's try a line with a Schoenberg-like thing mixed with a twisted Scott Joplin-like thing on the Farfisa organ. Something like this-" Jake played a quick line on his keyboard in Farfisa mode.

"I like that, Jake. Yeah. Put it in. Hey, you hear Randy settled with Solita for a cool mil'?"

"Man... Wish I'd been those kids' nanny."

"Oh no you don't." Bertie said, laughing with certainty.

"Better gab about that later." Even with the door closed, Jake looked left and right out of nervous habit. "Let's work on this next scene where Tip is surfing on molten lava on the surface of Europa. Whose moon is that?"

"Cowabunga, dude! Catch a lava-wave and you're sittin' on top of a world, huh? Uh, it's Jupiter's." Bertie was doing his best to stay happy. "Well, we at least can say we're working on a Tip Slyde film, huh?"

"You're right. We can at least say we're working-"

Randy opened Bertie's door and popped his head in with a smile. "Hey you two!" He chirped. "We're all cutting out for Joey's Memorial. We'll see you guys there. Oh, and add some spacey *pings* and *pongs* to the track for accent, will ya? Thanks. Dille's gonna be here to tomorrow to see how we're doing." He winked at them and reclosed the door.

"This place won't be the same without her." Jake coiled a dark brown lock in his right index finger for a second. Of Swedish and not Hebraic heritage, the young composer ironically resembled a yeshiva student studying to be a rabbi, from the top of his mop of tightly wound, bouncing curls, down to his round apple-cheeked smiling countenance and his slightly portly build and average height.

"And we were right in the middle of producing our *Horn Dog* album with her." Bertie shook his shoulder length mane of jet-black hair sadly. His sharp Mayan features scrunched up in stoic grief. "There's no replacing Joey Jabonno."

"Yeah, agreed Jake. "But she'd want us to finish that album."

About a year before, Jake, Bertie, Barter and Joey had been fooling around playing music after hours, singing improvised songs about lost love and hot babes. They were jamming for the most part, when Joey remarked: "Listen to us. We're just a bunch of Horn Dogs!" And then she started barking and went into this long solo that inspired the guys and the next thing they knew, they were recording songs and preparing to perform as *The Horn Dogs*, well aware of the double entendre of where they worked, without ever knowing the full ironic triple entendre of that name.

"Alright," Jake said, getting up. We better get going."

"Yeah-" said Bertie, getting up as well. "You know, I heard Randy was going to fire Joey the morning they found out."

"I heard that, too. C'mon. Let's go and get this over with." He looked out his window. "Randy and Tina just left. We better split."

Tina started chewing off Randy's ear on their way over to the memorial the moment he pulled out of the driveway, while he was thinking of ways to crash the car without hurting himself. He gave up trying to figure it out.

"Are you listening to me?"

"Half of Hollywood is listening to you. And I've got the windows up."

"That RoyBob character thinks he can subtly sway you on things. I think he's more friends with Jeffy than you. I wouldn't trust him. I know he doesn't work at the Horn, but because of Mei Ling, he's there a lot. You know I caught him playing buddy-buddy with Bamberger just because they're both Jews? Like that matters? Of course Noel couldn't care less. God there's so much bullshit around your company...I'm like choking on the fumes."

"Choking, huh?" Randy said in mock concern. "That reminds me," he thought to himself. "I need to get in touch with Avi."

Joey's memorial was held two weeks after her funeral. Jeffy had been the dutiful son and brother and brought his sister back home to Flint for her parents to lay her to rest in their family plot at the Sunset Hills cemetery. The funeral was private and quiet, somber and quick. The priest read a traditional Liturgy from the Old Testament and then the New Testament while Jeffy did his best to ignore it all and think of how he and Joey had their own gospel and their own ideas of what was next.

Despite being a private event at Sunset Hills, old Flint friends showed up at the Jabonno home to express their sympathies and condolences. Their homemade casseroles and lasagna made a mountain of the Jabonno kitchen table. One of the visitors was an old girlfriend of Jeffy's. He walked up to her and they hugged. "Melissa. Good to see you. Thanks for coming. I was thinking about us, lately. Do you remember going skinny-dipping in the principal's backyard pool at four in the morning on graduation day? We talked about getting married, running off to fame and fortune?" Jeffy was looking for anything fun and carefree to think of other than where he really was.

178

"To be honest with you Jeffy." His old girlfriend smiled at him sadly. "I hardly remember anything of those days, anymore. Sorry about Joey. You know I have five grandchildren now? And I got them for the weekend. I have to get back home. But it was great to see you and catch up on old times. You look great, considering... My condolences about Joey, again." She faintly kissed him on the cheek and without turning back said over her shoulder, "Bye Jeffy!"

He sat there thinking to himself how someone he almost married was now like Satoko the Abbess of Gesshuji in Yukio Mishima's *Decay Of The Angel*: She didn't remember fuck-all of their young love. Nothing. -None of the long conversations. -None of the embraces. No caresses. No whispers. No shared breathing. No gazes. All forgotten. As if they never happened at all. A cold bottle of beer broke through Jeffy's pity party. He looked up to see his dad offering him the frosty brew.

"Can you believe it, son? They still make Pabst Blue Ribbon! You know, Jeffy, it would really make your mom feel better under the circumstances if you'd stay with us tonight before you go back. Please? It's just for one night, son."

Feeling emotionally obligated to sleep in his old bedroom in his old bed in his old sheets his mother kept washing and changing once a week, he was so tired he gave in with a sigh and a smile and a nod to his father. As he stretched out on his old twin-sized mattress, his mind seemed finally still for once. And after everything that had happened in that one day from the funeral to realizing his old love didn't remember their old love, he was hoping for a decent night of sleep. As he drifted off, he thought finally he'd found a place of tranquility.

Instead he found himself at another funeral. A funeral filled with people he didn't recognize and did not recognize him. He wanted to leave. He looked everywhere for the door. There wasn't one. Anywhere. He went from one stranger to the next, demanding someone tell him how to get the fuck out of there.

The worst part was what happened when he went up to each of them yelling: "Where the fuck is the door? What the fuck is going on here? Hey answer me! Don't you know who I am?" Because when he pulled each stranger around to face him, he realized they were faceless - except for a mouth. And each faceless mouth he turned around gave its own answer in its own ghastly voice each time he asked:

"Don't you know who I am?"

"How many guesses do I get?"

"Don't you know who I am?"

"No. Don't you?"

"Don't you know who I am?"

"Literally or figuratively?"

Jeffy didn't want to ask anymore. He tried to stop. But he couldn't control it.

"Don't you know who I am?"

"Can you hum a few bars?"

"Don't you know who I am?"

"Does it matter who you are?"

"Don't you know who I am?"

"Don't you know I don't care?"

"Don't you know who I am?"

"Is this a trick question?"

"Don't you know who I am?"

"Can I see your ID?"

"Don't you know who I am?"

"Could you give me a hint?"

"Don't you know who I am?"

"Aren't you who you are?"

As things moved faster and faster Jeffy turned one last stranger around asking one last desperate time. "Don't you know who I am?" And as the stranger faced him he saw the face of Randy Root.

"Yeah. I do. Go look over there." Nightmare Randy pointed to the front of the room.

Instantly, Jeffy was looking over himself in the coffin and looking up at himself from the coffin - simultaneously.

Jeffy woke up panting in a cold sweat staring at the same ceiling he stared at as a kid, swearing one day he'd get out of that room and never return. That was as much sleep as Jeffy got that night.

Joey's memorial was held at a friend's house in Beverly Hills off Coldwater Canyon once owned by O.J. Simpson's lawyer, Robert Kardashian. It was part family reunion as all such gatherings usually are as well as part wake and even part row. Another friend with a local restaurant catered the affair. Many Hollywood notables passed through the house giving their respects. Jeffy stood there looking somber but still managing a brave, stiff smile, nodding and thanking everyone as they gave their condolences.

A large five by five foot photo of Joey at the age of 25, posing as the Indian Goddess Shiva on the Oracle's Vedic Tour was placed on a large easel with flowers arranged all around it. Her warm friendly, big smiling face was still young, bright and hopeful. She held a guitar in her own hands while her two mechanical middle fingers flipped off the camera.

The moment she heard about Joey's death, Mindy called Jeffy.

"Jeffy, I'm so sorry. You know I loved Joey. I know this is a hard time for this to happen. But I know-"

181

Jeffy hung up on her right there. Her call had come while he was sitting waiting for his flight back to LA at the very same airline gate he'd lost his laptop at O'Hare airport the last time he was there. An attractive middle-aged woman wearing earbuds sat down next to him. Her music was so loud, he could hear the song she was listening to: *Who Are You?*

"What's the matter, Jeffy?" John Lennon asked him. "Thought that was one of your favorite ditties."

"Shut the fuck up." He said a little too loud as the woman turned and looked at him for a moment.

"Now don't get cheeky with me, Jabonno. I'm on your side..."

"Oh yeah? Which side is that?"

"You know that early hit you had with your cover of *Help*? -Very helter-skelter, your version, by the way. Do you know why I wrote that mother? -Help! You need somebody. Not just anybody. You know you need someone. And that someone is me, Jeffy."

"You're helping?"

"Well who else are you going to discuss all this with?"

"I'm only talking to myself."

"That again? I thought we were past that. But Jeffo Jabonno, even if you were just talking to yourself, you'd at least be guaranteed there was one person listening. Though believe me darling, it is two. Now considering what happens tomorrow, you better keep it cool when you see the Root Of All Evil. The time will come to confront him. But not tomorrow, man."

"Tomorrow never knows..." Jeffy sighed.

"Good one!" Lennon laughed.

The memorial was held the next day literally hours after Jeffy had gotten back into town.

Most of the Hollywood crowd that knew Joey came to show their respects, dressed in varying shades and styles of black. The road-crew showed up. Scruffy, Philly Phingers, Keith Utz and Truck Copland were all there. Shaggy and June Lucey came together. Ricky Rudolph had flown in from New York just to attend the memorial. "She was the nicest one of the group." Ricky said to the circle he stood with. Everybody laughed and nodded in semi-somber agreement.

When Joey died, it threw a monkey wrench the size of King Kong into his plans to confront Randy so when they saw each other at the memorial, which was the first time they had seen each other since the tour, Randy and Tina were appropriately somber and comforting as the moment demanded. Tina whimpered, "I loved her sooo much." Jeffy was gracious about it, only giving Randy and Tina dirty side glances every so often.

Joey had become a big lovable, unkempt bear of a woman. She didn't exercise. She drank and ate heavy foods and did cocaine like she was still in her 20's. And menopause definitely didn't help. Jeffy was no stranger to partying. Neither was Randy. Forget Larry. "Party Animal" was her well-earned nickname. So when it came to thinking about advancing age - none of them did.

No one truly in the Youth Culture was raised to think about specific ages outside of birthday parties. So being in their 60's didn't really mean the same to them that it would if they had been working their whole lives on the GM assembly line back in Flint. Not in Hollywood. And damn well not in the world of rock n' roll. They, like everyone else in that world were accustomed to thinking they were going to live forever. They were accustomed to dating people half their age and younger without ever thinking about it twice.

That's the way it's been in Hollywood from Charlie Chaplin to the now. Celebrities are given so much in so many ways from acclaim to money to sex on a silver platter on regular basis that their sense of limits is blurred and in some cases completely erased.

The only time advancing age ever occurred to any of the Orifice Of The Oracle before this, was when some part of them, like Larry's hands, or Jeffy's back, or Joey's neck or Randy's ears bothered them after a performance. And more drugs were usually the answer to that.

As more and more people arrived to honor Joey, all the Horn staff started grouping with each other over an array of enticing finger food on silver trays set out in the dining room.

"Paulette," Mei Ling whispered. "Is it true, he was going to fire Joey? Actually," she added, "I heard he was gonna have Tina do it."

"Oh, darling-" Paulette smiled with a soft, velvety laugh and whispered low: "Tina will have him firing us one by one, mark my words. First me, then you, until everyone there is handpicked and working for her."

"That's what RoyBob's been saying."

"Oh yes, Mei Ling. RoyBob is right. No one is safe. She's been plotting to take over the Horn since before she was begging and banging at the front door to be let back in after Lacie threw her out."

Pockets of conversations were everywhere. Scruffy and Philly, Truck and the rest of the road crew had assembled their own little clique, including Ricky Rudolph, who always saw himself as a working class hero.Jake, Bertie and Jason Barter were standing nearby and joined them. They all stood around in a circle talking about everybody and all the gossip they knew about them.

"Man, it's really weird working on this Technotology thing just as Joey dies." Bertie spoke in low tones.

"Shit," Utz said, puffing on a cigarette. "Technos don't have no funerals."

"That's right," added Philly. "Those blokes don't believe she's dead mate. She's just...busy at the moment. You know, like: Please leave a message. She'll call you back."

"Talk about being busy at the moment - You guys hear Solita got a million from her case?" Jake asked.

"I heard Jeffy got his lap top stolen in Chicago." Jason added.

"Yeah, well word is Randy was gonna fire Joey the day she died." Truck said.

"You guys heard that, too, huh?" Bertie said, shaking his head.

Looking across the lawn to the patio Scruffy could see Mei-Ling hanging affectionately all over RoyBob. He nudged Philly and pointed at the two subtly with his chin laughing. "Wow." He said amused. "And we fuckin' thought he was gay, man. I put his name in my phone as *Ms. RoyBob.*"

Everybody stood in different parts of the house. -The living room. -The kitchen. -The dining room. -The den. -On the patio. -In the backyard. They were all innocently mulling about, munching on finger food, talking about Joey, talking about business. In a moment of required lucidity, Jeffy got up and addressed the gathering.

"Thank you all for coming. Joey would be moved to see you all here. I like to think that she is here with us at the same time she has risen as the divine being we've always said we all really are in our music. So let's not mourn her. Let's celebrate a meaningful and well-lived life. Here's to Joey!" With that, he raised a glass of Krystal champagne, Joey's drink of choice. The group raised their glasses in response.

"To Joey!"

Jeffy then invited the congregation to share their memories of Joey. He walked around listening to words of love and praise for his sister. He graded a few of them to himself at various levels of sincerity on a scale from one to ten.

"She was the heart of the Band."

"An 8"

"She kept the Horn together for years."

"A 9."

"Talented musician. Spirited performer."

"A 5."

"Excellent cook. Ever tried her sea urchin risotto? -Oh ho!"

"A 6."

"The backbone of the Oracle."

"A 7."

"Nicest person I knew in this fucked up business."

"Another 9."

"She was the realest person I know in this Town."

"Another 9."

"The world will never be the same."

"A 4."

"She'll be remembered throughout the ages."

"A fuckin' 2."

"I loved her sooo much."

"A Fucking Phony Cunt."

Larry distinguished herself by clearing her throat loudly to get everyone's attention and then in her inimitable style, grunted out her words for everyone to hear.

"Well, I'm not gonna get up now and say she was wonderful just to say she was wonderful or great just to say she was great. I'll just say she was someone I worked well with and if that's not good enough - you all can kiss my skinny white ass. Thank you."

Shaking his head, Jeffy had to admit as psycho as she was, nobody was more sincere than Larry Root. But he still didn't give her a ten. He didn't rate her at all. He was too busy spying Tara Thyme from across the room. She had just sauntered in adorned in a black and gold Chinese Cheongsam dress, complimented by her traditional gold silk neck-hiding scarf and elbow-length red velvet gloves. Jeffy embraced her. They hugged and she peck-kissed him.

"You know," Jeffy said, feeling very sentimental. "Tara, sometimes I wish we'd gotten married after your ex found us in bed."

Tara gave him a quizzical look. "He found us in bed?"

"You don't remember?"

"Oh yeah! Yeah... Of course! I'd been wondering lately why he and I split up in the first place. Yes. Thanks! That's right! I'd kinda forgotten that."

As people started to filter out, Jeffy, now taking in Tara's words, thanked her for coming, kissed her this time on the cheek and stomped into the backyard with Shaggy, as June stood and talked with a group including Paulette, Mei Ling and RoyBob.

"This should be someone else's memorial." Jeffy muttered under his breath, not meaning for Shaggy to hear that. "If I have to hear Tina Drekk tell one more person she loved Joey soooo much-"

"I felt like that when my Mom died." Shaggy offered in sympathy, ignoring any implication of whose memorial Jeffy was suggesting it should be. Jeffy just stared at Shaggy like he was the most clueless person on the planet.

"You have no idea what is happening, do you? I feel like I'm being erased from my own history by the Joseph Stalin of the rock world."

"Erased? What are you talking about? For Christ sakes Jeffy! You named the Band. C'mon, now."

"Yeah, Shaggy, Brian Jones named his band, too. -Look what happened to him. You saw that Golden Calf show where Root claims he did everything, didn't you?"

Shaggy didn't really know what to say. And as much as he felt a part of the group as a band and as people and especially as friends, he now felt completely out of his league and wasn't sure how to respond to the words that began spouting like a open fire hydrant out of Jeffy's mouth at the top of his lungs as he looked over and saw Randy and Tina talking with people he didn't recognize. They were laughing and carrying on as if they were at a party they were hosting.

All Shaggy could do was try to politely shush him as Jeffy unloaded like never before:

"Hey, speaking of everything that Randy Root did, did you know that Randy used to fuck *two eleven year old twins* when we first moved out here to Los Angeles? YEAH. HE FUCKED TWO ELEVEN-YEAR OLD GIRLS! He paid off their whore mother and had regular sex with these underage girls for years! Then he'd strut around the studio boasting how 'PUSSY DIDN'T GET FRESHER OR SWEETER THAN THAT!' AND HOW FUCKING TWINS WAS LIKE FUCKING IN STEREO! That's right! The great and all-powerful Randy Root Of All Evil would come to every rehearsal and every recording session back then going on and on about how great it was that his little girls DIDN'T GET PERIODS! And how great it was that his little girls COULDN'T GET PREGNANT! And ohhh, how cool was their mother not just to condone Randy molesting her girls, but to ACTUALLY BE OK WITH RANDY MOLESTING HER GIRLS, so long as he kept her compensated properly! Which the great Root Of All Evil thought was so fucking funny!"

Shaggy was shushing Jeffy so much, he sounded like a steam whistle. It didn't matter. No one at the house, including Randy or Tina could hear what he was saying. They heard him yelling and figured he was expressing grief over his sister. -Everyone but Ricky Rudolph. -And his pocket tape recorder.

Once the memorial had concluded, a flurry of prerequisite final phony goodbye hugs and goodbye near-cheek air-kisses and goodbye crocodile tears all adorned with passionate promises to always remember, uphold and love the memory of Joey Jabonno filled the air, as everybody left.

Jeffy went home that night not even remembering how he got there. He didn't remember the last time he'd actually eaten either. He wasn't hungry. He found himself sitting on the couch in front of the TV watching Whoopee Goldberg running around in a panic as she hears Patrick Swayze's voice as a Ghost.

Kelsey Grammar's voice in TV-psychiatrist guise started talking:

"It is generally discussed in academic and medical as well as philosophical circles that people who hear voices in their heads belong to one of two groups: Those with auditory hallucinations - And those with psychic communications. So tell us, which group do you belong to, Jeffy?"

Without even blinking, Jeffy answered, "I'm in the Orifice of the Oracle, asshole."

"That's telling the wanker." John Lennon said, now sitting next to him.

"Will you please be quiet?" Jeffy replied. "I'm watching something important."

The television was off.

Back at the Horn, Tina was finishing up some paper work. She'd already let Noel go for the day. The phone rang. "Hi, Tina? This is Melanie and Melody Mint? We're calling from Toronto? We're both on the line and need to talk to you?"

The Mint twins, in times of stress, had a nervous habit of up-talking: the post modern speech pattern in which the old 60s and 70s saying, "You know?" had evolved into a wordless upward inflection added onto the last word of every spoken sentence, resulting in it sounding like a question - you know?

"We saw the report about your nanny?"

"We didn't know you had young girls you adopted?"

"And he really likes young girls?"

"Are you asking me or telling me? Never mind, I forgot that's how you Canadians talk."

Tina listened to everything the Mint twins had to tell her. -Every single thing. -All of Randy's old favorite games from *Seesaw* to Merry-Go-Round. All the videos he'd taken of them nude modeling from ages 11 to 16. All the secret parties they had back in the day. How he paid off their mother with steady cash and a house in the Hollywood Hills on Blue Jay Way where George Harrison once lived. How she sold that at a nice profit. How she couldn't say anything after signing that Non Disclosure Agreement. But how they had found a loophole in theirs that allowed them to tell Tina. And how Randy had ruined their lives.

"We just don't want that to happen to your girls?"

When Tina hung up the phone, she immediately went down to confront Randy. "Guess who I was just talking to?" Randy opened his mouth to offer a guess but she cut him off before he had a chance, leaving his mouth an open invitation for flies.

"Yes. I heard about your bubble gum girls or whatever they were. You sick fuck. We're done! I'm leaving. I'm taking the girls. And I'm taking everything else."

Randy gulped, realizing that without any prenuptial agreement between them, he was fucked. He would lose everything. Not just a house. Not just the money. Not just the cars. He'd lose the Horn. He'd lose his reputation. He'd lose his career. He saw himself in a lineup with Weinstein, Epstein and a whole long suspect line of others who'd totally gotten away with it. He shook his head violently to rid himself of the image.

The only answer he gave Tina in defense of himself was, "Tina, be real! The 70s were a crazy, hedonistic time. Everyone was experimenting and exploring. I was exploring!"

"Exploring, were you? Well, you can go back to exploring where you'll be spending the rest of your life, as soon as I leave and take the girls, you sick fuck! Thank God they're away!" She stormed off slamming the studio door shut for effect.

He couldn't even use her cheating on him with Bela. He didn't even try. It didn't matter now. He was thoroughly compromised and he knew it. His emergency escape drawer next to his bed was starting to look mighty good in his mind. Without saying another word, Randy walked down to the studio and sat at his perch. Thinking for a minute and then grimacing with his eyes closed, he took a deep breath and pulled out his cellphone.

"Avi? Yeah. Where've you been? I thought you took care of the Girls."

"I did take care of them, Randy. I even went up to see them myself in Toronto. The Girls... You know they're in their late forties, early fifties now? Never married. Never had kids. In and out of drug rehab for years?"

"Yes. I'm aware. Now did you take care of them so they're happy and we're done?"

"I did. -Two-fifty K, each. They called it their retirement fund. And they signed NDA's so they can't go to the press."

"Well guess what? Those non-disclosures didn't stop them from calling Tina."

"Tina?? Those up-talking twats."

"OK, we're way past that now... Forget them. They're not the problem anymore. You know the problem... You know what? Fuck it. Do it. Set it in motion."

"Now? Are you sure?"

"Yes. Do it."

"There's no turning back from this."

"I know that. There's no turning back from any of this. -Do it."

"Look, in your state of mind, just be careful driving those Canyon roads up there. You know? Sometimes they don't find a missing vehicle down in one of those crevices for years."

"Avi, the only thing I want to know is when to file."

"Where are Bathsheba and Khungit?"

"They're at overnight summer camp for the next two weeks. Dog's in the kennel."

"Very good, my friend. I'll let you know if anything further goes down."

Everybody at the Horn knew long before Tina ever knew about Randy's criminal indiscretions. They all knew. -Except Jason Barter. And strangely, like Avi, who was actually paid for the service, they all felt obligated to protect him for the same reason everyone always thought he was so innocent looking. Something made them still want to protect him, and not because he was their main source of income, although in all honesty, that certainly played a part. But they also felt love, actual love towards him like a dysfunctional father that you know has done and is still doing wrong, but you still love him and something still makes you want to stupidly protect him.

When it came to Randy's indiscretions, that's exactly how his staff felt in a virtual Stockholm syndrome way. Everyone close to him knew, just like everyone in Hollywood knew about Weinstein. It was an Open Secret-as they call it there. But in a town filled with people dedicated to the proposition that "I'd rather be paid, than be right." What 99.9% of Hollywood's elites did in one twisted form or another was par for the Hollywood course. Kenneth Anger's Hollywood Babylon reads like a child's Golden Story Book in comparison to the reality of early 21st Century Tinsel Town.

In the Land Of Illusion where everything was built on pretense, it was easy to think virtually anything was OK to do. *"So long as you're not hurting anybody."* -was the rationalization. It was all make-believe in their minds. Nothing was really real. -Except money. So when a movie star walked out of a jewelry store wearing $50,000 in diamonds and emeralds without paying, she didn't think she was stealing. She thought she was given all that because she was given things like that all the time. A goody bag at any Hollywood event could be worth anywhere from $10,000 to $50,000 depending on the prestige of the event.

Haunted by his recurring Polanski dream, Randy spent a miserable night at the Horn giving Tina her space and pinning his hopes on Dille liking the Tip Slyde music. Dille was coming in later that morning to review the Technotology track. If he liked it, there was a good chance he'd be giving Randy a new full-length feature film Dille had teased him with, over lunches that spanned the length and breadth of Restaurant Row on La Cienega Boulevard from Lawry's Steak House to the Matsuhisa Sushi Bar.

"I have this thing in development." Dille would say to him in so many words from lunch to lunch. "My next important work I'm calling, and this is a working title: *Sweet Daddy God.* It's Groundbreaking. It's about this cat in the 1930s and 40s named Father Divine who claimed he was God. Had a massive following. -Early civil rights leader. I'm hoping to get Eddie Murphy for this. He'd be perfect. And whoever is in on this with me from music to food craft services stands to get an Oscar! Thing of it is, Scorch is busy on another project of mine." Then he'd sink his head down like he was telling a secret, wink and say, "The merchandising side of my films gets so crazy, Father Divine or really Eddie Murphy as Father Divine will even have his own action figure!"

When Dille came into the Horn that morning, he walked straight into Randy's studio, sat down and said, "Ok, play it for me." Randy played it for him. Dexter gave a nod of approval and asked for a flash drive.

"Do me a favor. Aside from the full mix, also give me all your music files, including the splits of every instrument, every ping and every pong put on the track so I can control it at final edit."

"I thought I'd bring all that to final edit myself. I'll be happy to be there for that."

"Well, Randy, I'd be happy not to have you there for that, to be perfectly honest."

Randy looked at Dille incredulously. "Wh-what?"

"Yeah. Thanks. That's it. I'll let you know if any other little things come up I can throw your way."

"Little things come up? Throw my way? What about that Father Divine project you mentioned? I proved myself on these test projects you gave me."

"Proved yourself? *Test* projects? This is it - if you want to know the truth. Your boys did this. I know how you work, or rather, don't work. What? You don't think I talk with Angelina Jolie or Easton Amberson or Kevin James or Tarantino? Your boys I would use in a heartbeat the moment they go independent. But you?" Dille started chuckling. "Why would I work with someone who even lies about his own building?"

"Lies? C'mon Dex, fun stories, maybe-"

"You know that cock and bull story you tell everyone about Frank Lloyd Wright? Ever heard of Dr. Rattrop or Charles Luckman? Yeah, Luckman's widow called me about doing a film about his work and one of the buildings being the Horn. She even showed me the blueprints. You should have heard what she said he used to call this place!"

Randy tried to sidestep that. "Anything my guys did, I directed them to do, Dex. All that work reflects me."

Dille looked at him and smiled. "Yes. In a way you're right. All their work does *reflect* you.

"C'mon, Dexter. Give me a chance to show you I can eclipse anything you'd ever get out of Scorch."

That made Dille laugh. "You know, normally I wouldn't even waste my time telling someone this, but you are special to me. Derek Scorch is a fine composer. He focuses on the work himself. -Him and him alone. -No one else. Sometimes he's even his own arranger. And he never spends my time and money working on his own hobbies in edit sessions."

"Hobbies? Dex, you yourself said I was gifted in that *Shoot* interview. I'm telling you, man. That Father Divine project was made for me. I mean the guy claimed to be a God, Dex. That's a perfect fit considering where I come from musically. Who better? C'mon. Give me a shot."

"I'm giving that project to Byte Wurst'nBark of Global DoggKilllas Incorporated. To be blunt, he's edge." Then Dille went in for the kill: "Randall, I've enjoyed our dining experiences. Thank you. But frankly, you were a fresh, spoiled, petulant asshole at your height and now you're a rotten, phony spoiled one.

"Oh, you're very Hollywood. You tell all the right bullshit stories. But I will never hire you for anything more than the crumbs I've already thrown you. You know in a way, as much as he's a blaring asshole, at least Jeffy's an honest one."

Randy wasn't used to someone, outside of Tina, being so honest with him in such a condemning way. It literally froze him in place as he listened to Dille go on.

"And just because I say I think someone is gifted, doesn't mean I like them or want to work with them, any more than you wanted to work with me on that telecast back in '84. And yes, you can beg off on that televised abortion all you like. You think I've forgotten that week? All the shit YOU said behind my back? Yeah, Jabonno's a horrid control freak, yes, but what, Randall, can't you smell my *Swish Lube* that I still wear after all these years?"

Randy couldn't take it one more second. "Why don't you just ask me to suck your dick, then?"

"Because I'd be afraid you'd say yes just to get the job, honey. Besides, this has been much more fun. But now it's done. And I'll even give you that the Horn O Plenty produces some very fine work like I said in that interview. But you're no

Derek Scorch. -Toodles!" With that, Dexter Dille took the flash drive Jake handed him with the Technotology score and all its splits and left the building. Forever.

"Fuckin' fruit." Randy cursed after him. "-All that effort. -All that time. -All that groveling. -That fuckin' Jabonno." Then his mind went elsewhere, remembering something he'd almost forgotten to do. "Hey Mei Ling!" he yelled from his perch. "Has anybody seen Tina?"

The next morning, Jeffy got a call from Paulette at the Horn. "Randy would like you to come pick up Joey's personal effects. Could you come today?"

"He couldn't afford to have them delivered?"

"He asked me to call you to pick them up, Jeffy."

"Fine. I'll be there as soon as I can."

It was an especially hot, dry, muggy LA day.

On the way to the Horn, Jeffy had turned on the radio. *Who Are You?* was playing. Thinking he was switching to another station - he instead turned the radio off.

"Hey There, Hep Cats and Cool Kitties! I'm Johnny L. with all your favorite hits on KUNT radio and our FM sister station KOCK Rock! And this next number is dedicated to that burning, yearning question: The classic cry of the over-the-hill faded rock star, actor, celebrity knocked out of their orbit and headed straight for the black hole of professional oblivion. The sad query brayed and belched and howled from the Hollywood Bowl to the Sunset Strip. -From the Sky Bar to Dodger Stadium. -From the Playboy Mansion to Disneyland. Echoed in airports, fine restaurants and five-star hotels throughout the world and translated into a UN of languages.

"Do you know it yet? The cry has been uttered, muttered, hollered and yelped by the has-been and the never-was since saber-toothed tigers blindly jumped onto

Woolly mammoths trapped in the La Brea tar pits. Can you dig it? Do you know what I mean? I'll give you a hint:

"In Español, it's 'NO SABES QUIEN SOY?'
In French, it's 'TU NE SAIS PAS QUI JE SUIS?'
In German, it's 'WEISST DU NICHT WER ICH BIN?'
In Japanese, it's 'WATASHI GA DARE DA KAWARANAI?'
And in English, it's OUR NUMBER ONE HIT WITH A BULLET!"

A single electric guitar started strumming in the key of C playing C, G and F chords in a common punk progression. Jeffy's own voice started to sing over the radio. "When did I record that?" he asked himself.

"DON'T YOU
KNOW WHO I AM?
CAN'T YOU SEE I'M A STAR?
I'VE BEEN LOVED BY MILLIONS! / I CAN SHOW YOU THE SCARS!
I DESERVE TO BE FIRST! / I DESERVE TO BE HAILED!
I'M THE BEST-YOU'RE THE WORST! / I SUCCEED AND YOU FAILED!
DON'T YOU KNOW WHO I AM? / CANT YOU SEE I'M A STAR?
YOU SHOULD KNEEL AT MY FEET! / WORSHIP ME FROM AFAR!
JUST DO WHAT I SAY! / BECAUSE I DON'T GIVE A DAMN!
I JUST WANT WHAT I WANT! / DON'T YOU KNOW WHO I AM?
DON'T YOU KNOW WHO I AM? / DON'T YOU KNOW WHO I AM?
DON'T YOU KNOW
WHO I AM???"

"-And that was *Don't You Know Who I Am?* by Jeffy Jabonno! Yes, dear listener, we've been getting a lot of requests for that one, lately."

While Jeffy was on his way to the Horn, Randy was conducting an interview in Studio Zero.

"It's a myth that Larry's home burnt down in a meth lab fire or for any other nefarious reason. She has this obsession with fireworks and that's how her house accidentally caught on fire."

"Yes, but didn't she also shoot rockets and roman candles into her neighbor's house, burn that to the ground and set some passerby's hair on fire?"

"Well, first off, it was the Fourth of July. Secondly, her neighbors were out of town and she thought she saw a prowler. But that investigation is still underway. So I really can't comment on that. What I can comment on is what a legendary guitarist and talented composer Larry Root is."

Larry looked into the studio behind the reporter so only Randy saw her. He shooed her away with a quick sweep of his eyes. She left the Horn muttering curses, headed for beer and sulking. The strange dynamics between Randy and Larry enabled Randy to control Larry almost like a Doberman Pincher he could call off at will, except when a stage they were performing on was stormed. In the years following the Band's nadir, Randy had thrown bones to Larry, keeping her alive by having her pick up his cartoon work for which she was simultaneously grateful and resentful.

Jeffy pulled into the Horn's back parking lot. Tarzan presented himself naked on a branch above Jeffy's car trying his best to upset him. But Jeffy was beyond these things. Jeffy looked up at the tree dweller seeing him as a car valet and threw him his keys. "Hey, good to see you again, Mr. T!" He said to a thoroughly confused King of the Jungle. "This shouldn't take long!"

The reporter, changing gears decided to go in a totally different direction. "OK, here's something fun: I heard you came up with this tale you told about how the multiverse must have one planet out there where we're all like *Jesus*? An Earth where Jesus wasn't crucified so we're all rocking out with Jesus power? An alternate you and me and everybody else, all walking on water, turning agua into wine, the whole bit on another Earth somewhere out there? Wow. Now that is pure

Orifice of The Oracle at its best. And you came up with this for the annual Oracle convention called the Divine Intervention? Is that true? Was that your idea?"

"Well, sadly I couldn't make it there in person this year, I'm sorry to say. So I came up with that brain candy for the fans. I like to think of all my ideas as fun keys to unlocking doors in the multiverse, you know?"

As Jeffy entered the Horn, he climbed up the multi-colored Lucite stairs, each step lighting up red-orange-yellow-green-blue-violet in succession as he took one by one. He stared at himself into one of Root's circus mirrors mounted on the wall and saw someone else completely different. He stopped for a few seconds and asked his image "Who are you?" To which his image answered: "Don't you know?"

Randy was going into humble-innocence mode. "I've been blessed that people respond to the things I do and create. In fact, I just learned the Children's Wholesome Entertainment Association will be holding a dinner in my honor, celebrating my contributions."

"Congratulations!" The reporter beamed. "That has got to be so gratifying. Feeling the love of so many young children-"

"Oh, you can say that again, pal!" Jeffy burst into Studio Zero, swinging the door open so fast, the reporter jumped up from the couch.

Randy looked at the visibly shaken reporter. "I'm sorry for this. We're obviously having a family squabble. I'm sure you know Jeffy Jabonno. We'll have to finish this later. I'm sorry. Talk with Paulette and we'll reschedule. -Hey Paulette! Please reschedule our friend here. And has anybody seen Tina yet today? Anyway, let's finish this up later. -Thanks!" The reporter left, closing the door. Randy turned right around to Jeffy. "WHAT THE FUCK, JEFF?"

"Oh, I'm sorry. Is there a law somewhere I don't know of that says I'm forbidden from bringing up anything out of the encyclopedia of Randy Root fuck-ups while you're conducting a very important interview where you whitewash everything for the public?"

Randy tried to calm Jeffy down. "Listen, I know you've been through a lot lately-"

"Through a lot lately? You're systematically shaking me loose from the equation that added up to US, Randy. *-To the Orifice of the Oracle.* OUR creation!"

"Hey, it's not my fault that you've squandered all your chances. Or that people blame you for the demise of the Band. I mean, don't you get it? People *want* to believe I did it all by myself. It's easier. You complicate things. You always did. That's not my fault. I'm not doing that. It's just that people prefer seeing it that way. That's why you and I remember things differently."

"Oh, what utter horseshit! You're doing this!"

"I'm doing this? Really? This whole Dille jerk-off was your brilliant doing! You're the one who came in here with this great tour that Dille was shooting. And what does he do? You can bet he shot us at our worst. Found every opportunity to insult us and use me. And then jerks me around even more on these fucking shit projects he deliberately used me on to save his golden boy Scorch from getting his delicate hands dirty. Thanks to *you*, Jeffy!"

"It was the only way to get you to tour any more, you selfish fuck!"

"You know what? Even if what you're claiming was true, *and it isn't*, you can't do anything positive or productive anymore with the history of the Band anyway. Not like *I* can. You might as well let me have it all anyway and let me make the most of it. I'm the one who can still do something *with* it.

"But guess what!" Randy went viciously on. I do have an idea, for you, Jeffy." Randy was madder than he had ever let himself get before. "Tell ya what. You want to do more touring? Just start a band called *The Victims Of Circumstance*! Now there's a name that really suits you."

"And who the fuck do you think *you* are? A Derek Scorch? Ha! You're nothing more than a Tin Pan Alley hack who steals!"

"You and your high-handed arrogant political bullshit in the Band. Bullying everyone, especially Skippy. That's what killed us. Forcing that crap down people throats. Nobody cares! When the fuck are you gonna get it, that all we are anymore are nostalgic novelty action figures only an aging demographic group of old farts relates to? Don't you get it? We're over. We're old hat. Yesterday's news."

"Then why the fuck are you rewriting and making it all about YOU?"

"And how am I doing that?"

"Oh man... How are you *not* doing that? I saw your Golden Calf interview. I heard your lies. You worked my sister to death and now you're killing me!"

"What I'm saying in these interviews is how I remember it all, Jeffy. You're imagining things." He turned his back to Jeffy. "And now, you're boring me."

"Really?" Jeffy stared at a new display shelf Randy had recently installed over the client couch featuring his own original MegaHorn. "Boring you, am I? And I'm imagining how you literally stole the MegaHorn from me? -My Megahorn that I designed? The one you called old hat and part of our old monkey suit, putting it down constantly? But look! Now you have it as a shrine! Gee how'd that happen? When everybody on the Tour told you what *genius* it was and you decided then and there, that you remembered doing it all by your fucking self?" Jeffy grabbed the MegaHorn out of its display case and turned around now facing Randy sideways.

"Here, Motherfucker! You want it so fuckin' bad that you have to lie?? Here, you fucking thief! -IT'S ALL YOURS!!"

Jeffy hurled the MegaHorn at Randy's head as hard as his forty years worth of bottled-up rage, anger and resentment could propel it, and as Randy turned to dodge it, one little razor-sharp lip of a wing ran right across his neck and sliced open his jugular before he even realized what was gushing onto the floor. Randy looked puzzled, turned to look at Jeffy in disbelief and then blacked out. Both Paulette and Mei Ling ran in and tried to help, but nothing could resuscitate the legendary Randy Root. There weren't enough towels in the Horn to deal with the deluge.

The police arrived right afterward. An officer spoke first with Paulette. Then he walked over to a frozen Jeffy as a stretcher with Randy covered in a sheet rolled by.

"Come with me, Sir. You're under arrest."

"Take your hands off me! Don't you know who I am?"

"Yeah. You're the guy who killed Randy Root."

"It's only fair." Jabonno replied, staring at nothing. "He killed me first."

*

The news reports flew fast and furious with clever spins on the Band's name and their music. Jeffy was charged with voluntary manslaughter as a result of a *Sudden Quarrel* - as defined by California law. He was facing a maximum of eleven years in prison.That is, until he was placed under 30-day psychiatric observation and judged unfit for trial. He was then sent to the moderate-security Pleasant Valley hospital prison in Fresno with periodic hearings every three months.

Ricky Rudolph's piece on the Orifice of the Oracle: *Rock Of Aged - Cliffs For Thee - A Crash Course In Post Modern Idol Worship* was published in the Times several months later, earning him a shelf full of journalist awards. He brought a copy of the piece with him when he visited Jeffy, feeling the story wouldn't be over until he did.

When Rudolph walked in to the hospital visitor's room, he saw Jeffy dressed in jeans, an Oracle t-shirt and white slippers, sitting by himself twisting a piece of blank paper into a cone.

"Jeffy, hi, how are you? I wanted to show you what I ended up writing about The Orifice Of The Oracle. And I want you to know that I know better than anyone what happened and what you were going through. I'll do whatever I can to help you."

Jeffy looked at Ricky, first not seeming to recognize him. Then a look of familiarity slowly came over his face as he nodded and took the paper and skim-read the article focusing on the last few paragraphs:

"In a town paved with the dreams and aspirations of those countless souls who fell for false prophecies and broken promises, a great band arose blaring a wake up call that the general masses soon dismissed and forgot, except as nostalgic fodder. Youth opens a credit account in the Bank of Human Comedy & Vanity and leaves Old Age with the bill.

"In the end, my experience following a rock band I grew up listening to and idolizing became an enlightening object lesson: Getting to know your rock n' roll heroes is a risky enterprise. Rock Gods quickly become frail tiny human beings prone to life's pitfalls as much as any of us mere mortals - and often far more. -Especially in a mindset such as Hollywood's. Where the altars of self-adulation are kilned from the ashes of those who dared to touch the sun and were burnt to a cinder.

The Orifice of the Oracle fell victim to it's own philosophy as Gods who literally forgot who they were and fell back into their own mortality - as they had cleverly said about all humanity. And just a block or so down from where Randy Root had his Horn O Plenty Productions, (the de facto headquarters for the Oracle in its last years), the first superstar organic spiritual vegetarian restaurant, called the Source, brought forth another divine entity in the 70s called Father Yod, who decided to hang glide off the 1,300 foot cliffs of Eastern Oahu without any experience. He crashed on the beach and died nine hours later. Which proves that even Gods have limits.

Just ask Zeus how he's done lately. Or Flotsamheimer's Technotologists and their electro-Godz only a mile down from there. None of that is new. Just ask the Ghost of Aimee Semple McPherson. -Or the ghost of Aleister Crowley, if you dare. And after a while you're just counting fallen Gods, which in Hollywood could be a lifetime career. And then you come to realize after actually bearing witness to not just their frailties and foibles, but their perversions, their abuses, their trespasses into the taboo turned normal, that the personal fetishes of your childhood heroes cannot help but change your outlook on life - and change You.

"You are left with the conclusion that the entire Town is guilty. Whatever crimes and excesses the powerful committed - everyone knew. Everyone always knows. You have to be complicit to survive there. That's what the Town itself taught and still teaches. You were taught to believe (you had better believe) as Tina Root once said to me: 'In this Town you learn quick if you wanna make it- it's better to be paid than be right.' And now, it's not only a Town anymore. It's a mindset. -Of the entitled. -Of the privileged. -Of the celebrated. It's a sickness. Like a seething, undulating giant gelatinous blob of viral hypocrisy consuming the city. But this is not an indictment of individuals, but rather of a culture. A culture built on pretense. A culture so ingrained that those in it can no longer tell the difference between freedom and limits, right and wrong or reality and fantasy.

"So while others will scoff at this and write their own clever little cynical pieces about the "Orifeces of the Orafools," and all that low-hanging fruit, I write that you must separate the artist from the art. This is no less true for them than it is for Chaplin, Mozart, Disney, Picasso and an endless cavalcade of stars. If the art itself is to survive, there has to be sunlight between the creator and the created. Few people look at a Charlie Chaplin film or a Picasso painting and judge it by saying, 'God what a bastard he was in his personal life therefore this movie stinks and that painting sucks!' And time provides that sunlight. So, in the future, when 'Flip It Off' or 'Blow It Out' or any one of a number of their hits are played anywhere you find yourself - think about their flight - and not their crash. It'll be a far more rewarding journey."

Jeffy put the paper down and turned to Ricky. "Well I guess this proves there really isn't any such thing as bad press. I hope you win a Pulitzer."

"I've been nominated." Ricky looked around the room, leaned in close to Jeffy and lowered his voice. "Jeffy, after everything that's happened, I have to ask. -Do you know anything about the disappearance of Tina Root? I know you've been asked this. But *I'm* asking..."

Jeffy looked Ricky right in the eyes. "Ask the Root Of All Evil. -He made me disappear."

Ricky smiled sadly, looked down and then looked back at Jeffy. "I'll look into when your next hearing is and come out to speak on your behalf, if you like."

Jeffy looked at him blankly and echoed his words. "Speak on my behalf..."

Ricky sighed as he stood up. "It was great to see you, Jeffy. Really great."

"*See me*? That's funny! After all the times the Root Of All Evil used to say I wasn't there, *Abracadabra: Here I Am!*" He forced back an almost uncontrollable urge to laugh that wrenched his face as he watched Ricky head for the door.

"Hey!" he shouted. "Have you heard my new hit?" Then Jeffy began singing:

"DON'T YOU KNOW WHO I AM?

DON'T YOU KNOW WHO I AM??

DON'T YOU KNOW WHO I AM???"

Ricky stopped at the door, turned and listened to Jeffy sing the same line over and over. He thought for a moment, smiled, nodded, gave Jeffy a thumbs-up and left.

The co-founder of The Orifice Of The Oracle, co-writer of half a dozen of its charted hits, the co-designer of its trademark MegaHorn and once a God, stopped singing. A few of the other patients and their confused visitors clapped. He closed his eyes and saw a kaleidoscope of thousands of fans all rushing to crowd around him as he heard John Lennon whisper softly in his ear:

"Well done, Jeffy, old boy. Now everyone will always know who you are."

-END-

ACKNOWLEDGMENTS

To Anyone And Everyone I've Ever Worked With.

In The Land Of Illusion You Can Get A Contusion For Thinking The Glitter Is Gold
So Be Of Great Care As You Sashay Through There 'Cause You Could Find That
You Were Just Sold

★

Made in the USA
Columbia, SC
02 May 2021